THE KEYS:
TWISTED TALES FROM AUNTIE'S ATTIC

Drew Bittner

David Disspain

Leon J. Cooper

Sherin Nicole

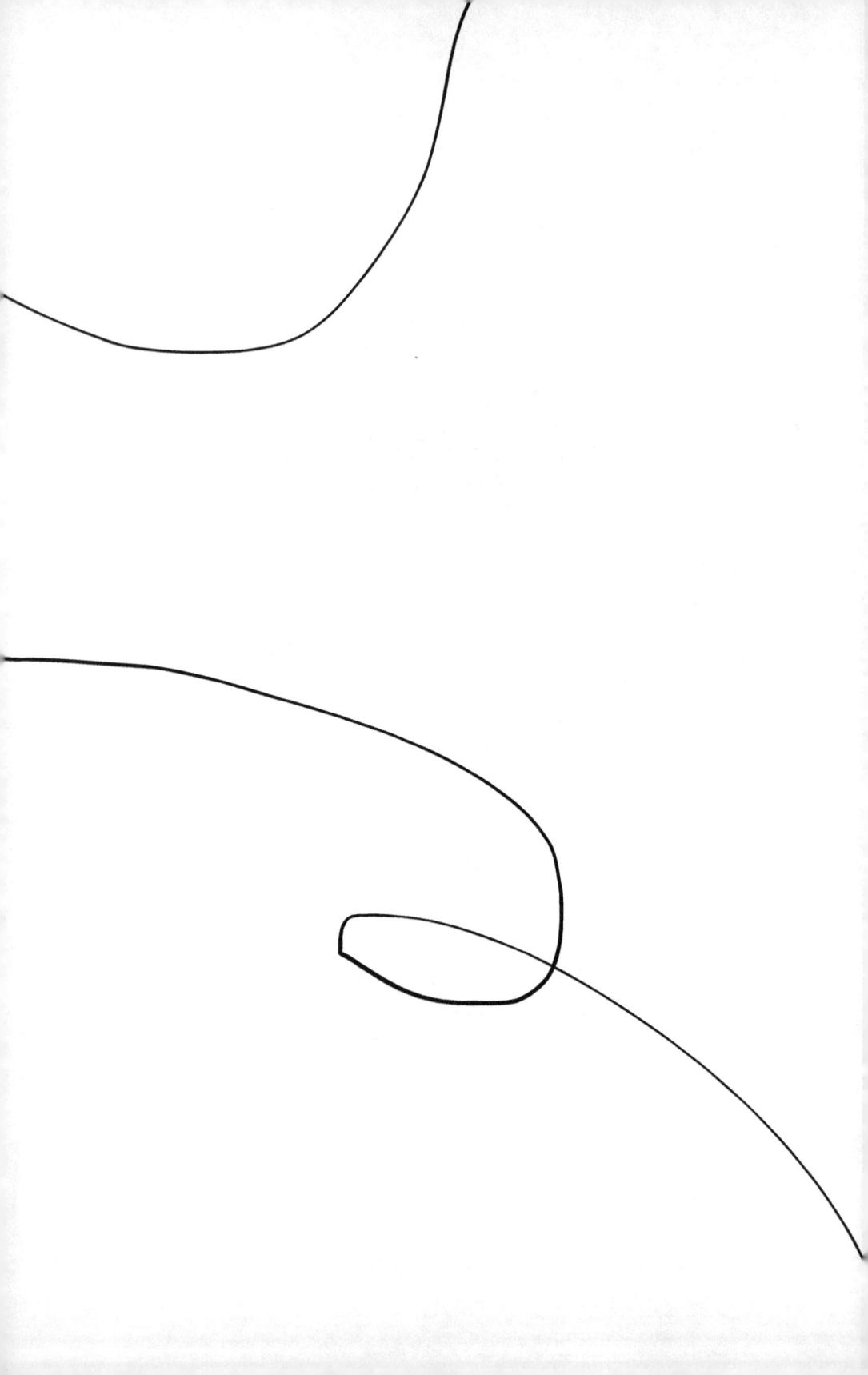

THE
KEYS

Library of Congress Cataloging-in-Publication Data

Sherin Nicole, Leon J. Cooper, David Disspain, Drew Bittner, The Keys: Twisted Tales from Auntie's Attic

Summary: Four wickedly imaginative authors explore one idea: you have unlocked the world of Auntie's Attic. A key is in your hand. White as bleached bone and slick as lies, your key unlocks a storage room. Inside you'll find an object that could lead you anywhere, but wherever you go, you cannot return.

Edited by Mira Singer
Designed by Sherin Nicole

Illustrations by Sumit Roy, akar.std, Alice Brereton, Ananyo Chatterjee

ISBN: 978-1-939282-51-4

Published by Miniver Press, LLC, McLean Virginia
Copyright 2023 Nell Minow

First edition October 2023

FOR LEON

Contents

Introduction: Turning THE KEYS - Drew Bittner   I

From the First   1

(Unit 219) Bidding - David Disspain   3

(Unit 222) IQ - Leon J. Cooper with David Disspain   11

Three Missing In Prank Gone Awry   26

(Unit 888) Fair Exchange - Sherin Nicole   29

(Unit 333) Perfect - Drew Bittner   45

Chronicle Reporter Gone Missing   57

(Unit 111) I Got It from My Mother - Leon J. Cooper with Drew Bitner   59

(Unit 233) Bear With Me - Drew Bittner   77

The Final Meeting of the Urban Legend Hunters Club   94

(Unit 1618) The Refraction Principle - Sherin Nicole   99

(Unit 18) Nirvana - David Disspain   117

In Search of Auntie's Attic   145

(Unit 446) Win Big Prizes - Drew Bittner   147

(Unit 03) The Misuse of Grimoires - Sherin Nicole   157

Crossroads Weekly Gazette   162

(Unit 379) Outwit, Outplay, Outlast - Leon J. Cooper with Sherin Nicole   167

Closing Time - Drew Bittner   208

(Unit 5011) The Apocalypse Plurality - Sherin Nicole   211

(Unit Unknown) Cypher - David Disspain   215

Remembering Leon   III

   Who Was Leon Cooper?   IV

   Music and Stories. A Remembrance of Leon Cooper   V

   The Physics Of Leon   VII

Acknowledgments   IX

INTRODUCTION:
TURNING THE KEYS

Drew Bittner

In the beginning…

No, let's start with…

Once upon a time, there were four writers: Sherin, Dave, Leon, and Drew, each one somewhere along the path of being a writer. Given that we're all sociable folks (mostly) and wanted to be part of a writing group (definitely), we agreed that we could meet up, talk, and give it a try.

Four of us got together in the café at Barnes & Noble in Clarendon, Virginia. I was the only one who knew everyone else and I had no idea if this ensemble would jell, but I was hopeful. So we ordered our drinks at the Starbucks counter, grabbed a table, made introductions, and everything clicked. Sherin, Dave, and Leon took to each other as if they'd been friends for years. A circle of friendship was born.

Then we asked ourselves, "What now?"

We each had stories in some stage of development, and we were all willing to share them for mutual critique, but somewhere along the line, we wanted more. Why not write new stories for an anthology? (I think it was Sherin who had the idea for a book, having had novels published already.) We liked the idea—us guys were game for sure—but what would be the premise? Was there a central theme around which we could write stories?

I've had storage units for several years, in all sorts of places. Some are wonderful, modern and brightly lit and air-conditioned, while others are barely more than shacks with a dubious lock on the door. TV shows have been made about people opening up and selling off the contents of unpaid units. Nobody really knows what lies inside those mystery boxes until they're opened…which gave me an idea. What if our stories all involved a protagonist getting a key to a storage unit—and whatever is inside changes their lives dramatically, for good or bad? Seemed like an idea that could generate lots of stories.

And when I pitched it to the group, they agreed. We would go off and write our stories, then figure out a location. We knew it would be one place, not a different facility in each story, but…well, that "one facility" turned out to be interesting in and of itself, and it became a character on its own.

I think it might have been Leon who suggested simply "The Keys" as the name for the anthology, while Sherin supplied "Auntie's Attic" as the facility's name. Dave pitched that the place would look different from story to story—not a function of age or when the story was set (as far as I was concerned, they were all set "now") but because the place would change, like light through a prism, depending on who perceived it. Some people would know the place, others would swear it had never been there before. It would be a mystery unto itself, and one we wouldn't even try to solve.

We wrote several stories each—I abandoned my first idea, as the execution was proving far too dark even for my sensibilities—and then gathered to go over them. We were making excellent progress, and then COVID hit. The pandemic shut down our gatherings, pushing us onto sporadic web chats and email exchanges, but we made some headway even so.

Then Sherin, who was the unflagging advocate of this becoming more than a writing exercise, said she was actively promoting it to publishers. Our collective hopes rose—and soon, we learned that we had a publisher. Miniver Press wanted our book. Now all we had to do was…everything that comes after writing.

But the stories were there. We picked and chose, then added some additional vignettes to flesh out the setting and the concept, and then got to work rewriting. The premise worked; our stories ranged far and wide in the realm of the fantastic but were connected by that common thread of a humble storage facility where strange things awaited those with the right key.

Turn the key, open the door, you never know what you'll find inside.

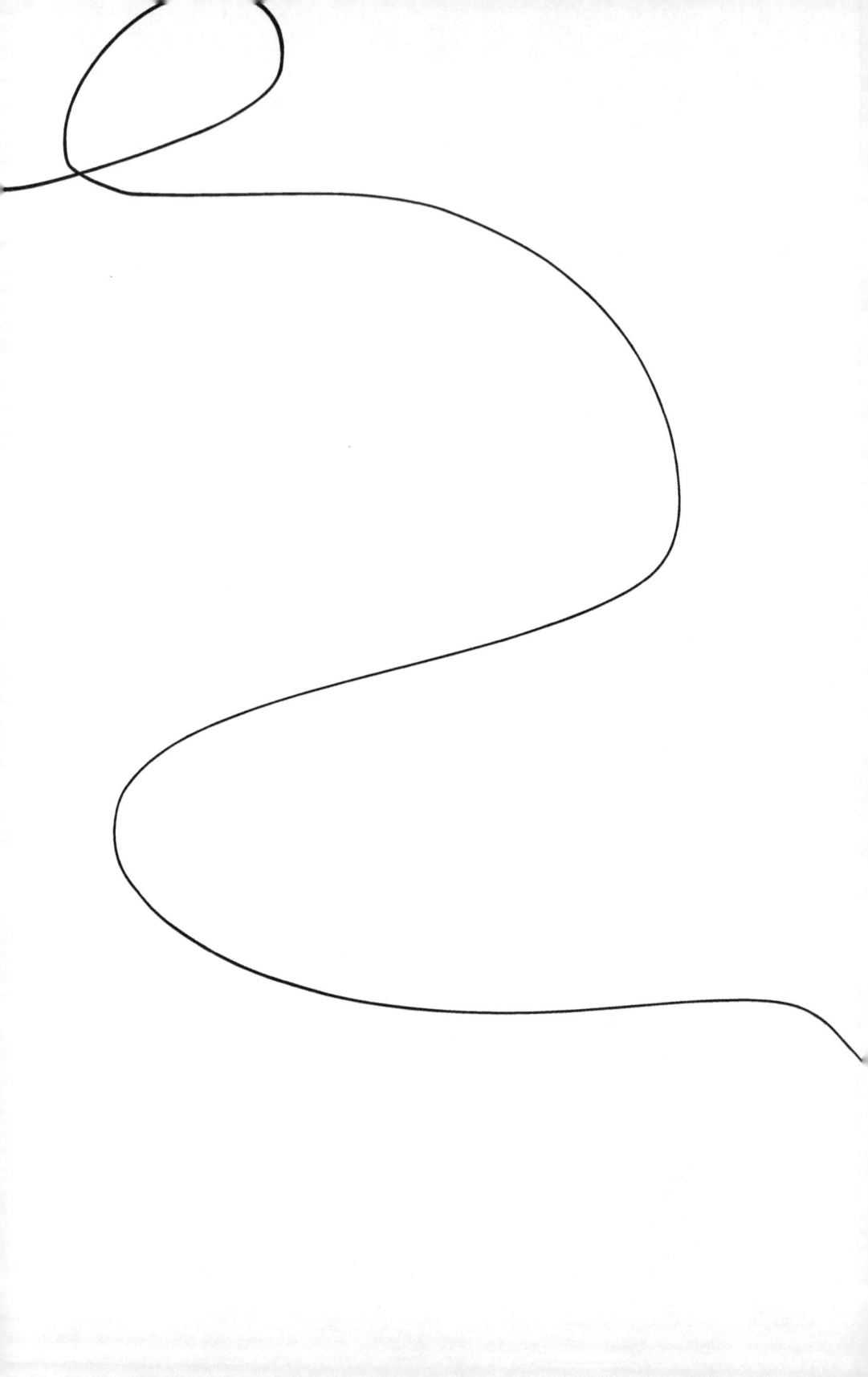

FROM THE FIRST

Come, children, listen. What must be known is this. Rather than question what came first or questing to be first (as humans do), we must first speak of "reason." Nothing can exist without purpose. ***Statement of proof: Emptiness cannot be empty without the possibility of being filled.***

D'you see? The Creator must exist because there are ever things to create. The Creator is why emptiness is and is not. The Creator is why fullness is and is not. This is good.

Therefore, rather than questioning what came first, or questing to be first (as humans do), understand this: Neither the chicken nor the egg claims precedence. Hunger interceded. Thus, the chicken and its egg, or alternately the egg and its chicken, are real. To eat, to be eaten, to prey. A chicken is simultaneously all and ever. It is a predator now because raptors roamed. Purpose outpaces reality. Each tumbling lock, every cause and effect required for the fowl's evolution happened in a snap. And everything needed to fulfill its future snapped into place instantaneously. Hunger did that. It gave the chicken a reason. ***Statement of proof: This is true. Your bones know.***

Therefore, it is natural to extrapolate that doors became real as soon as there was someplace to go. This is logical. This is true. This is untrue. Purposes are stacked, as sure as odds, or Jenga, or women in the '70s—each with varying degrees of "futz around and find out." Doors may lock something inside or keep something out. Still, doors are an effect. The cause is the key. ***Statement of proof: There is nowhere to go unless you unlock the purpose of going anywhere at all.***

Across the multiverse, the various Albert-Steins (Ein, Zwei, and Vier) have written, "Nothing happens until something moves." Still, some firsts cannot be. ***Statement of proof: If a door ever leads to nowhere, evermore will be unmade.***

Tell us, child, for we must know: What would be the purpose of that? The Keys will not allow it.

–Translated from Oracle Bone Script by Sherin Nicole
Rumored to be inscribed across nine Keys
Origin: Undiscovered

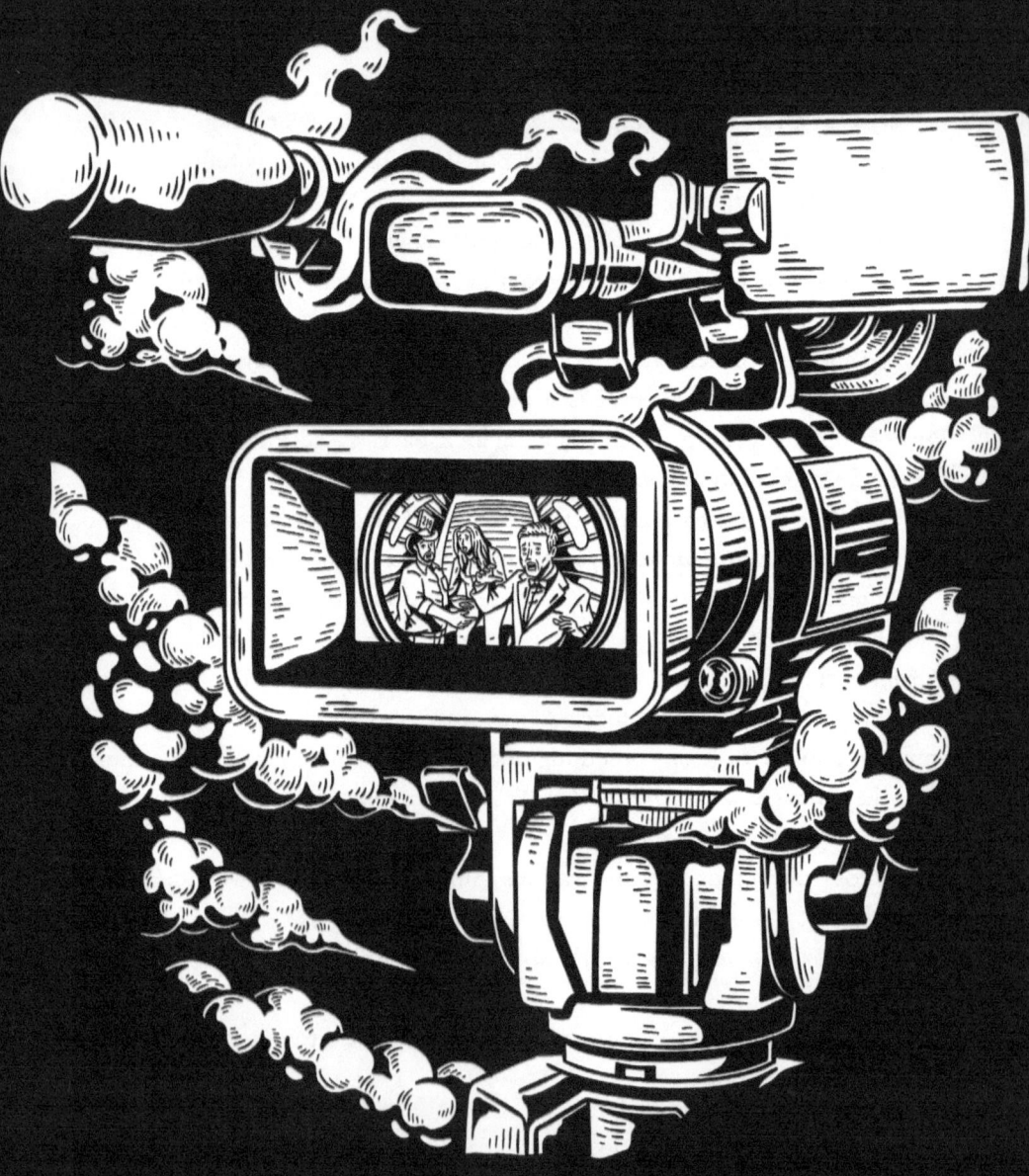

(Unit 219) **BIDDING**
by David Disspain

"Ladies and gentlemen, welcome to Storage Unit Battles. I'm your host, Tommy Murdock, and on today's episode, we're here in Crossroads, Virginia at a beautiful old facility called 'Auntie's Attic.' Today we have one of our SUB favorites, and former tournament of champions winner in 2018, Fred 'Buster' Jakes here to bid on today's unit. Buster, are you locked in for today's bidding war?"

"You bet, Tommy. We've toured the grounds and we feel we got a good look in the sneak peek, so we're ready to roll here."

"Fantastic, Buster. Let's meet one of your opponents today: she hails from Massapequa New York and has been in our tournament of champions twice, finishing in third place last year—Christa Mapp. Christa, you've been one of our elite players coming up fast through the ranks. A lot of folks think that now's your time to break through and bust up the 'Buster' himself today. How are you feeling today?"

"Feeling mean, Tommy! Feeling mean! I'm ready to take on both Buster and Clyde today. I think I have a few tricks up my sleeve that might surprise them. We came to win today!"

"Outstanding, Christa! Outstanding. OK, folks, it's time to meet our third competitor today: Clyde Addelson. Clyde is a former National Pickers Champion and although he's new to SUB, he's been making a name for himself by outbidding the likes of SUB champs Sid Jamison and Elaine Freydkin, and two weeks ago in Charlotte North Carolina, he took down current SUB champ Jeff Bell. This is going to be a knockdown, drag-out fight with two of the best today, Clyde. I hope you brought your A game!"

"You bet, Tommy! Buster and Christa may be two of the best, but we're ready to rock and roll and get the 'W' here today!"

"The man has some good old-fashioned quiet confidence, folks. It's the quiet ones you have to look out for, am I right? Alright, let's get down to business. If you've never seen the show before, the concept is pretty easy. Our three competitors will bid on the contents of what's in Unit 219. The one who outbids the others will win the keys to the unit, and we'll watch as they open it, and see if it was money well spent, or a complete disaster! Now, there's a fine art to bidding on units like this, so we try to give them some help and let them tour the facility, talk to the owners, and interview them about the usual clientele. After they've asked all their questions, and are comfortable, we actually open up the door to the unit twelve inches, and give them a one-time-only, fifteen-second sneak peek at the contents inside. The sneak peek is always the most critical part, so we'll show you the sneak peek footage after we have a winner and the locker is opened. No sneak peeks for you! All three of our legendary contestants have already talked to the owner and had their sneak peek, so at this point we're ready to start the auction. So now let's head over to the auctioneer for today's bidding battle! Take it away!"

"Thank you, Thomas. Miss Mapp. Mister Addelson. Mister Jakes. You have completed the interview and you have had your preview look into Unit 219. Are you ready to begin the auction at this time?"

"Yes sir."

"Yup."

"You bet."

"Very good. Now by process of random number selection, Mister Addelson has the benefit of the opening bid. Mister Addelson, what is your bid?"

"Eight hundred dollars, Mister Auctioneer."

"A very strong, confident bid. Well done, Mister Addelson. What do I hear from you, Miss Mapp and Mister Jakes?"

"Nine hundred."

"Nine hundred from Mister Jakes—very good."

"One thousand."

"And we have one thousand from Miss Mapp."

"Eleven hundred."

"The bid is now one thousand, one hundred dollars. Thank you, Mister Addelson."

"Mister Auctioneer. I have a proposal."

"Very well, Miss Mapp. We shall halt the bidding at one thousand, one hundred dollars to hear your proposal. You have the floor. Please state your proposal for the record."

"Mister Auctioneer, I'd like to propose that I will pay both of these gentlemen one thousand dollars cash to drop out of the auction right here, right now."

"Miss Mapp. Buying out a competitor, or competitors, is something that has never been attempted before on Storage Unit Battles."

"I've read the rules, Mister Auctioneer. There's nothing that states that it's not allowed. Someone has to be first, right? Might as well be me."

"Miss Mapp. The auctioneer well and duly salutes you for your creativity and for your bold and creative thinking. The offer now stands and the proposal is hereby submitted to your competitors. What say you, gentlemen? Miss Mapp has offered you the sum of one thousand dollars to cease the bidding. What say you?"

"Make it fifteen hundred and I'll take it."

"We have a counter offer! Miss Mapp, Mister Jakes has countered with an offer of one thousand five hundred dollars. Do you accept the counter proposal?

"I accept."

"Very well. Mister Jakes has accepted the sum of one thousand five hundred dollars to cease his bidding on Unit 219. Mister Addelson? Do you accept the proposal as well?"

"No, Mister Auctioneer, I don't. I think we're still at eleven hundred, right?"

"Indeed. You are correct, sir. Miss Mapp. Mister Addelson has rejected your bid for purchase and the prevailing bid is one thousand one hundred dollars. Do you wish to continue the bidding?

"Yes, Mister Auctioneer. I'll increase my offer to twelve hundred."

"Mister Addelson?"

"Fifteen hundred."

"Two thousand."

"Mister Addelson, Miss Mapp has increased the bid to two thousand. Are you willing to go higher?"

"Three thousand."

"Miss Mapp? Do you wish to increase your bid?"

"Thirty-five hundred."

"Thirty-six hundred."

"Miss Mapp?"

"Take it."

"Very good. Sold! Ladies and gentlemen, we have a winner. Mister Addelson has purchased the contents of Unit 219 for the sum of three thousand six hundred dollars."

"Alright, folks, there you have it. Christa came in with the surprise offer to buy her competitors out and it partially worked. She's walking over now. Here we go. Christa! Wow. That was amazing. We've never seen anything like that before. You said you had some tricks up your sleeve, but that was truly a first. What do you think?"

"Man, I really thought they would take it. Did you at least think about it, Clyde?"

"Hell yes! Walk out of here with guaranteed money? That was smart. Really, really smart. I'm using that in the future!"

"Aw man, don't steal my move!"

"I'm totally stealing your move!"

"Excellent game, Christa. We'll see you in a couple of weeks in Wichita. Thank you very much!"

"Thanks, Tommy. Good luck, Clyde!"

"Thanks."

"Okay! Let's talk to the winner since he's right here. How are you feeling, Clyde?"

"Feeling pretty good. That went a little higher than I wanted it, but I thought, if she's willing to buy us out, she must be feeling pretty strong about what's inside. That pushed me out a little further than I wanted, but I have a great feeling about this one too, so I'm pretty happy, Tommy."

"Alright, folks. We're going to take a second while our competitors sign off on the arrangements here, and while we wait, let's take a look at the key to the unit. This one is very unique, so we thought we'd take a moment to examine it here with you. As you can see, it looks like one of those old-fashioned skeleton keys from days gone by. It's really heavy. Heavier than you'd think. Look at these fine etchings or carvings on the side. It's all very intricate and detailed, certainly like nothing we've seen on our show. It almost looks like Latin or Italian or something inscribed on it on the side there. My producer even said we may want to call in the Antiques Caravan people to take a look at it. It's a rare thing when the keys themselves are potentially valuable. Alright! It looks like the auctioneer has signed off and ratified the purchase. Mister auctioneer?"

"It's settled. The agreement has been authorized and accepted by all parties and they have confirmed with their signatures. We have reached a successful conclusion and we are ready to proceed."

"There you have it, folks. Signed, sealed, and delivered. Clyde? Are you ready to take a look at what's inside Unit 219?"

"I sure am, Tommy! I sure am!"

"We are too. We'll be back after this break for the big reveal! Stay tuned!"

"Cut. We're clear."

"Let's head on up to the locker. Jesus, Clyde! What if she got you? Thirty-six for this crappy little place out in the middle of nowhere? I think you got taken to the cleaners, my friend."

"Eh…Maybe. Thing is, units out here, who knows what could be inside? Back on Pickers, we bought a unit in rural Georgia. Had about ten grand in stuff from World War Two in it. Phil Sebring bought a locker in Yonkers with an authentic Civil War musket in it. Ended up selling it to a collector for about seventy-five hundred. Even that pinball machine I got a couple of weeks ago ended up selling for almost fifteen thousand. Who knows what's in this one?

I'm waiting for the holy grail: first edition Superman number one. It looks like there's a box inside that might have books or comics in it."

"Holy crap. That would be awesome."

"Hell yes, it would!"

"Mister Murdock? We're all set at the unit. Are you ready to resume?"

"Sure, Charlie. Has the B-roll been sent over to graphics?

"Yes, sir. They'll cut that in after the commercials so the audience can see the sneak preview when we're done with the reveal. We can do the voiceover when we get back to the hotel tonight."

"Awesome. Just count me down whenever. You ready Clyde?"

"Yup."

"Cameras ready? Sound? Everyone? Okay, good. Ok Tommy, in five, four, three…"

"Thanks for staying with us! We're standing outside Unit 219 and Clyde Addelson is about to find out if not taking the guaranteed money was a brilliant maneuver, or if he was just plain outmaneuvered. Are you nervous, Clyde?"

"Nah. More like excited to see what's inside."

"We are too! So, let's go ahead and take a look. Anytime you're ready, Clyde! Let's see what treasures are inside after you won today's Storage Unit Battle!"

"You got it? What's wrong?"

"Key seems to be stuck."

"Stuck? Didn't we just have the thing open an hour ago? Do you want me to get—"

"Oh, got it? Okay, we'll edit that. You guys ready? Okay, go ahead, Clyde."

"Alright, ladies and gentlemen, as you can see, Clyde has the locker all the way open now and he's beginning to go in."

"What is that?"

"Terry, get your light on that. Where's the flashli—"

"Oh my god, what is that? Clyde! Are you—? Is that blood?"

"Oh, holy shit!"

"Get out. Run! *Run!*"

"What's go—?"

"Run, Charlie! Run!"

"Oh my god!"

"Let's get the fu—"

…

…

illustrated by
Sumit Roy

(Unit 222)

IQ
by Leon J. Cooper

Excerpt from recovered Audio File 890-4589652-3/2548WB

Subjects:

Peters, Benjamin—Case file 890-23A-WB
O'Donnell, Andrew—Case file 890-161C-WB
Recorded: 2078/08/08—13:53 PM

Begin Playback:

"The exams are coming up soon, Ben—is Billy ready?"

"Yeah, he is, I think. I'm afraid he might not test well, though."

"My little Riley tells me he's really smart."

"Yep—that's what I'm concerned about."

"She's got a little crush on him. It's kinda cute. Listen, there's a way, if you're interested—I know a guy."

"What's that going to cost us?"

"You know what it'll cost, but at least—"

"I know, I know. How long do we have to think about it?"

"Today's Friday, which gives you the weekend to run it by Jodi. I need your answer by Monday morning, otherwise, I have to offer Janet Calloway the opportunity—her kid shows promise as well."

"Alright, then. Thanks, Drew."
"No problem. And good luck."

End Playback.

References:

O'Donnell, Riley—Case file 890-161D-WB
Peters, Jodi—Case file 890-22A-WB
Calloway, Janet—Case file 890-1A-RZ

"Mom, what does this word mean?" Billy came out of his room, holding his reading tablet with both hands in front of him. Jodi looked carefully to examine the word that he indicated on the screen.

"Beò? I don't know. But what should we do when we come across a word we don't know?"

"L.I.U.I.T.D.," came the boy's confident reply."

"Right. Look it up in the dictionary."

Billy happily flipped over to the languages portion of the tablet as he walked back to his room. Jodi watched his retreat and turned her attention to Ben when their son was out of earshot.

"Do you think this is for real, Ben?" Jodi Peters, Ben's wife, bit her nails as she asked the question. She had bitten all of her nails down to the nubs at this point. Her eyes, beautiful and soulful and brown, displayed every bit of her anxiety as they pierced into his green ones.

Ben knew the truth, of course; this was not necessarily on the up-and-up, but it was the only real choice, or the best of all choices, bad or good, that they could make. "Yes, honey. I've known Drew since we were kids. Our little crew used to run around and do everything together. It's the best choice that we can make for Billy."

She didn't believe him. Her inner lie detector had its sensitivity running on full, and there was something in his voice that indicated he was not telling the truth, the whole truth and nothing but the truth—rather, he was hiding something, maybe something big, maybe something small, but something nonetheless, and that raised her hackles.

She didn't know that she was doing it, but she was standing with her arms crossed, rocking back and forth, using her right foot as a pivot.

It's how Ben knew that she thought he was lying, or at least hiding something.

He looked over at the oven, which was cooking dinner from the ingredients that had arrived that morning. It was an advantage of modern technology and their status; the Ministry of Health & Welfare, the State entity for which Jodi worked, delivered a bag full of food each morning to their living quarters with the ingredients for a nutritious breakfast, lunch, dinner, and snacks, based on the residents' metrics and dietary needs. Then they placed the ingredients in containers, selected meal options, and the stoves and/or burners cooked the meals automatically, applying seasonings and condiments to their own pre-programmed settings.

He didn't really need to check on the meal as the oven produced a sound, indicating that dinner would be ready in less than five minutes—another beauty of the current tech was that you weren't ever going to burn a meal.

He turned his attention back to his wife, who was now embodying full-blown anxiety—not a trait he would have ever expected to see in his queen of a woman, and certainly not a trait that he would normally have expected from an employee of the Ministry of Health & Welfare. Most people who worked for that organization were the calmest and coolest people whom you could know; they were oh so cheerful that you just wanted to strangle them in their sleep.

But year after year, and day by confounding, frustration-filled day, he had watched, in silence, the transmutation of his wife from Warrior Princess to Worrier Princess. He glanced at the medicine sitting in view of the communications console. He couldn't help but wonder if there was something regarding her body chemistry that couldn't be regulated by diet alone. There weren't that many people in society anymore, but the Ministry of Pharmacology usually had solutions for people for whom simple nutritional tweaks didn't work. Better living through chemistry was still a thing, and it was still a big thing; the engine of society chugged along, and it chugged along best when everyone was productive and happy. All of the metrics provided by the Ministry of Statistics bore that out. The drugs always came prepackaged, in discreet shipping materials, tailor-made and precisely prescribed based on reported symptoms and cataloged physiology, but she had never leaned into the mindset of artificial happiness and stopped using the patches regularly long ago. She said she wanted Billy to be raised by a mother and not a zombie. Nearly every day she surreptitiously destroyed the medicine and used her position to avoid the periodic tests that required full blood and toxicology screenings. He couldn't help feeling a little guilty that he hadn't tried harder to convince her to use them as instructed. If she were ever caught, the State would step in and move to correct her condition, first by gentle reminder, then followed by less and less gentle methods.

She pressed on. "Are you sure about that? I mean, Billy is so…"

He cut her off, knowing what she was going to say, knowing why she worried so damn much. "I know, I know. I'm not gonna lie, this is risky as hell, but it's our only real option. The boy loves books and not TV—he's not normal.

"And you know more than anybody else that we shouldn't be talking about this openly," she murmured with a slight tilt of her head towards one of the many hidden cameras they'd discovered.

He pulled her close and embraced her. Partly because she always smelled fantastic to him, but he also wanted to give them a little additional privacy.

She whispered in his ear. "How long do we have to decide?"

"A day and a half. Drew needs to know by Monday morning, otherwise, he has to move on."

"Okay, then."

The oven's bell sounded, indicating that dinner was finished, and they could remove everything and start eating in another three minutes.

"Billy! Dinner's ready!"

"Okay, Mom!"

Billy, the light of their life, set his bookmark, paused his screen, remembered to mostly wash his hands, and made his way to the dining room.

They ate their prepackaged dinner together, like they always did, after which Billy went to his room to read, and Ben and Jodi watched television until 9:30 pm, at which point the thirty-minute warning came via dimmed lights. They retired to their bedroom sleep chambers, and after their sleep pods provided them a massage, chiropractic adjustment, and second massage, an odorless, colorless gas put them out quickly—no such thing as insomnia in the New Society. The Ministry of Applied Sciences and Statistics showed that citizens who slept well and whose bodies were kept in optimal shape were much more productive. As full citizens and professionals, they were provided with an apartment in one of the most coveted parts of the city, designed for comfort and ease. During the night, cleaning would come from disinfectant spray from the ceiling, and a silent room-cleaning robot. Come the next morning, the Peters family would wake up to a clean, fresh-smelling 1,000-square-foot apartment, provided by the State; for a family of three, this was considered more than ample space.

They were the fortunate ones; rank certainly had its privileges.

2078/08/12

The box arrived early Tuesday morning, wrapped in tissue paper and a cardboard box, at Ben's office at the Ministry of Education, compliments of Drew's office at the Ministry of Science & Technology.

He wondered how the package made it to his desk in the first place. Drew O'Donnell must have had some serious pull, even more than he claimed. Somehow he was able to get a priority code for the package, or it was delivered in a manner where it got past the advanced screening and security scanners. He'd seen the holo-videos about people who got overambitious and questioned packages with that type of code being relocated and redesignated as noncitizens that very same day. The threat of noncitizenship was an incredible stick in a world where the supply of carrots was exhausted.

He fought with himself over opening it then and there or waiting until the end of his day to bring it home and unwrap it in front of Jodi. He had been up to his elbows in lesson plans. Despite his love for his job and his desire to do good work, he knew his position was well on its way to becoming obsolete. The New Society wanted its citizens to be smart enough to operate the machines, but not enough to create or design new ones. The machine intelligence takeover had taken decades, but statistics proved that everything functioned far more efficiently with AI making the major decisions. People were distracted to their liking, well fed, healthier, and, though at first loath to admit it, happier. Once happier and comfortable, the citizenry cared less about who or what was in charge and did their George Jetson–like jobs just so they could get to their leisure time. Soon enough, the AI algorithms would set the curricula and metrics, guiding the children online, establishing benchmarks with the goal of full citizenship after the requisite two years' military service.

He also wondered if maybe Drew was a spy, and this was a test; that was always a possibility. The fact that they'd known each other since they were teenagers really didn't mean that much; State spooks were so well trained that you didn't know, even when the State knocked on your door. The State had long since mastered the art of never revealing information on its assets during their investigations of crimes, regardless of scale, reusing them as needed, or "retiring" them when necessary.

He decided, after much pondering, to wait until he got it home to open it with Jodi watching. He had made up his mind some time ago; it was now a matter of getting his wife on board. She was becoming more mercurial of late, increasingly less trusting of anyone, even him, making their situation more tenuous.

At the end of his workday, his thighs were chafed and sore from rubbing them for more than half an hour with worry. Finally, he scooped up the package and prayed that he'd make it out of the building with it; Drew had assured him that it would be okay, but he had seen what happened to people trying to leave the building with contraband of any kind, as small as a pen, as large as a computer.

All he had to do was play it cool; that was why Drew sent the package to him, rather than to Jodi. He sent it to Ben at the office, as Ben told him that sending it to their home would mean that the concierge, also known as the nosiest man in the building, would ask a bunch of questions and gossip with anyone who would listen, and even with those who would not. They were both certain he was a State informer.

"What's in the box?" Jodi's delivery was calmer than usual, evidence to her husband that she was having one of her better days—a great relief to him. He hoped that with the stress of Billy's examination behind them, her good days would come more frequently.

He rubbed his neck, considering how all this would play out. "Our best chance for Billy."

"So, in other words, you decided for us?"

"We had to let Drew know yesterday, so yeah, I decided for us."

"I told you, I needed more time."

"Time is a luxury that we don't have, Baby Girl. The boy's test is on Saturday, so we needed to take care of this immediately."

"I know, honey, I'm just so damn scared."

"Me too, Babe".

His unspoken thoughts reigned in his mind as they studied the package from Drew. Our "best chance for Billy" is likely our only chance for Billy. Why did we have him in the first place? Because the New Society needed more children, and because they rewarded couples for becoming families with better jobs, better accommodations, more credits, more travel options, etc. And because Billy turned out to be an absolute gem of a kid. I hope to the God-I-No-Longer-Believe-In that this works. "Let's open this and see what we're dealing with."

He unwrapped the outer box and cut through the tape, using his thumbnail as an opener. Inside was a wooden box. When he opened it, there was an old key inside, with a couple of pieces of paper. One contained an address, and the name of a facility called "Auntie's Attic."

The other was a handwritten note:

Ben & Jodi,
  You need to do this no later than Friday.

Go to this facility, find Unit 222, and you'll find what you need to help Billy in there. I couldn't put it in this box because you never know who's watching—well, you do, but you don't know who else is watching.
Best of luck to Little Billy,
—Drew

Ben's mind rapidly oscillated between suspecting he was being set up and trusting his childhood friend with his son's life. *Let's hope that Drew took care of things like he said he would, and that I'm not walking into a trap. No real choice, is there? Dammit.*

2078/08/14

Ben hopped on public transport, his destination was a town named Crossroads in what used to be Virginia, which was still in the habitable part of the New Society.

He disembarked when the bus got as close to the facility as it would get, and he walked the rest of the way, guided by the box's GPS.

He came upon what appeared to him to be a whole lot of nothing: a large, nondescript, empty field, reminiscent of the fields on which kids and grownups alike would have played baseball twenty years ago, which ramped up his anxiety to a level that his wife experienced on a regular basis.

It was one of those times when he found himself feeling truly empathetic for Jodi; he couldn't imagine feeling like this all day every day.

When he came close enough, a proximity sensor activated, and he was startled by a door appearing. He wondered for a fraction of a second why he hadn't seen this facility from the street, before he realized that this must be one of the Ministry of Science & Technology's "cloaked" facilities. They were rumored to be all over the country, at least near the few remaining populated areas, invisible to satellites, radar—you name it. Under normal circumstances, he'd have hesitated or looked around in squirrelly suspicion like the shady people in propaganda holo-videos, but that was something for which he did not have time, and he knew better than to do that. Without the slightest hint of reservation, he opened the box, pulled out the key, an old school version, seemingly made of bone and coated in some kind of grease, inserted it in the lock, and rotated it one hundred and eighty degrees clockwise.

He heard simultaneously a metallic *click* and a series of beeps, after which the door opened.

The facility looked like one of those from his grandfather's time: cement walls and floors, the unmistakable smell of Curtis Brand™ Cleaners in the hallways, corrugated metal doors (painted orange in this instance), and old-school fluorescent lighting on the kind of timers that you had to rotate in a clockwise manner—mechanisms from a better, vanished time.

Following Drew's directions, he walked briskly and ended up in front of Unit 222 in just around two minutes. With rapidly increasing apprehension, he inserted the same odd key into the lock. He heard the exact same click and series of beeps as when he opened the outer door. He surmised that it was someone's way of knowing who was accessing the unit; someone, sitting in a room somewhere, was probably recording this. It was a matter of not making any movements that might be deemed suspicious; as long as he looked like he knew where he was going and what he was doing, he was more likely not to attract attention and be flagged for questionable activity.

The room was five feet long by five feet wide; it might as well have been two by two, as there was only one object in it:

Another small box, about the size one would put a ring in, sat atop a small table, which had once been a podium.

He opened the box, and there was a single white pill, and another small note inside, which read:

Give this to Billy the morning of his test.
Make sure that he takes it.
Tell no one.

He locked up behind him, exited the facility, and prayed all the way home that no one from the Ministry of Safety & Security was paying too much attention to his activities, at least until Billy's fate was determined.

"How are we going to give it to him?"

Jodi had bitten her nails, each and every one of them, all the way down to bare skin, drawing blood from some of them. Thirty years ago, she'd have chain-smoked her behind off, but cigarettes had long been banned by the Ministry of Health & Welfare.

Ben regarded his once-gorgeous wife with great sadness; despite her best attempts, she was slowly but surely turning into someone bedraggled and unrecognizable to him. He wondered how long it would be before the anxiety and worry fully took over. He responded with a surety that he did not truly possess, the kind that he affected when he went to the unit, hoping she would be too locked in her own head to notice. "The best two options are to either A, slip it into his breakfast, or B, grind it up and mix it into his juice. I'd go with the juice option, since we know he'll finish it."

"What's this pill going to do to him?"

He massaged the back of his neck. "It's going to do two things: first, it's going to counteract the effects of the drug that they give him to be compliant. He'll be relaxed, of course, as expected, but it won't register in their screening, or so Drew tells me. Second, it will, for about a week, in case they want to randomly retest him, change his IQ enough for him to fall back into the acceptable parameters."

She didn't trust her full voice, so she whispered. "Do we really have to do this? What if he just naturally is in—"

"Range? Are you kidding me? You know the boy's IQ is gonna be off the charts. There's no way on Earth that they're going to let him live with the kind of score that he's likely to produce. This is the only chance for him, Jodi, and you know it."

She sat at the edge of the bed, rocking back and forth, eyes darting to and fro in panic, arms folded, biting her nails, tears streaming without relent down her cheeks. She knew that their son was too intelligent; no matter what she and her husband tried, they just couldn't get his head out of those damn books, they just couldn't get him to be a normal kid, they just couldn't keep him *safe*.

She brought her face up to Ben's, resigned to their collective fate. "Are we ever going to see him again?"

He sat down with her, enfolding her tightly in his arms like a Venus flytrap. When he trusted himself enough to use his voice, he drew a deep breath. "Probably not. He's either going to score too high, at which point they'll inject him, and he'll go quickly, or he's going to score just high enough to live, at which point the Ministry of Science and Technology will take him away. Either way, this will be his last morning with us."

Jodi didn't want to wake their son up with her crying, but she couldn't stop herself, clutching her husband's arm with both hands and sobbing uncontrollably. Knowing that they were being watched, Ben forced her head into his chest, muffling the sound, hiding her tears and worry as they hoped that their sweet, beautiful, and gifted boy could get a little more sleep before everything changed for good.

2078/08/16

"Billy! Breakfast's ready!"

In their greatest acting performances ever, Ben and Jodi went on as if nothing in their lives would be the slightest bit different after the examination.

They ate breakfast, their wonderfully wonderful son put on his uniform, and two members from the Ministry of Education picked him up promptly at 8:35 a.m.

2103/05/09

Twenty-five years later, Ben Peters found himself strapped to a gurney at his local hospital being administered an injection, but almost immediately afterward, the workers had all but forgotten him. Only the robots in the facility kept on working. The human hospital staff were instead transfixed by breaking news and images of brutal and disturbing footage on every screen in sight and likely on every mobile device across the New Society. Newscasters had interrupted every broadcast as it became known that a coup against the

State was underway. Live images of explosions, open warfare in the streets, and pillars of smoke rising from fires all over the Capitol complex were being shown from every available angle and perspective.

One by one, the insurrectionists were being identified by AI extrapolation of facial and biometric information compared against the database of young geniuses that had been executed after testing too high on the examination. Their names and faces were being shown against the backdrop of disturbing and violent combat footage. New names and pictures popped up rapidly on a split screen, showing captured video images of them now versus the photographs taken the day of their examination.

But the young geniuses had not been executed as the State had claimed. Thousands of them had been hidden away, one by one, for decades, by Drew O'Donnell and the Ministry of Science & Technology. They were now in open defiance of the State, they were well organized, and they had a plan to overthrow the New Society, which they were executing flawlessly.

Ben lay there, helplessly watching the robots and listening to the hospital workers cursing and yelling when State police were gunned down, and cheering loudly when any insurrectionist was killed. Unable to see the monitors from his perspective, he glanced around and realized this was the same hospital that Jodi had been taken to twenty-five years ago when she managed to commit suicide in open defiance of the dictates of the State. She had never gotten over them taking Billy away, and the resentment and anger in her grew to a point of no return. The New Society was cruel and inhuman to those who publicly humiliated them, and they spent hours mutilating her corpse trying various surgeries and procedures to resuscitate and revive her, just so that they could put her on trial and execute her their way, but mercifully for her, they were unsuccessful. Since then, the State had found itself frustrated by a lack of ways to punish him for her act; his wife was dead, and he was, by his own right, an exemplary citizen. Multiple investigations had not turned up any useful evidence, so any attempt to demote him to a low-status position would have done more harm than good to the State's reputation and public image.

But today, he was finally "aging out" of society, so the petty and vindictive State was taking advantage of its mandates for older citizens, and finally getting rid of him. The public statement read: *"As a reward for a lifetime of loyal service to the State, he will be administered a painless lethal injection and honorably cremated immediately afterward."* What had not been shared publicly was that the injection was actually a carefully curated amount of sulfuric acid and he was going to experience an unmentionable amount of pain before they rolled him to the incinerator. It had taken them a long time, but he was going to pay for Jodi's suicide after all. He could feel the liquid beginning to burn him from the inside out as he imagined Jodi and Billy laughing and eating food around their table like they had done hundreds of times before.

Yelling at the monitors and lashing out, an angry staffer shoved Ben's gurney violently, slamming him against the wall and breaking his reverie. After he settled and stopped, he could see one of the monitors from this new vantage point. On the screen were several armed individuals of the rebellion, executing State officials on the wide white steps of the Capitol. Other staffers looked on in shock and horror. Ben lay there transfixed as the face of his lifelong friend Drew O'Donnell showed on the screen. The camera was too far to pick up any distinguishable audio, but Drew was clearly mouthing something over and over along with several others.

A sudden explosion shook the camera and the feed went black for a moment before switching to another angle, further back from the scene. An AI-controlled drone strike had struck the Capitol steps, killing the insurrectionists, the aftermath fiery and bloody. The staffers cheered. Ben's eyes filled with tears as he struggled against the growing agony in his veins and from watching his friend perish.

A robot took control of his gurney and wheeled him towards the conveyor belt. Unceremoniously it shoved him onto the moving treadmill and continued its programming with others in the hospital corridors. He could still see a reflection of the monitors in the thick glass doors to the cremation chamber and he watched as the building to the Ministry of Control came on the screen. The building erupted in flames as a huge explosion tore it apart, leaving nothing but smoking ruins. The robots' displays went dark as they ceased to function, and the staffers all slumped in defeat and began to sullenly disperse.

In his last few seconds of consciousness, he bore witness to the final, violent end of the AI regime and the birth of a new human one, but it was the figure holding his rifle victoriously overhead, directing the rebellion that brought Ben the most pride and gratification to these last moments of his life. Emerging from the smoke was a man in his mid-30s, whom Ben recognized as his son, but whom the newscasters were calling by the name of William Beò, was out leading the revolution.

Tears of pride streamed down his face as the conveyor belt mindlessly delivered him into the incinerator. He hoped to the God-That-No-One-Believed-In that this would be worth it.

The thing he heard as he last drew breath and drifted off into universal consciousness as a citizen was a chant, first fairly loud, but growing fainter as pain and death increased their grip on him:

"Here comes William Beò."

THREE MISSING IN
PRANK GONE AWRY

July 16th, 1973
By Franklin Rush

Crossroads, Virginia. Three students from Crossroads High School have gone missing after a practical joke apparently went wrong at a nearby self-storage facility. Deborah Hastings, 17, Frederick Alcorn, 16, and Robert Massey, 17, have not been seen since late Friday night after they attempted to lock their classmate, Jonathan LeQue, 17, into a ground floor unit at Auntie's Attic. LeQue told police and reporters that the other students had wanted to play a joke on the teen by locking him into a unit, then pretend they had left the facility before returning to release him a short time later. They pushed LeQue into the unit and closed the door behind him, then used a padlock they brought with them to lock him in. But the pranksters never returned and have not been seen or heard from since. LeQue spent almost seven hours in the unit before being released by a staff member, who wished to remain anonymous. When questioned, LeQue explained what had happened, even admitting he initially found the prank amusing but had no knowledge of the whereabouts of the other three teens. Searches of the pranksters' homes have revealed that none of the three returned home that evening. If you have any information regarding the missing teens, please contact the Sheriff's Department or the Crossroads Weekly Chronicle.

From the Collection of David Disspain
Source: The Crossroads Weekly Chronicle

illustrated by
Alice Brereton

FAIR EXCHANGE

(Unit 888)

by Sherin Nicole

Every morning she woke up on a wet pillow. Wetter than tears and saltier too. This morning a silver ring lay on the pillow beside her. Close enough to kiss her nose. So shiny she could see it, even in the dark minutes before dawn.

"Rejected again." Rolling onto her back, she whispered, "Breathe, Amaya."

Her bedroom smelled of brine and sea breeze. The scent brought back memories, the haze of sleep faded, and a familiar ache returned. Everything, except her body, hurt.

When Amaya reached for the ring, her hand shook. Trembling fingers skimmed across the soaked pillow, but she refused to look directly at it. She kept her gaze on the ceiling while she lay on her back.

A brown water stain, in the shape of a Caribbean Lily, continued to bloom on the white paint overhead. Each morning, since the day her brother was taken, a new claw-shaped petal seemed to reach down. Amaya imagined the stain would eventually lift off the ceiling and swallow her during the first rays of sunlight.

She sometimes wished it would.

Her disappearance wouldn't make the news the way her brother's had, but it would be sweet clickbait: *Woman Swallowed In Bed by Eldritch Horror*.

Something slimy slid across her palm and she opened her hand to stare at the ring. A tendril of deep green seaweed had wrapped itself around the silver.

Amaya sat up. The clash of slick green and shiny gray, the stink of seaweed, and the sting of rejection sent bile rushing to the back of her throat. She threw the ring, the same as she'd done with every other rejected item before it. It landed in the corner of the room, clanging against the heap of pretty things that had collected there: the black pearl Amaya's granny discovered as a young diver; a rosary Amaya had crafted from the broken antiques she and her friend Bernardo thrifted; the sapphire bracelet Daddy had slid onto Mama's wrist in lieu of a ring. Precious things, huddled together, crusted with salt, covered in dried seaweed, and refused by the lady who lived beneath the waves.

Her brother's first camera was the only thing missing.

Something different glinted against the pile of rejected objects this morning. It was dull. Not bright but disturbingly pale. And the energy it emitted was wrong. Dead wrong. The key did not belong to her or any member of her family. And she knew, instinctively, she did not want to go to the places it led.

Amaya picked up the key by its neon-colored keychain, using only two fingers to minimize contact. She rushed to her bedroom window, opened it, and threw the key out—the way she used to skim stones on the waves at the wharf. The damn thing bounced on air, dodging raindrops, and disappeared. Without falling.

Breathless, Amaya leaned against the wall beside the window and tried not to chip the paint with her nails. "I want you back, it can't be any other way," she sang quietly to her brother, but the lyrics faded.

One foot at a time, she walked away from the window. The damp in the air warned her she'd be trapped inside her apartment today, but the rivulets of gray rain, forming mosaics on the glass pane, confirmed it. Amaya didn't deal with the rain. She had enough problems with wet things she couldn't control. She'd lost her job because of her aversion to water, but she'd also kept her sanity. Some small part of it at least. Although her family—the ones she called the aunties and the cousins and the silent uncles—would disagree. They'd convinced themselves she'd gone mad, *yeah*? To absolve themselves of any responsibility to help rescue her brother.

Forget that. The bed needed to be stripped of the seawater-soaked pillows. Amaya did this on autopilot, part of a morning ritual that kept her from thinking. Shake the pillows out of their covers, put the inserts by the window to dry, roll the top and flat sheets off the bed, then wash it all together, again, to keep the colors uniform. She stuffed the entire mass into the washer, already thinking about what needed to be done next. Her hair. Because the drying salt would damage her thick fluffy curls. She managed to bathe in as little water as possible. She'd become good at it and on some days she used cotton balls soaked in peroxide. The habit had hardened her skin over time, but she thought of it as a kind of armor. That made her feel better, although Amaya knew she wouldn't win her battle against the waters. *How could she fight the first-mother?* She couldn't. She only hoped to make a trade.

"Give me my brother back," was more than a whisper, this time.

The rain meant she couldn't go down to the docks, but since her granny, Yaya, and her granddad, Poppa, had worked themselves into wealth and given their descendants the freedom to choose the shape of their days. At some point, Amaya would choose a new precious thing to sacrifice to the sea. For now, she'd go downstairs and hang out with Bernardo.

To get to Bernardo's bodega, which wasn't a bodega because he came from Brazil, Amaya used a back staircase just outside her flat. She owned the building. Bernardo owned the corner store and paid her rent to keep it there. He'd told her many times to call his shop Mercadinho Maresias or a mercadinho, but she kept forgetting and he kept forgiving her for it. He said her *Americanness* turned every other culture into a buffet of unrecognizable slop.

The insult made her giggle, mostly because her fellow Americans proved Bernardo right regularly. And the truth, no matter how cold, gave Amaya comfort. So, she spent more time with Bernardo than she did with the aunties, and the cousins, and the silent uncles. Almost as much time as she'd spent with her brother. Aamir.

She shared an unbreakable truth with Aamir too. Being twins, even fraternal ones, had made it hard for Aamir to lie to Amaya. She saw the lies swirling around his head, swarming and stinging.

As twins, they had been gifted with the ability to look past the fabric of the human world and into the realm of the Loa, the Orisha, and the jumbies. Yaya called it the Hidden World, and Mama said they'd been born with veils, thin membranes of the amniotic sac called cauls, over their faces. That's what gave them *the sight*. Whether truth or family lore, the twins couldn't tell.

Aamir had said Amaya's lies formed storm clouds over her head. He'd imagined self-made lightning bolts striking her down for talking shit. He'd laugh so hard whenever he said it, so hard she'd roll her eyes and leave whatever room they'd been in. Now he'd gotten the ultimate payback. Aamir had left the room, in truth.

Those thoughts didn't help, so Amaya shrugged into a sweater with jeans tight enough to be skin and jogged down the stairs.

She busted through Bernardo's door so fast he jumped. His customer, Mrs. Sandoval, clutched her pearls and scolded Amaya in Spanish. Something about ghosts walking in shadows. Amaya didn't know for sure, but her presence always seemed to whisper of spirits and the dead to the elders. Nothing new there. Nothing wrong there either. Mrs. Sandoval would die soon, asleep in a chair with a tiny dog named Frodo on her lap.

"Oy," Bernardo said in greeting. "Todo bien?"

Amaya shook her head. No. It wasn't all good. Another day, another rejection. But Bernardo seemed to guess already.

After Mrs. Sandoval left, Bernardo tapped the wooden countertop he stood behind, pushing a massive jar of dill pickles to the side. A collage of his favorite places in Brazil covered the counter from edge to end. It had taken two days to compile the photos and pour epoxy over their work to preserve it. It'd been worth it. The collage gave the mercadinho a story. Amaya hopped up onto the counter and sat on top of an image of sand and sea.

"They ready yet?" she asked, breathing in the scent of cheese and tapioca flour, knowing the answer before he replied.

"The meatballs or the pão de queijo?" he asked. The dark sepia of his skin made Bernardo's smile more brilliant.

"Gimme both." Amaya held out her hands, palms up and ready.

"No." He laughed, turning his back. Ruining his refusal by peeking over a shoulder with a brilliant flash of smile. "You're going to make a mess out of it."

"I won't."

"You eat them wrong." Another quick glance over his shoulder.

"I maximize the deliciousness." She believed that.

Eventually, he relented. Not because she held any sway over him, she didn't believe that, but because the meatballs were going to burn and his customers would rage if they didn't get their fix.

Bernardo used a pair of tongs to lay the meatballs on a tray underneath the heat lamp in their display case. It reminded Amaya of the Jamaican shop two streets over and the way they stacked hot patties and coco bread. There the colors were golden: turmeric crust with spicy beef or chicken tucked inside; buttery bread steaming. Here ground lamb mixed with onion, garlic, fresh cilantro, and cinnamon glistened with fat and smelled amazing.

Next, Bernardo brought out his pão de queijo—crusty, fluffy Brazilian cheese biscuits that melted on your tongue. Amaya swung her legs over the counter, grabbed one of each treat, popped the top off a pão de queijo, jammed a meatball inside, and shoved the goodness into her mouth.

She only stopped moaning when the volume on Bernardo's silence turned up to eleven. Wiping her lips, Amaya held her hands up in apology.

Her friend refused her with a stare. "Those aren't cheeseburgers."

"Not even Brazilian ones?" she mumbled around a mouthful of food.

He wanted to laugh. Amaya could see it in the tremors around his firmly pressed lips. The time she spent with Bernardo gave her a break from the memories that weighted the rest of her life. But the laughter she and Bernardo shared, just because they could, inevitably conjured up the phantom of her brother.

Amaya and Aamir had teased each other the same way she and Bernardo did now. And the *used to* of it, the past tense of it all…it hurt.

She jerked her gaze away from Bernardo's, shredding the moment, and regretted it. Bernardo held a singular place in her life. No visions of his death had ever come to her, even though Amaya knew how everyone else would die. Which is how she knew her brother still existed, somewhere.

The absence of death in her relationship with Bernardo usually gave Amaya peace. She guessed or maybe hoped she would *give-up-the-ghost* first and thus be there to welcome him into the spirit world. Or perhaps he would live forever. Amaya usually liked that idea, but today Bernardo's potential immortality made her miss her brother more.

She spun her body. Scanning the shop for a distraction, Amaya jumped down on the opposite side of the counter from her friend. Forming a barrier between them.

Bernardo came to the rescue, again. Then again, probably not. "This came for you this morning," he said, sliding a clamshell-shaped box across the counter to her. The box had the deep luster of a black pearl.

It intrigued Amaya. She didn't like it. "Came from who?"

Bernardo seemed resigned when he answered, "The rain blew it in."

Amaya cursed a long steady snap of expletives that crackled with nervous energy.

Rather than deal with the box she asked, "Who is this?" Her fingers glided over the collage within the countertop, drifting away from the cold luster of the clamshell. Her gaze found the image of a woman with dark skin, wild dreadlocks, and a crown of shells cascading into a veil over her face.

Bernardo went back to laying out the cheese biscuits. "She is the goddess Iemanja, the one who knows." Looking as savvy as the goddess, he tossed the tray aside. That done, he laid his palms flat on either side of the Iemanja's image and leaned forward to stare at Amaya.

She'd amused him. She saw it in his smile at her attempt to turn the counter into a barrier that could never stand between them.

If Amaya wanted a distraction, she'd made the wrong choice. The same as with the offerings she took down to the docks on days when it didn't rain. Her choices never brought her what she wanted.

She tried again. "The goddess Iemanja," she repeated.

"Yes, Iemanja is in every molecule of the waters from my home."

"Is she the one who keeps rejecting me?"

"No, my goddess belongs to Brazil," Bernardo said as he turned to ring up a customer. "She is the one who sees, like you see, but for her, it is the future, the path that must be walked. In Brazil, Iemanja is the ocean and the rain that returns to it."

The words were love and devotion in a tangle. Amaya snarled. Bernardo stood silent. His jaw worked while he considered the sudden tightness in her shoulders and her jutting cheekbones.

"I'll go with you," he hesitated, "if you want."

Amaya snarled again, unable to keep her anger at bay. The helplessness of her situation burned. And so she flicked the top of the clamshell open and found what she expected: a key. Not bright but disturbingly pale. Cold and slick and wrong to the touch. Hanging from a keychain the color of pickled lime.

Bernardo decided not to speak on the key. Not yet. He had other things to say.

"The goddess you're dealing with, I don't know her name. I call her Rainha do Mar but maybe she is Mami Wata too."

"Mama? No. She's not a mother. Not the kind you mean." Amaya turned her back on him, crossing her arms as protection against her thoughts.

"Then why are you raging like a child?"

No venom. Only a truth he knew she needed. Bernardo liked giving her what she needed.

Decision made, he grabbed his wet yellow raincoat from a rack behind the counter and stomped up the stairs, shedding droplets. He came back down almost immediately, carrying Amaya's tartan plaid cape with its waterproof hood.

Amaya's arms dropped to her sides, allowing Bernardo to help her into the cape. "How do I persuade her?"

Bernardo leaned closer to catch the quiet words. "Ahh my 'Maya, I don't know. When it comes to the gods, you either pray or you beg. You can't keep your dignity."

He looked at the illustration of Iemanja. His heartbeat filled his ears and the pendant beneath his shirt pulsed. Bernardo wrapped his fingers around the vial of ocean water suspended on a golden chain…and he knew what needed to be done because his goddess told him.

He tugged Amaya behind him, headed for the front door of the mercadinho. And because she trusted him, she followed. When they got there, he turned the sign to closed and locked up behind them.

As they trudged through the thick gray rain, Bernardo kept Amaya talking. "You could start with a kiss," he said, "A kiss is a conduit. Or maybe you can entice her with love. Love created your problem—maybe love will be the fix."

Bodies rushing by on the sidewalk buffeted Amaya. Somehow the small violence of the contact made her feel better. "How could I possibly love her?"

The young Christie sisters brushed past Amaya and Bernardo on either side. The sisters would have stopped if they'd recognized Bernardo beneath his hood—their crush on him made them freeze and blush each time he smiled. Amaya glanced back at the look-alike sisters once they'd passed by. The pair walked arm in arm while arguing over who should hold their shared umbrella and cussing each other. The Christie girls wouldn't die for a long time. Amaya knew. When they did go, it would be within a week of each other. It wasn't clear which would go first. Not that it mattered. Neither the oldest one's husband nor the younger one's wife could hold them once the first one moved beyond the veil.

Bernardo and Amaya took a light rail train and two buses to get to Auntie's Attic storage facility. The trip seemed overly long and they spoke very little, but they got there. The sign at the gate read: *Well Kept Storage For Needs Big And Small.*

Now they stared at the corrugated metal garage door that led into Unit 888. They had no idea when they'd started holding hands. They didn't question it either. There was enough happening. The shared warmth felt too good to worry over repercussions.

Bernardo scanned the tightness in Amaya's spine and saw the corner of an image tucked into her back pocket. "What's that?" He reached out and tapped the edge of the photo, careful not to touch her in any way that went too far.

Amaya reached around to the seat of her jeans. She hadn't put the photo in her pocket but she found it there each day. She could change her clothes as many times as she wanted; the photo would still show up inside whatever pocket it chose. If she didn't have pockets, it would tuck itself into her waistband or inside the cups of her bra.

She handed the photo to Bernardo. While he looked at it, Amaya watched a middle-aged man as he smoked a Black & Mild. The man leaned against another storage unit, his wafting smoke undaunted by the rain. Yet the box of slender cigars wouldn't be what killed him. Amaya knew. And she didn't like it here. Auntie's Attic—the name seemed so benign, much like the beautiful yet poisonous lily slowly spreading across her bedroom ceiling.

In the photo, a tall red-brown boy stood on the left. The boy playfully squeezed the shoulder of an older aunty with long gray-white braids twisted up into a bun on top of her head. On the right side, a younger Amaya wrapped them both up—her auburn-brown arms squeezed the boy and the woman into laughter.

"See how different we are, even though we're twins?" Amaya said. "My yaya, she's the one in the middle, she used to call us cinnamon stick and vanilla bean. She'd say, 'Aamir-boy, come here and blow on Yaya's coffee—it needs cinnamon in the mix.' Or, 'Little girl, come stir this cake batter with a finger or two. The vanilla gone, you know.' And then she'd cackle. But she wasn't funny." Amaya laughed, the sound encrusted with salt.

"You and your twin brother look the same to me." Bernardo barely kept himself from tracing his fingertips over the knuckles of her hand. "One heart beating for two bodies. Maybe that's why Aamir couldn't stay."

He thought she'd get angry. Instead, she deflated. "And you want me to love this goddess, this Rainha do Mar? How do I do that, Bernardo?"

And then Amaya surprised him by gently taking the photo from his hands and tearing it into pieces so tiny the rain whisked them away. The dismal confetti drifted on the breeze.

Bernardo wasn't sure how to deal with Amaya's actions, so he didn't.

"I dunno," he whispered. His attention shifted to the key hanging from the pocket of her cape.

Amaya looked down at it too. The wetness at the corner of her eyes wasn't rain, and the tightness at the corner of her lips wasn't anger.

"We've all got our own ways of loving, my 'Maya," Bernardo said as he took the key and opened the storage unit for her.

The corrugated metal door rolled up with a *thunk* and *hiss* repeated several times over. When it had opened fully, the sound of seagulls escaped the darkened unit. And the scent of saltwater rushed forward, an assault that burned their nostrils.

Amaya walked in first, gratefully finding a light switch without too much effort.

"My way is food." Bernardo kept talking as the lights came up. "Others love with gifts. And some do it from so far away it hardly looks like love at all."

The lights flashed on. They'd stepped into a museum. The storage unit couldn't be called anything else. The damp, salt-encrusted space held the story of Aamir. Every object that represented the life he lived had been collected here, neatly cataloged, labeled, and displayed.

Amaya trembled.

What is this?

How does this place exist?

Her hands ran through her curls, her fingers snagging here and there. "Look at this place!" she screamed. "There's nothing I can give Rainha do Mar. There isn't a single memory she'll trade with me because there's nothing left she hasn't already taken."

Amaya leaned against the shelves, resting her head on driftwood, but she quickly recoiled. The photo that appeared in her pockets, the one she'd torn to bits, was now framed on the shelf in front of her with a placard:

> The Younger Years: Aamir, Yaya, Amaya
> The twins (aged 12) enjoy an afternoon with their
> beloved grandmother

The vial of ocean water beneath Bernardo's shirt pulsed again. "There must be something. Something she hasn't already rejected and can't steal. Something only you can give?"

Amaya sagged against the driftwood shelf again—this time the photo felt like the only thing she could hold onto. "You ask like it's easy. These choices. These rejections," she spoke so low Bernardo leaned closer, his body encircling hers. "It's not a matter of choosing this thing or that, Bernardo." Her voice caught on every other word. "The things I offer her aren't precious to me because appraisers smile when they see them." Amaya heaved on a deep exhale. "Do you even understand what treasures truly are for my family?" She pushed away from him. "No. You can't."

"Teach me," he said. "Don't turn your back on me while pain cuts through your spine."

Amaya whirled to face him, her anger electric in the frizz of her hair. Bernardo retreated, a little.

"Yaya's black pearl," she began, pointing to the precious thing that had somehow left its corner in her apartment and appeared inside storage unit 888. "The rosaries we made from broken bits." She pointed again to the part of the unit where the rosaries hung. "The jewel the color of where the sky and the sea kiss...the way my parents used to..." Amaya pulled the bracelet off of a stand on the shelf, knocking its placard to the floor. Another ragged breath escaped. As she fought for calm, Amaya cradled one more precious thing that somehow no longer belonged to her. "In order to give these treasures to Rainha do Mar, I had to cut them out of my flesh. I had to choose which chunks of me to lose. And to bleed without losing myself."

Rain slammed against the metal walls and splattered the salty white concrete floors. And the goddess, who usually spoke to Bernardo through the waters of Brazil, remained silent through the thunder.

"Let's go home, Amaya. Please. Give yourself time to think," Bernardo pleaded. "Rest and the path to Aamir will clear up."

She looked up at him, wisps of hair breaking free from her bun. His words seemed to crush her. He would have taken them back, but exhaustion reflected in her eyes, weariness dulling the usual shine.

"There's no quiet place inside me and no quiet place for me anywhere else," she said. "What is home now? Where can I go to rest?"

One obvious answer came to mind: death.

Bernardo hoped she didn't think of that. But he knew her, and he knew Amaya thought of it often, and he feared she would try it one day.

Maybe today.

And after, he wouldn't make "Brazilian cheeseburgers" anymore.

Amaya picked up the picture frame and her thoughts drifted away from Bernardo. "I have to go."

"Where?" he asked, doubting she meant alone in the rain.

"To end this," she said, before she stumbled out of Unit 888, leaving Bernardo to the storm for the first time.

Aamir had said, "Go ahead to the battlegrounds or wherever. I'll be at the reopening of the docks."

Amaya hadn't even hugged him. Her obsession with history had lured her back onto the metro trains, leaving her brother on the platform. He took his camera down to the harbor but he also texted photos of the angular wooden architecture and the functional art of each dock.

He probably hadn't noticed the raggedy man who'd chosen to make his discontent heard in the rat-a-tat splatter of a semiautomatic weapon.

The terrorist had been perfectly American in that his ancestors emigrated to Oregon in the 1930s. Perfectly American in his pale skin, denim eyes, and dishwater blond hair.

Aamir had fallen off the dock onto a stretch of man-made beach. His camera hit the water. It had a hole in it, so it sank. Aamir landed half in, half out of the tide. Blood and sand, salt and screams. Amaya saw it in the darkness of the nap she took on the train at that same moment.

Her brother was perfectly American in that their ancestors sailed from the Caribbean to Canada in 1805. They emigrated to the US in 1895. Alongside those who came here from Dominica and Barbados, their bloodlines linked to those who'd been here from the first. An Ojibwe great-great-grandmama, a Lakota grandfather—Wakan Tanka knew their names. They were perfectly

Black American in their brown skin, and topaz eyes, and dark coiled hair that turned sandy at the temples in the sun. Aamir might've died that day because of and in spite of his *Americanness*.

But Aamir, like those who'd been forced to pluck cotton and mill sugar, must have made a deal with the gods to survive.

He must've promised the water goddess anything she wanted.

Must've seduced her in his undeniable way. Because Rainha do Mar gave him seawater in place of blood and pulled him into her arms.

Amaya knew—saw it with vision doubled by the twin bond.

Rainha do Mar sent a wave crashing down on the domestic terrorist. He'd swallowed bullets as she crushed him. Later, the patrol found that raggedy man's body wrapped around the pilings below the docks.

They thought they'd recovered Aamir's body too.

When they'd ushered Amaya into the morgue and showed her, she saw nothing but seaweed over a driftwood skeleton. That was the magic Rainha do Mar had spun to make humans see a man. Driftwood and seaweed. Not Aamir's body at all. Amaya was glad until they'd whispered "crazy" behind her back. The aunties said it. The cousins couldn't see past Rainha do Mar's spell.

"She gone mad, you know?" They sucked their teeth.

Yes, mad in the Caribbean sense and crazy in the American one. That's why Amaya's hands still shook. She'd become infused with a steady undercurrent of *mad-ness*. The aunties and the silent uncles loved her but they didn't have the faith to search for a nephew only Amaya knew still lived.

She pushed past her memories, stumbling down the stretch of beach where Aamir made his bargain with Rainha do Mar. Or Mami Wata. Or whichever name the goddess chose.

"What do you want?" she asked the sea. No answer. "Take this." Amaya threw the key into the waters first, glad to be rid of it. But she flung the glossy photo of Aamir and her and Yaya next. The waves leaped to catch both and swallowed them down.

The rain slowed.

"Breathe, Amaya," she told herself.

Maybe this time the trade would be good. The waves might part and carry her brother back to her…Instead, the tide laughed like a bell inside a buoy. Amaya reached into her pocket. Her favorite memory had come back to her, draped in seaweed. But the key didn't return.

She left the beach and climbed up onto the dock. Staring down into the water she hated, she stood at the edge for a countdown from eight. Seven seconds later, she jumped.

No one saw. The waves sucked Amaya into Rainha do Mar's realm too fast. The goddess rose from the fathoms to meet her. Bernardo's goddess, Iemanja, and Rainha do Mar might have been cousins, perhaps sisters, but one could not be mistaken for the other. Rainha do Mar's skin changed from sunlit brown to seafoam green depending on the direction she swam. Her hair could be called green, black, or blue. Or all three, as it danced in the undercurrent and melted back into the water at the tips. The lower half of her body took the form of a sea serpent, although Amaya suspected the goddess could take any form she chose. Beautiful seemed a wasted word for Rainha do Mar— unfathomable and terrible suited the goddess better.

"Amaya." Rainha do Mar's voice rasped in the sound of air escaping from beneath the waves. "Your brother speaks of you often—as often as he makes love to me."

"Take my life," Amaya said, refusing to play the game. "Fair exchange is no robbery."

"Your life?" The goddess seemed perplexed. "What need do I have of your life? I am the seas where leviathan dwells. I am rain. And the waters in which your cells multiplied within the womb. What need do I have for the momentary pulsing of your heart?" Rainha swam a circuit around Amaya; dorsal spines caressed human hips.

Panic, first because Amaya had thought the trade would finally be made. Second, because she was drowning. On lips numb with cold and dark, she gurgled, making one last attempt at a bargain.

"Then I'll give you my love. The love I have for my brother, and for Bernardo. For the aunties. For the cousins and the silent uncles. My love of history, and planetariums, and the color green."

The goddess inclined her head.

Amaya struggled with the sea in her throat. "And I will give you my memories. I'll forget the ones I love and replace them with you. It will be you and not my yaya who says, 'Come here, vanilla bean girl.' It will be you who laughs at me when I try to lie. Not Aamir. You who gives me advice in the mornings and bakes me pão de queijo."

Rainha do Mar floated upward, bringing herself nose to nose with Amaya. The woman tried but could not hold the gaze of the goddess. She looked away. The goddess grabbed her face. Seashell pink talons hooked into brown skin. Rainha do Mar drew closer still…too close…and took Amaya's final breath with a kiss.

A kiss is a conduit.

Bernardo's words echoed through Amaya's consciousness, even while the kiss of the goddess made her drunk.

The sweetness of the exchange amazed Amaya, even while water filled her lungs and she did not drown. Would never drown. She couldn't be blamed for calling it a win. Aamir would live and she would forget the risk of a love that could be lost to the sea.

"Deal," the goddess said. "Fair exchange is no robbery."

He woke up in a bed wet with tears, and salty, too. "Breathe, Aamir," he whispered. A key lay on the pillow beside him—bone colored and yet dully gleaming. He didn't like it. Next to that he found a photo. Close enough for the images of his yaya and his twin sister to kiss his nose, triggering an ache so strong he lurched out of bed.

"Amaya?"

No answer.

A lingering dream of the sea left a kiss of brine on his lips. Aamir shook his head. He couldn't think. Couldn't remember what went wrong. He breathed in the sharp scent of saltwater and copper blood.

As the haze of sleep faded, an emptiness filled his chest.

"I want you back."

illustrated by
Sumit Roy

(Unit 333)
PERFECT
by Drew Bittner

Clay Devereux considered his latest work. The composition was brilliant, the use of color—in some places harmonious and in others not—was bold, the dynamism was undeniable.

So why was he so dissatisfied with it?

"Ugh. I wish I'd never taken up a damn paintbrush," he groaned.

Cissy looked up from her magazine. Her eyes lit on Clay, then the painting, then back on Clay again. "You say that every single time, and then it sells for fifty thousand," she pointed out. "I get the whole 'tortured artist' thing, I do! Being an unpublished writer in her mid-thirties gives a certain perspective. But you, darling, are on top of the art world. Everyone loves you!"

"Not everyone." He nodded to the issue of ARTODAY on the coffee table. "They didn't love my last gallery show. Said I was," he made air quotes, "'falling back on the same old familiar style that got me noticed fifteen years ago.'" He snarled in disgust. "As if any of those hack reviewers made it out of first year in art school!"

"Want some tea? I made some a little while ago."

Clay's shoulders slumped. "Yeah, sounds good." What stung was that the review was dead on. He *was* falling back on what had worked before. He growled in frustration, feeling that gnawing dread of being...

…out of ideas. Out of anything to say with his art.

Out of a career, basically.

Cissy brought back a mug of steaming tea with honey, the way he liked it, and he tried to evaluate his latest project in a more positive light. Sure, there were hints of "Incident," his groundbreaking work, the one that had gotten him noticed. And maybe a little of "Process in Reverse," or "Chalk Outline of Icarus" if you squinted a little bit. And…

"Goddamn it, it's like a montage of my whole fucking journey," he sighed.

"No, it isn't! You're too close to this to see it," Cissy insisted. "Why don't you go for a walk? Clear your head and come back refreshed."

Clay nodded, still glum with the weight of self-condemnation, and grabbed his jacket. "I'll…I'll be back in a little bit," he mumbled, locking the front door behind him.

Cissy set down the mug and then considered the painting as objectively as she could. Finally, she shook her head and said, "You're in a rut."

Clay liked that his house and studio were out in the country. The closest neighbors were not all that close. Heck, going to get the mail was enough for a good start on his steps for the day. Walks of a few miles out here weren't uncommon at all.

So he meandered, leaving the road to amble down a street he hadn't noticed before. Lost in thoughts of how to try and combine colors and strokes and perspective in a new way, he only resurfaced when he was standing opposite a storage facility at the end of the side road.

He frowned. Had this always been here? He was sure he knew this area better than that, to have some storage facility appear out of nowhere. It didn't look new, exactly, but it was nothing like the shabby, rundown places he had seen (and used) in his early days, before he had enough space to store his own work.

"Auntie's Attic, hm?" he mused, studying the sign. "Well, that's certainly…something."

I am running out of room for the junk I haven't sold, he thought. Maybe it'd be worthwhile to rent a spot for a few months, reorganize all the stuff…

He walked across to the office and stepped inside.

The guy behind the counter looked up and smiled. "Hey there. Interested in renting a unit?"

Clay smiled back. "I might be. What do you have in small, climate-controlled spaces?"

"I can do a five-by-five for eighty a month," the guy said.

"Sounds pretty good."

"And we give you the first month for a dollar," the guy added.

"Sold!"

Clay did the paperwork and paid the guy one whole buck, after which the guy passed him a key to unit 333—which he said was in the main building, not one of the two outlying ground-floor side buildings. He offered to guide Clay to the unit but the artist was still in a wandering-by-himself state of mind and said he could find it fine by himself.

He walked into the building and up the steps to the third floor. His nose twitched at the scent of ozone (*is there an electrical short somewhere?*) and maybe a hint of incense. It was a bit like patchouli, the kind his ex-girlfriend would sprinkle around their place. Clay relaxed, buoyed by a happy sense-memory, and soon he found unit 333. He unlocked the door, slid it open, and considered the space inside. It was very ordinary but clean, and he liked that. Yes, maybe clearing out the studio would help clear his mind as well.

Cissy offered to help, but Clay was able to load two boxes of six canvasses apiece into the pickup and drive it back to the storage facility with no problem. "I might be getting into my middle years, but I can haul canvas around all day," he told her, huffing a bit as he pushed the second box into the truck's bed.

"I see that," Cissy said, voice rich with loving sarcasm.

"Be back soon." While Clay started the truck and headed out, he thought that sometimes, fate gave you just what you needed, when you needed it.

He would have cause to revisit that thought in a different context, of course.

He pulled into Auntie's Attic, used the code for the electric gate that the counter guy had given him, and drove to the main building's front entrance. There was an elevator there, something he had managed to miss the first time, and soon the two boxes were on a flatbed hand truck and on their way to storage.

Taking the key out of his pocket, Clay had a moment of...not doubt, precisely, but more like *what's this in my hand?* The key felt strange this time. It had been an unremarkable steel key when he had been there before, but now? Now it looked unsettling.

The key had been maybe an inch and a half long before, but what he held was easily three inches long. What had been stainless steel was not, having become a chalky white stone that left pale smears where he touched it. It also had a faint scent of decay, as if it had been left in a compost pile overnight.

He almost dropped it. Touching the thing, much less holding it, made him want to soak his hand in sanitizer.

"Get this over with," he told himself. He didn't expect this weird key would fit into the lock, only to be surprised when it did—and worked! The door slid open, a bit less easily this time, and Clay looked into his storage unit for the second time.

Had the light been at a different angle last time? That didn't seem possible, since the fixtures certainly hadn't moved. But it did seem like there were shadows and patches of darkness that hadn't been there before. And...what was that shape in the middle? Clay fished out his cell phone and called up the flashlight app, sending a bright beam into the gloaming of unit 333.

"Well, that wasn't there before," he said, looking at an easel with a canvas set upon it.

He wondered if the counter guy was pulling a prank on him. He could easily have Googled Clay Devereux and found out he was a well-known local artist. But when would he have had time to run to an art supply place, buy this stuff, come back, and set it up? Clay hadn't been gone all that long. And he couldn't have had a prank like this prepared in advance—that didn't make sense at all.

Whatever.

Clay moved his two boxes into the storage unit and then looked at the canvas. It was snowy white, very high quality, and the size he liked best (24" x 36"). Just looking at it, he had ideas for what he might do, what images he might set indelibly upon this pristine surface. It was…

It was perfect.

He took the canvas with him, locked up the unit with the disturbing bone-white key, and headed to the office. By the time he got there, Clay was ready to unload a barrage of "How dare you?" on the guy, bombarding him with questions about invasion of privacy and so forth.

Clay's storm cloud of indignation dissipated when he saw the BE RIGHT BACK! sign in the office's window. He looked around, wondering if he could spot the guy anywhere, but no such luck. He waited a few minutes, checking his watch, then finally gave up. He could call later, after all.

Driving home, he kept sneaking glances at the canvas on the seat beside him. It was so exciting! He had ideas for an exotic landscape, like the kind in Spain he and Cissy had seen on their honeymoon. Maybe a bold figure crossing that landscape, like Don Quixote or El Cid? Or maybe not a Spanish theme at all, but a Middle Eastern desert with an oasis and…oh, the mind boggled at the possibilities.

"All done?"

"Yeah, but it was strange. I found this in the unit when I got there," he said. "And the key was…" He reached into his pocket and took out the key, only to find it had reverted to being an unexceptional piece of steel on a wire loop. "…was, um, nothing. I put the boxes away and brought this back, because, well, look at it!"

"It's nice," Cissy agreed.

"Nice? It's perfect," Clay said. "I want to start a new project right away."

"Now? I mean, sure, but I thought you weren't totally done with the last one."

"Oh, the last one is trash and we both know it. I can do something amazing with this canvas, I'm sure I can, and I want to get started right away."

"Okay then. I'll call you for dinner."

He shut the studio door behind him and Cissy, with a shrug, went back to her magazine.

The sun had been down for some while when Cissy finally knocked on the studio door. "Hon, it's dinnertime. Hungry?"

"No," came the muffled response from within. "I'm still working. Go on without me, I'll make a plate later."

Cissy ate dinner, cleaned up, and watched some television well into the night, half-expecting Clay to appear at any moment. But he didn't, and eventually she was so tired, that she turned off the downstairs lights and went to bed.

The next morning, his side of the bed was untouched.

Cissy frowned. What, he hadn't even come to bed? He *never* did that, not even when he was on a huge deadline. Throwing on a robe, she went downstairs. There were no dishes, dirty or clean, from last night and the food was where she had left it for him. He hadn't eaten, either. She went to his studio door and knocked. "Clay, you didn't come to bed or even eat dinner? Are you okay?"

The door opened in a rush, startling Cissy. Clay glowered at her, the white canvas shining untouched behind him.

"Cis, I'm busy, okay? I...I have a real feel for this one and I can't do the work if I'm being interrupted. Just let me eat and sleep when I need to. Don't..." Clay deflated. "...Don't worry, I'll be fine."

He shut the door.

Cissy didn't see him the rest of that day or the next. She found some evidence he had been out, in the form of breadcrumbs and a jar of peanut butter left open in the kitchen, but he had not been to bed—at least, not in their bedroom—and his studio door remained resolutely shut.

She could hear loud music playing at intervals, then silence punctuated by muttering and even shouted curses. Clay had done this before, it was part of his process, but the peaks and valleys of these random noises struck her as somehow more ominous.

Finally, she couldn't stand it any longer. She knocked but got no response. Quietly, she opened the door. Clay was lying on the floor of his studio, unconscious, a brush in hand. The canvas was where it had been, without a single stroke of paint on its gleaming surface. There were pages torn from his sketchbook, studies in pencil of what he might paint, and all of them seemed interesting. Several represented a real breakthrough in terms of his approach to his work.

Why had he discarded them?

Cissy gathered up the castoff pages, more worried than ever. Clay had never gone through so many attempts to conceive a painting; this was unlike him.

"Hnh," Clay snorted, then blinked. He fixed bleary, bloodshot eyes on her. "Wh-what are you doing in here?"

"Clay, you've been locked away for two days…"

"I said not to disturb me," he snarled, dragging himself off the floor. "I'm working! I need to be free to think, not distracted with stupid things like dinnertime and bed and all of it! Dammit, Cissy, you're weighing me down with mundane bullshit and I can't breathe!" He trembled with rage and pointed at the door. "Get out! Go away and don't pester me! I have to finish this! Go!"

Cissy gaped at the raving thing her beloved husband had become. With tears welling, she nodded and backed out, only to have him slam and lock the door behind her. After a minute, she got her phone, made a call, then waited for the cab to pick her up.

Clay turned back to his béte blanc.

"It's just you and me now," he whispered. "No distractions, nothing to get between us."

The canvas' pure white surface caught the light, reflecting it into Clay's face like sunlight off water. As if it was trying to respond.

"What will it be? I thought landscape," and he set the canvas on the easel lengthwise, "but maybe it should be a figure out of myth or history," and he set the canvas back the way it had been. "Something abstract, like Picasso?

I'm just...unsure. A canvas this perfect deserves a perfect image. I...I need to think. Now that she's gone, I can finally do that. Yes, finally."

He grabbed his sketchbook, found a blank page, and went at it with a singular frenzy. Line after gray line marked the paper, an image taking shape as it was transferred from his mind's eye to his hand to the page. Art students would have been silent in amazement, as raw forms were bypassed in favor of finished line work. Irritated with its imperfection, Clay tore out the page and let it fall to the floor, only to begin another.

Nothing was perfect. Nothing was worthy of the canvas's unnatural perfection.

Clay tried over and over. The floor was soon covered in a thick layer of discarded pages, any one of which might have launched the career of an artist. Any dozen of them might have ensured a solid, even lucrative career. All of them together would have led to a coffee table book and lasting fame.

Brilliant, maybe. But none of them were perfect.

Such is the tyranny of genius colliding with expectation.

Cissy finally called Tom. She had lost count of how many times she had tried Clay's phone, but it had been a lot. Too many times, honestly, but she didn't want to face going back. If he had been so terrible before, how bad might he be now? So, reluctantly, she called Clay's closest—and maybe only— friend.

"You okay? You look sad."

She looked up into Tom's weathered, kindly face. Clay's mentor and agent had been part of their lives long before they had married, and if anyone could help unravel what Clay was going through, it would be Tom.

"I'm worried about him. Again." She sighed. "I don't want to see him if he's going to yell at me and...and accuse me." Grabbing for tissues, she dabbed her eyes. "But I don't want him to kill himself over a fucking canvas either."

"It's odd even for an artist," Tom confirmed. "They can be obsessive and work-addicted and all that, but suicide-by-paint is unusual."

"If he was painting on it, it'd be one thing, but he can't even decide what to paint."

"So you said. You think it's still untouched?"

Cissy nodded. "I'd bet you a hundred bucks. It's wrecking him, trying to figure out what to paint on it."

"We can drive over and see. Maybe even stage an intervention."

It took a moment, but she nodded. "Okay, let's call a few people and see what we see."

Cissy unlocked the front door and the small contingent walked inside.

"Oh my God," she mumbled, holding her nose. The inside of their home was trashed, as badly as if a fraternity had thrown a party and not bothered to clean up. Two pizza boxes, countless beer cans, torn magazines. Furniture overturned, curtains pulled down.

"This doesn't bode well," Tom said. "Let's go to the studio."

They picked their way across the living room to the back hallway. The studio door stood open. Inside, Clay was sitting on the floor, staring at the canvas.

"Clay, can you hear me? It's Tom. We're...we're all worried about you."

Clay's head turned toward Tom. He was gaunt and spent, eyes reddened and underscored with dark shadows. His chin was dark with a half-grown beard and his hair was lank and greasy. His filthy clothes hung on him and he smelled awful, clearly having not bathed in several days. It was almost a parody of an artist's vitality burned away by unfulfilled passion.

"Tom," he croaked. "I...I know what I have to do."

Cissy leaned close. "You need a hospital, Clay."

"Cissy, I...I'm sorry. I'm sorry for what I said. But I finally figured it out. I finally know."

Tom snapped his phone shut from calling an ambulance, then said, "Well, go ahead and tell us, Clay. What did you figure out about this canvas?"

Tom's question was answered two nights later when his exhibition had its opening night.

"I don't think my brushwork has ever been so…sublime," Clay said, admiring the canvas. "And the choice of colors, well, that was a genuine struggle, but the choice of subject guided me in the right direction."

Those gathered around the artist nodded sagely, stealing glances at his masterpiece as if to match his words against what they could see for themselves.

"There are many who say it's impossible to marry subjects as diverse as the immortal quest for meaning with something as mundane as a diner, but I like to think I rose to the challenge." Clay's lips curved in a grin that was (as one witness put it later) "deeply disconcerting." "I mean, a battle for the soul of man taking place in an Illinois grain silo? Where did that inspiration come from? And the clouds above, each representing one of the cardinal virtues of mankind…ah, it overwhelms me now, just thinking back on that flash of…well, I'm not too proud to call it 'genius.'"

"Is…is it finished?" Cissy turned to see Franklin Thorpe, a local art collector, peering at the work in confusion. "Is he talking about what he…but why would he display…? I don't get it. Maybe it's just me…"

"It's not you, Franklin," she assured him. "It's…not you."

Cissy drank another glass of wine. She'd had hopes, the last week, that he might—wake up, maybe? But every word dashed those hopes with greater cruelty.

She had come to realize—and start to accept—that maybe he was lost for good.

"Has any artist ever tried to encapsulate the grandeur of Mother Nature and the shabby pettiness of humanity, juxtaposing the two in such a way?" Clay asked his circle of listeners. "I think using black and white exclusively was a stark decision, but it paid off handsomely. Such bold strokes, such dramatic flair—oh, I think this is one that will be talked about for years to come. Decades!"

Tom moved next to Cissy. "He has no idea, does he?"

Cissy shook her head, wiping away a tear. "Not at all. He's…been like this for days."

Tom turned to look at the canvas, as he had a hundred times in the past week. Since that day when they found Clay and the canvas, he and Cissy had walked into a scene out of an artist's worst nightmare—or so it seemed at the time. Now he wondered whose nightmare it was, really, and whether he might somehow wake up from it.

ARTODAY called it a "stunning triumph of subtlety and subversion." The reviewer admitted that he hadn't thought Clay Devereux still had inspiration like this in him, and that this one work alone would establish him as a true legend about this century's painters. (And it did.)

The gallery opening was a monstrous success. The gallery owner later said that attendance was triple what they had anticipated, and the offers for the work dwarfed anything he had ever received. Several bids were private and confidential, made by people who were immensely wealthy and famous. Clay held off on a final sale, however, until the gallery show had fully run its course. He spoke about this masterpiece to any who would listen, though many of the interviews were later combed through for signs of the madness that had claimed the artist.

Clay Devereux was found dead two weeks after the painting had been sold, having drunk nearly a gallon of paint.

The inevitable, untimely eulogies and obituaries featured this work alone among his many masterpieces.

Nobody who saw the exhibit came away unmoved, often profoundly.

Sitting in a room by itself upon a simple easel, the work known as "Perfect" was displayed for three months to world acclaim.

Hardly anyone was crass enough to say that it was just a blank canvas.

Because it was perfect.

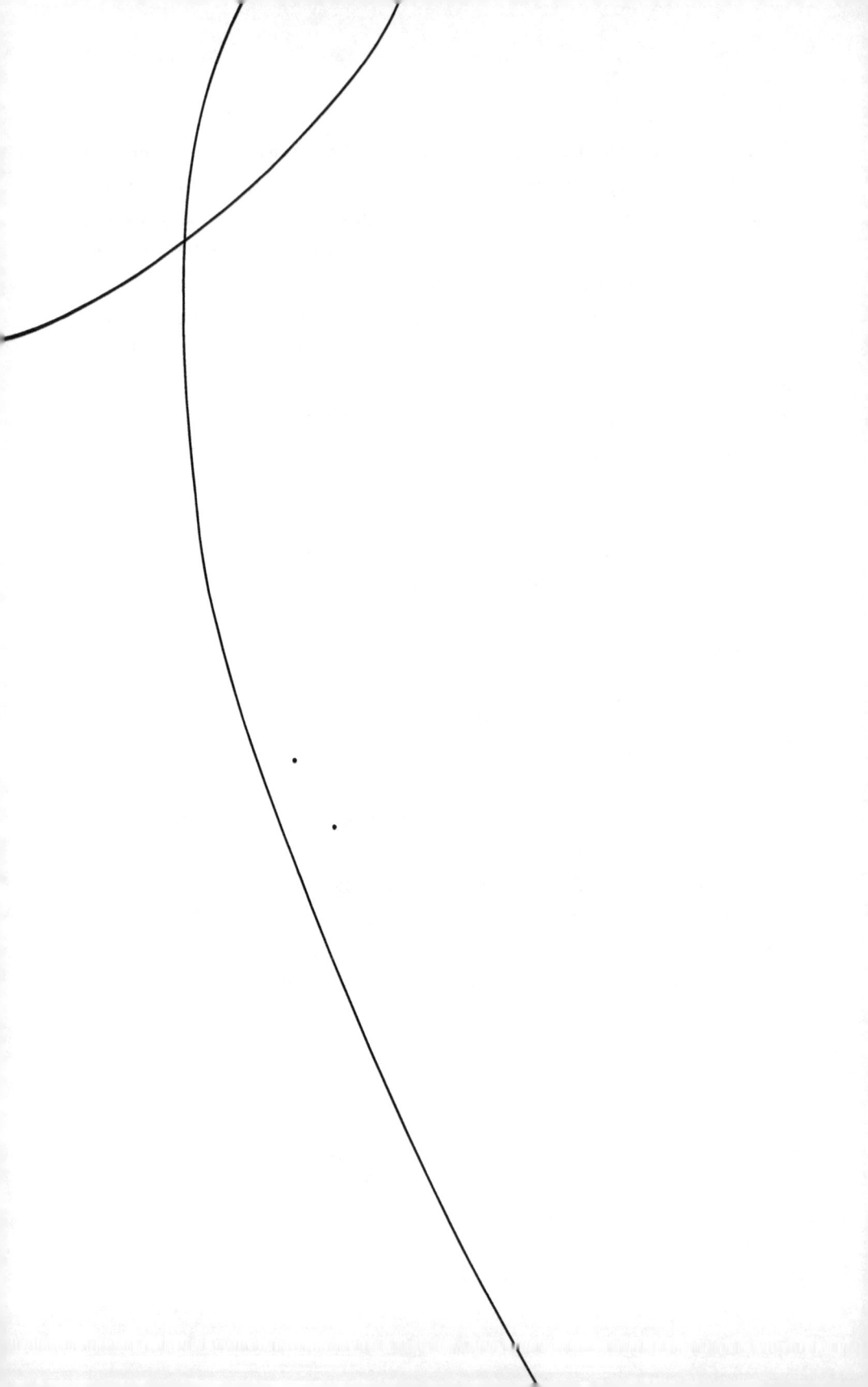

CHRONICLE REPORTER
GONE MISSING

August 2nd, 1973
By Scott Nichols

In a bizarre twist to an earlier story from July 16th of this year, the Crossroads Sheriff's Department confirmed today that our own Franklin Rush, a reporter here at the Crossroads Weekly Chronicle, has been confirmed as missing. Rush began investigating a story regarding three missing teens from the local high school after a practical joke went awry at a local self-storage facility. Mister Rush was continuing his investigation of the story and did not return from a scheduled interview with an unknown and as of yet unidentified source. Staffers here at the paper and Mister Rush's sister are cooperating with authorities regarding his disappearance. This paper, and its editorial staff, are all dedicated to finding Mister Rush, and we will provide any and all updates to this ongoing story.

From the Collection of David Disspain
Source: The Crossroads Weekly Chronicle

illustrated by
akar.std

(Unit 111)

I GOT IT FROM MY MOTHER
by Leon J. Cooper

To you who are now reading this:

There are things I must explain to you while I am able. Judge me, because you *will* judge me, only after you read what I say here. My time grows short so forgive me if I race over important details.

My mother passed away last month at the age of sixty-eight; I miss her so very much, as does my sweet little angel of a daughter, Lissa. My precious baby lights up—sorry, it's still so raw to me—lit up like a candle in the presence of her magical Gamma, and doesn't understand why she can't come over, or why we can't go to see her anymore.

On that day, I lost my friend, my mentor, my shining example, the world's greatest babysitter, someone who loved me unconditionally, the one person who knew me better than anybody on the planet, and so much more; to this day, it hurts so damn much. I also lost someone I thought was crazy. Who prepared for the end of the world, kept far too many secrets, and ultimately...well, that's skipping ahead a bit too fast. Let me think.

Okay then.

Of all the things she told me that I wish I had listened to, I wish that I had taken to heart more carefully the speech she gave me when she turned the box over to me.

You see, I was young.

I knew more than she did about just about everything, I was sure of it.

She was worried about everything under the sun. If it were hot outside, she'd be the one slathering me with sunscreen like it were mayonnaise on a club sandwich. If it were cold, she'd have me in so many layers of clothing that it took half an hour to get it on and off. Rainy? Ample supply of umbrellas. She kept hand sanitizer in tiny bottles all over the place. The woman was insane that way. Now that I'm a mother myself, I get it a little. Okay, maybe more than a little.

I didn't realize the depths of her insanity until I was ten, and I was allowed to go by myself to my friend's house. My friend's basement *wasn't* filled from floor to ceiling with paper towels and bathroom tissue and surgical masks and hand sanitizer and personal protective equipment and medical kits and baby wipes and ramen noodles and canned goods and powdered milk and juice boxes and can openers and boxes and boxes of MREs and foods with a shelf life of at least five years. Sure, she had a gun locker with more than a dozen guns and enough ammo to hold off a zombie apocalypse for a good two months, but that wasn't unusual, considering where we lived. My mother went the extra mile of having two flamethrowers, and a full well of gas in the backyard, like you see at gas stations. My father passed away when I was two, so she couldn't blame it on him.

There's a photograph that hangs in my apartment that my mother took of me and my father back when I was Lissa's age; he was holding my hand, and we were both smiling without having to say "cheese." We were in Old Town Alexandria, and he had bought me a hot dog from a stand just off of the river, which I was holding as my mother operated the camera. He cut it into very small pieces and fed it to me because I ate fast back then and might have choked. She liked telling me that story, that my dad was a superhero not by making a bunch of big gestures, but by many small ones. She loved the things daddy did that showed us that he was always thinking of us; I suspect she never remarried because there would never be another man like him. Daniel Danforth set an impossibly high bar.

Almost every time I walk past that photo, I want to have a hot dog. On occasion, I do…and I cut up little bits for my daughter to nosh on.

I don't remember his voice or the way that his hand felt as it encompassed mine, or the way that he mussed my hair or kissed me on the forehead or swept me up in his arms and swung me about while I giggled, or any of the things that my mother told me about, so I make believe that I do; it's comforting to me, even though it's not based on any of my actual memories. Mom's memories of him are good enough for me, or at least they have to be. Thanks to my mother, I remember him as a truly wonderful man, who loved me more than anything in the whole wide world.

I think maybe, now, I idealized him a little too much. I mean, he was gone, Mom was here. It's easy to feel that way—easy to project all the good onto the fairy tale, all of the bad onto the real.

My friends would often complain about how demanding their fathers were, or how they were always working and never attended their recitals or plays or tennis matches, or how they ran off with some other woman and abandoned them, and the jealousy would get the best of me and I would always want to shake the living hell out of them and yell at them.

As bad as those things were, at least they were lucky enough to have had their fathers in their lives, to varying degrees.

I often catch myself crying when I see that picture, for reasons that I know and reasons that I don't. Staring at it, every line of that face was etched in my memory, but it was barely more real to me than a movie star's picture torn out of a magazine. Only the emotion I felt made it real, made it something I held on to like a drowning person with a life preserver when Mom was too much to take.

I hung a similar one of Lissa and me right next to it.

One day when I was about thirteen, maybe fourteen now that I think about it, I was rummaging through her closet, and among the decades-old clothing relics I found all the way in the back, there was this blood-red hooded robe made of silk with little gold accents here and there; it was soft to the touch, smooth and eye-catching. The robe came with a cape, which I found hilarious and yet a bit scary.

I'd never seen it before. It was exotic and…I was a kid, okay?

It took both of my older brothers to pull her off of me when I came into the living room to show her how I looked dressed in that robe. I still can't believe how deftly she leapt over the couch to tackle me. Like she was some kind of jungle cat who'd been loosed in our living room. That apparition, her and that flame-red hair and green eyes and crimson lips contorted into a surreal expression bounding towards me, is one that will be with me for as long as…well, it'll be with me for a long time. Maybe.

She was even more upset with me when she noticed the stains from the sandwich that I'd been eating when I fished the robe and cape from the closet.

She grounded me for a full month. That was the *only* time that I had to serve a full term of being grounded.

With so little to do, I spent most of my time texting and using FaceTime with my friends and eating. I must get my metabolism from my father; I can eat pretty much whatever I want without gaining weight. Plus, I ran track in high school and college, so that helped. It pisses me off that Mom was genetically blessed to the point that I would catch my boyfriends staring at her behind, or her legs, or her boobs as she walked by on her way to the kitchen or the living room or anywhere, as I sat there looking like a stick figure in comparison. You can't imagine how disheartening that feels. When my imagination really lets go, at some point, the rubber bands holding me together might snap, and I'll be as shapely as she was, or at least that was my hope.

I'll always be thin, like my father, a magnificent weed.

I know that every girl competes with her mother in one or many ways, but most of them win by the time they reach my age. I couldn't help but think, a 40-year-old guy, given the choice between me and my 68-year-old mother, would go for my mom—clearly not the greatest thing for one's self-esteem.

Was it so wrong for me to want to try, even in such a small way as wearing a robe from her closet, to compete with her? To even…*be* her, a little?

That's what I remember thinking, anyway, when I slipped on that silky, blood-red wonder of a garment and strutted out into the living room to find…well, I already said that. A month of being grounded, no appeal, no reprieve.

But the robe incident did have one silver lining.

That was the weekend I learned that not only was my mother part of a cult, but she was its leader.

They were, to all outward appearances, a yoga and meditation group; for all the years that I had known these women, I never would have guessed otherwise. They came over routinely with their rolled-up yoga mats, inside which they hid their robes, went down to the basement, locked the door, played their weird music, and chanted, which I thought was just some New Age-y stuff. My brothers and I would sometimes try to figure out what was happening down there like we were some detective agency, as we thought that it was weird that they would lock the basement door just to do yoga and meditate; try as we might, we never solved the mystery.

It was also the weekend that she showed me the box for the first time. The key to this mystery was literally handed to me.

It was made of dark wood with reddish undertones, polished to a high glossy shine, with these ornate carvings on the outside. They looked like a bunch of symbols that I couldn't quite understand, not exactly like hieroglyphs, but more like some kind of religious symbology. (Granted, I never studied that stuff in high school or college. I was a marketing major, but I did get straight A's all the way through school. I think my father would have been proud of that fact, or at least I hope so.) The box was probably a hundred years old, maybe even older. Inside it was a key, wrapped in plastic, sitting on a red velvet cushion; I never have and never will again see a key quite like it. It was lightly coated in something that felt like chicken grease, and the head of it felt like bone, with the letters "LS-DD" carved into it. I found that interesting, in that my name is Denise Danforth and my mother's maiden name was Lenore Stewart.

Just opening that box, and touching that key for the first time, made the little hairs stand up all over my body.

"It's time for you to hear some things, Denise," my mother told me.

And we had a talk. Perhaps the first one in our entire lives.

"Denise, this box—now mine—belonged to your grandmother, and her mother before her, in a line unbroken for generations we can't even count," she said. I held it, trying to imagine the weight of history contained in my hands. This thing was *that* kind of old, and it even had a bit of an odor to it, not the pleasant smell of cedar or perhaps oak, but more of something dead, like maybe lettuce gone bad.

It was really off-putting.

"It is the duty of our Order to ensure the box is kept safe," she said next. "Each trustee takes her turn and it is mine now. The box is to be polished on the first day of each quarter of the year." She gave me a long, serious look. "You remember when you and your brothers were fooling around in the basement and I nearly hided the lot of you? Well, I keep this box under lock and key beneath the basement floor."

"I-I see," I stammered, struggling for something to say. Something wise, something to show I was worthy.

"Someday," she continued, "there will be a ceremony. You will become the trustee, keeper and protector of the box. You will then be allowed to wear the red robe, with permission this time," and here she allowed herself a self-conscious grimace—it had only been a few days since the "robe incident," as I already thought of it—then continued, "and inherit my responsibilities."

I understood what she meant. I would be their leader then, which meant that I'd get to wear the stylish cape, and they would take their cues from me.

I tried hard to play it down, but if I'm being honest, it was an unbelievable rush to know that one day, I would be in charge of something as important as this.

"There have been times when the box almost fell into the hands of…of men," she said, her expression growing somber. "Denise, this is the most important thing: the box must never be seen or held or opened by a man. Ever."

"But why?" I asked.

"Because men can't be trusted. They would misuse this and cause ruin for us all," she said, with such bone-deep conviction that I shivered, once again fearing I wasn't up to this.

I mean, even without knowing what lay inside, I couldn't agree more. The patriarchy has afflicted the world since biblical times. Since before.

"You must swear," she said, her eyes large and dark and deeper than our well, "swear an oath and you will be struck dead if you ever reveal the existence of the box to a man. Swear!"

Like I said, my mother was insane, but it didn't mean she wasn't right. That notwithstanding, I came to believe that I would indeed be struck down if I spoke of this outside of the Order, as absurd as that might sound.

"This isn't an idle thing, Denise," she said. "The Order has failed twice. The first time…" And she told me a story that put ice in my bones. I won't share it here. But if you know history, the echoes of that failure resounded for hundreds of years. People only think they know the true horrors of the Black Death.

The second failure precipitated a conflict between the English Plantagenets and the French House of Valois, but that was only the *start* of it. Again, if you know history—in this case, the history of the great wars of Europe—suffice to say that generations of wars were fought and millions of lives lost in the fallout of that original conflict…which was *our* fault.

"Both failures utterly decimated the ranks of the Order," my mother said. "We rebuilt over time, but the great seers of our Order warned us then that there were only *two* chances left. And if we failed, there would be a horrific ending to all things."

At the age of 14, I was awash in both confidence and anxiety. I thought I knew just about everything I needed to know, so I was intractably skeptical. *Of course*, I thought that she didn't know what she was talking about. I don't know if I was ever what you'd call completely rebellious in my youth, but I did feel the need to challenge my mother.

That also was how I came to understand why my mother had freaked out so hard when I dressed up in her robe and cape and why my older brothers never knew that these items existed. After the living room incident, they made jokes about it once, and Mom shut that down so *fast*. In time, the day I found and wore the robe (for the first, inappropriate time) ceased to have any special meaning, like a few others in the history of the Danforth family.

The only other thing I remember from that weekend, because it felt so out of place, was right after my mother put my own red robe around my shoulders. It wasn't a formal thing, I wasn't part of the group yet, but it was a Moment. We were in her bedroom, with the door locked and the shades drawn. In the dim light, her eyes seemed large and especially soulful. She looked at me with—forgive me if this sounds improbable because it was— tenderness. Glancing at the bedstand next to her bed, she gazed at the picture of her and my father on their wedding day.

"I wish you had known him better," she said softly. "He was such a good man. If anyone could have understood the burden our family carries, the responsibilities, it might have been him. He was…he was special, Denise. I hope you know that kind of love in your life."

And my stomach fell, because without knowing it, she'd put her finger on an important puzzle piece of my life. A missing piece, one shaped like a man who'd been gone from that picture for far too long.

I hadn't known him well enough. Maybe if I had, things could have been different.

On my eighteenth birthday, I was granted membership into the Order. There was a ceremony, I swore an oath, and I was given my own red silk robe, which slid over my body as if it were meant to, like the hands of an intimate. Given no advance warning but simply told, "Come with me" by Mom that afternoon, I hadn't expected to spend my birthday like that. However, the night made up for it. I went out with my girlfriends to Richmond and used our fake ID cards to go to a few bars and have a few drinks and maybe meet some cute guys. I look older than most girls my age, so I could have gotten in without being checked, but I have friends who will probably look like teenagers until they're thirty.

Thirty-year-old men hitting on me that night felt a little creepy, but I looked like I was in my mid-twenties and my friends had gotten in, so it was understandable.

I got so wasted and horny that night that I almost let slip that I was the newest member of a cult led by my mom. I reaffirmed that I had better watch how much I drank, and to make sure to lock away that little piece of my life, pun intended. This was something that I couldn't even tell my best friend Janet; I love her to death, but the girl could never keep a secret, even if you pinky swore her to it.

From then on, once per month, we donned our robes, rolled out our mats, lit a bunch of carefully arranged candles, and sat while listening to my mother as she read from this super old book. (All I know for sure is that it wasn't a Bible and it wasn't Latin my mom was reciting—beyond that, I got nothing.)

After that, we chanted, words that didn't make the slightest bit of sense to me then but that I committed to memory over time, and then drank red wine. My mother and the other women of the Order helped me to become fluent in this language over time, which filled me with a sense of pride and purpose.

When the meetings ended, we talked about ordinary things and enjoyed each other's company just like we were an actual meditation group. They were great women, some doctors and nurses, some lawyers like my mother, some in real estate, some who ran businesses from their homes, and others who took care of their homes during the day. Having the Order in my life took some getting used to, for sure, but after a year, it felt like it had been this way my whole life.

Years passed.

Until a decade or two ago, we used to be able to hold meetings and practice self-defense outdoors at night in the woods that were on one member's property, but that was before drones flown by bored suburban kids became a thing. These days a video of women doing yoga followed by an hour or so of "Crouching Tiger, Hidden Dragon" would have gone viral in no time.

We thrive on anonymity, and we hide in plain sight.

My mother told me that every ten years on November 11, she has to take the box with the weird key in it and go out to some storage building called Auntie's Attic in this middle-of-nowhere town called Crossroads. She has to go to Unit 111, insert the key into the lock, open the unit at precisely 11:11 a.m., and recite words that she'd committed to memory. The last time she went was on 11/11/11, ten years ago. I was not a member of the Order yet; I just noticed that she was in a mood when she came back from there.

She wasn't her normal batshit-crazy self for a few days afterward.

The thing you have to understand about my mother is that when I say that my mother was "batshit crazy," I mean that she was by my and my brothers' standards. Lenore Stewart was, to the general public, a fine upstanding woman, and a pillar of the community.

She was an attorney who specialized in mergers and acquisitions, she donated time and money to charity, she played golf and tennis at a local country club, and she had men coming at her every way they knew how to: she was easy on the eyes, with her fire-red hair and green eyes and perfect lips and little need for makeup and ample bosom and swell of her hips and great legs. She was a catch, the kind of woman about whom men write songs and poems, or jokingly refer to as "the unicorn of trophy wives": beauty *and* brains. She had at least a dozen smiles, each one of them more disarming than the next.

Lenore Stewart could sell you a box of air and convince you that you needed it.

One man who pursued her as if it were his job told me that she reminded him of Lee Meriwether, an actress who played Catwoman on the old Batman television series.

I could see it.

I told you before about the food and weapons she had stockpiled in her house. Today we'd call her a "Doomsday Prepper." Lenore was ready for some real end-of-the-world type stuff. She kept books on how to turn household waste into fuel, how to make homemade wine, how to do any number of things in case the power or the internet went out. The first time I asked her why she did this, and she looked at me as if I were the biggest idiot on the planet. She stressed to me that we had to hope for the best, but always, and she meant *always*, prepare for the worst.

It took a while for all of that to sink in, but it was fun to call her "Lenore the Lunatic." (Behind her back.)

My oldest brother Pete came up with "Literal Lenore," because when she told you that she was picking you up at a certain place at a certain time, heaven forbid you weren't there at *that certain place* at *that certain time*. Her standards did him some good, though; living up to her standards helped him get through medical school and when he started his own practice.

My other brother Andrew came up with the nickname "Lenore the Lunatic," telling Pete and me that no one else's mother did what our mother did. Andrew was big on taking polls of his friends, Pete's friends, my friends, pretty much everyone he met. He was a bit of a fanatic himself, with his constant data collecting and statistical measures; it's no wonder he works for the Gallup Corporation now.

We used to giggle in private about those nicknames we had for her.

God knows what nicknames she came up with for us.

Looking back, I guess I'm more my mother's daughter than I imagined I would be. I don't know how I feel about that.

Nana used to tell me that Mom was an impossible child who gave her and Pop-Pop fits, but grew into a truly great woman; Mom told me that Nana was a rigid taskmaster who tried to prepare her as early as she could to assume her role in the Order.

When I close my eyes, I can still smell and taste Nana's mashed potatoes, which she made with string beans and pork chops and applesauce; she was magical when it came to her German dishes. While Pete and Andrew fought over the pork chops and Mom acted as referee, I would eat the mashed potatoes and string beans until I thought I would explode, and Nana would smile and wrap me in her arms and hum the songs that she loved.

She always smelled great, and she had a wonderful singing voice.

Time passed. Then the unthinkable happened.

Mom was hit by a drunk driver a month ago. She was a little tipsy herself, so it's not as clear as one might think who was at fault, though it looked like she had the right of way. Witnesses at the scene blamed the guy, I think mainly because of the Confederate flag, "All Lives Matter" stickers on the back of his pickup truck, and the "14" and "88" in black ink tattooed on either side of his neck. It turns out that he was on his way to scare some protesters and he was running late. He was indicted quickly, and I was in court to watch as much of his trial as I could.

I haven't said a lot about who is in the Order—on purpose—but we can pull strings. One of the Order prosecuted him; another is the clerk who schedules the cases. He went before a judge who's also one of us.

The trial lasted a day.

Kurt Wagner will never draw breath as a free man ever again, and that doesn't upset me in the least. Call me vindictive if you want.

Mom told me that one day I would have to make the trip to Crossroads to do the recitation. We drilled and drilled and drilled what I was to do and say from start to finish.

There were to be no mistakes, and there was absolutely, positively, no margin for error. Remember those two more strikes? I did.

Mom was every bit the taskmaster that Nana was.

I don't like this next part.

My mom Lenore died of a bacterial infection that she picked up while she was in the hospital; she was 68. My eldest brother Pete is 44, my brother Andrew is 42, and I just turned 26 in August. It seems that my mother needed to have a daughter, if for no other reason than needing someone to carry on for her. I am comforted by the fact that I was not an "Oops Baby."

We gave her a nice funeral; even if she hadn't had good insurance, it would have been a good event. My brothers do pretty well, even with kids in college, and I'm a year out of grad school, with a job in pharmaceutical sales, a 2-year-old daughter, and a boyfriend with commitment issues, so none of us are hurting for money. I think that she would have liked it—the service I mean. All the women from the Order were there, most with their significant others and children in tow. Plus, the flowers were beautiful, and the woman who did her hair and makeup did a great job.

And, at that point, I became the official Keeper and Protector of the Key and the Book.

This morning, I came out to the facility.

It was a nice enough place. It was clean, smelling faintly of Curtis Brand™ Cleanser. Everything seemed to work as it should, the air conditioning functioned properly, and there was no evidence of spiders, mice, rats, or worse that I could see or hear.

I gave myself enough time so that there was no way that I would be late. I practiced the speech on the way to make sure that I had it locked in; from start to finish, it took about three minutes.

On my way to the unit, I saw what appeared to be some people wheeling an elderly man who struck me as a soldier, based on his bearing, into an elevator. I wondered to myself why these people couldn't go to the unit and bring whatever was in there to him. In the midst of that brief reverie, I bumped into an attractive Black woman who looked about my age, and who seemed to be mesmerized by some kind of multi-tiled mirror that she was holding in her right hand and which could have easily been mistaken for a hairbrush. She was too far gone to even have noticed, but I apologized anyway.

This place might have been cleaner than I expected, but it made up for that by being ten times creepier.

I stood in front of the unit at 11:06, donned my robe and cape, and took the key out of the box. It smelled just as bad as before and felt just as greasy. As I rubbed my thumb over the head, I noticed that the engraved initials had changed from "LS-DD" to "DD-LS."

My daughter's name is Lissa Shelton.

At precisely 11:11, taking a firm grip on that unsettling key, I opened the door to the unit…which was completely empty. My mouth dry and needing a large drink of water, and my body trembling, I had never felt so nervous in my life. It felt like fifth grade and we had a play. I froze up and couldn't say my line until Ms. Grier gently prompted me. The other parents laughed, and I turned beet-red and cried on the spot and vowed that it would be the end of my acting career.

With a deep breath, I took precisely three steps as rehearsed, closed my eyes, and started to speak. I was maybe ten seconds in when a mist appeared before me; I could feel it up against me, but my mother had told me to expect that, so I kept going just as Mom taught me. The words had to be recited in an exact sequence; stopping was allowed, as long as the sequence of the words was not broken.

The mist spoke.

Mom had warned me that it would; she warned me that it would probably sound familiar and that it would try to distract me to make sure that I flubbed the incantation.

"Hello, Denise."

It was not a familiar voice to me; it was deep and measured. I kept my eyes closed and kept going.

"I'm sorry I wasn't there for you, Pumpkin."

Dad?

"Daddy loves you. I just wish that I had gotten to see you grow into such a beautiful young woman."

I opened my eyes, my mouth agape. "D-Dad?"

Oh, NO!

The most handsome man I'd ever seen stood before me. He was tall, thin but well-muscled, with beautiful eyes and a smile that melted hearts, or at least mine.

He looked exactly like my father did in the photo on my apartment wall.

Mom warned me.

She *warned* me.

She warned me.

I'd blown it.

I had *one* job.

I fell to the floor as if my leg muscles had stopped working and started to cry. Just like I did back in fifth grade when I couldn't remember my line. No one had saved me then and no one would save me now.

He was no longer handsome. He was sin ugly, rotting from the inside out, and he looked as if he were a couple thousand years old, you know, like one of those people whose faces kinda sorta remind you of trees, where the deep cracks look like bark.

He spoke again, his yellow eyes burning their way into me. "You have your mother's nose. And her eyes. She and your ancestors were able to keep me at bay for centuries. I just had to wait for the right circumstances, and what happened? Your father dies without you knowing him, and your mother dies before you were ready. What an incredible stroke of luck! Thank you for releasing me. And now, if you'll excuse me, it's been a long time coming for me to spread Famine across the world."

"Mom told me the box could never be revealed to a man," I demanded. "Why?"

He smiled, a tooth dropping from his rotted mouth. "Because men make wonderfully effective partners," he said. "They did the last two times, anyway. Maybe this time as well."

He ambled past me like a zombie from any one of a boatload of series that you'll find on any number of television networks. I tried to grab him, but my hand went right through his arm, as if he were a ghost, or simply malevolence in the shape of a man.

I heard a horse whinnying behind me. It was a thing of beauty, well groomed, shiny, and black, with hungry eyes.

As he mounted the horse, he extended his hand; as he did, he turned back into my father, ruggedly handsome and magnetic.

I had to take his hand; he was my father, after all.

A girl needs her father, doesn't she?

Doesn't she?

In that instant, I no longer felt like a twenty-something woman.

It was as if I had suddenly accumulated a millennia's worth of knowledge. Everything inside of me felt as old as dirt, which made me wish to avoid any mirrors for fear that I might resemble a millennia-old tree.

We rode off, with me wrapping my arms around him, digging myself into his back, me crying and him laughing. I don't know if he was laughing at me (I'm pretty sure that he wasn't), or laughing because he was finally free to do what he was meant to do, but I will remember that laugh until the day I die, which will probably be much sooner than I expected.

Or I'm already dead, and I *am* Famine; that's probably more the truth.

Everything we come across that's normally green is now brown and dead.

That's because of me and my father. I wish I could withhold the terrible power I wield but I can't, and soon enough I won't want to. If I could still cry now, I'd never stop. And if there's a Hell, I deserve damnation for my moment of weakness.

In moments of rest, dismounted from the horse amid vistas of devastation, I've tried to call my ex Kurt to ask about my daughter Lissa. I couldn't get through to him, likely because I *am* dead.

I also tried to contact the Order; same result. At some point, they'll receive the fourth box—the power of fate made manifest, it will simply appear in their midst one day soon—and realize how truly screwed we all are.

This is the third time that the Order has failed.

More to the point, *I* failed them. I'm going to be forced to fight the women who were my sisters for eight years. If they can last that long.

If they fail to stop us, their dead bodies will rise under our control, killing crops, polluting the air and water, and making all things ready for the creation and delivery of the next box.

I hope Lissa will be stronger than I was when her time comes, and that she'll be more like her Nana or her great-grandmother. The burden of keeping these boxes will remain in our bloodline, with Lissa set to inherit a responsibility I failed

I'm not one who prays, but I pray that Kurt is up to the task of raising Lissa.

I hope that when the Order comes to explain all of this to my daughter, she will realize what her duty is, and that she will do it.

I hope that she'll be strong enough to withstand the temptations Death will offer her. That's the last one, you see, and the only one left. It will be up to her.

I hope she doesn't hate me.

I'm so sorry, everyone.

~Denise Danforth

illustrated by
Sumit Roy

(Unit 233)
BEAR WITH ME
by Drew Bittner

Swear to God, the first sound I hear is her slippers scuffing over threadbare carpet. What a way to start the day.

"Norton! Get your lazy ass out of bed, you bum!"

God, I hate that old bitch.

"I swear to God, Norton, you're going to find a job or you're out on the street. You hear me?"

And her scuffing feet go the other direction, fading into merciful silence. Until:

"Swear to Jesus, Norton! The want ads are waiting, not that you'd get hired anywhere. It's almost eight o'clock! Early bird gets the worm, dumbass. Mr. Pookie says so."

If there's anything I hate more than my great-aunt Hortense the Horrible, it's her goddamn teddy bear, Mr. Pookie. It's just a teddy bear, I know that—pint size and button eyes. Hell, it's even kind of cuddly. But she *talks* to him...and apparently he answers back.

From the first time I caught his black button eyes glaring at me, I knew Pookie hated me just as much as I hate him. Hell, if I didn't know better, I'd swear he knows I'm just waiting for Hortense to kick the bucket so I can help myself to her "estate," such as it is.

It's all my own fault, really. See, two weeks ago, I'd been out drinking when I found this key...

I'm at O'Malley's, my favorite watering hole. The bartender on duty, Morley Sherk, gives me the side eye when I ask for another double. The other guy, Joe, wouldn't be doing that. Joe's a stand-up guy, even treats me to a round now and then. I owe him probably a grand or so by now, but he's cool.

Not Morley. Damn drink-slinger thinks he's God's gift to hard-drinking working stiffs like me. Or I would be a working stiff if I had a job, the right break, anything. But no, good ol' Norton Rideau ain't got none of that.

I slap down my last ten on the bar and he serves me anyway. I knew he would.

But since that was my last ten, until I can bum more bucks off my hateful aunt, I have to nurse it. My lips barely feel the burn as the whiskey slides past and down, stoking the fires inside that haven't gone out in fifty-one years...and I hope won't go out for a whole bunch more.

My thoughts are fuzzy.

I just need a break. Some luck. Something to give me a helping hand...

My hand brushes against something in my jacket pocket. I reach inside and feel something cold and slightly moist, something that feels...well, I bring out some kind of key, with a tag wired to the end. It tells me it's from some storage place out in the godforsaken end of town.

How the hell did I wind up with a key to some storage unit?

I hadn't been gambling in the few spots that still let me in. Had Hortense put it in my pocket by accident? No, that wasn't like her. She never did shit like that.

Well, it was here now. Maybe I'd go check it out. The night was still young and I felt like I could drive. I mean, I probably shouldn't drive at all—not feeling as buzzed as I did—but I could manage, y'know, a little. And besides, there weren't a whole lot of cops down where this storage place was.

"Auntie's Attic, huh?" I swallowed the last of Sherk's not-generous pour and stood up, wobbling only a little. "Morley, ol' pal, I'm off to see what this key opens."

"Maybe it'll be a million bucks," he said, wiping a glass.

"My luck, it'll be empty," I said, walking out into the chilly October night.

I drove, weaving only a little, and got to the storage place faster than I'd expected. It looked brand new, lights shining on black asphalt, a trim and freshly painted office building to one side, and an electronic gate. I was at a loss for that one until I flipped over the tag and found a series of numbers, which I punched in (because why not, right?) and lo, the gate opened like Jesus leading a parade into the Pearlies. I drove until I found the central building, marked with 100-1199 on its side, and took the elevator (which I was relieved to see was as brand new and clean as the place outside) up to the second floor—to unit 233.

The lights were strong here, old-school fluorescents, but when I took the key out of my pocket—I don't know, they flickered or something, and the place…looked different. Like the walls were gray one second, then white. Clean, then dirty in the corners. Little stuff. Ehh…maybe I just hadn't paid attention. Just for a second, you see, but…like a mask had slipped and been put back in a hurry.

It had to be the booze.

I found unit 233 and put the key in the lock. With one twist, it opened, I slid the door aside…and found him.

A teddy bear, maybe all of a foot tall, wearing a red bow tie that went well with his rust-colored fur. He was sitting on a stool as if waiting for me, his black button eyes fixed on the door.

I stepped into the unit and shone my cell phone's flashlight all around. The bear (and his stool) were the only things inside.

"You're what I get? Huh. Figures. I need a lucky break and I get some moth-eaten bear. Well, c'mon…" and I read his name off the back of his bow tie. "Mr. Pookie. Maybe you're worth a ton on eBay or something."

I locked the unit and dropped the key back in my pocket. It might be handy to have a storage space out here away from Hortense. Handy indeed.

I tossed Pookie into the trunk of the car and started for Hortense's place. I didn't want to live there, you know, but hey, I'm sort of between things and she has extra rooms and needed someone to help out and I do plenty of that. So keep that judging look off your face, okay?

Got home and dragged the bear inside. Hortense was waiting, like she always does. She's got goddamn radar about when I'm about to walk in.

"Norton, you're late. Have you been drinking again? I can smell it on you from here. Smoking too, I don't doubt. And…well, who is this?"

I handed her the bear. "Says his name's Mr. Pookie. You want him? He's all yours, Auntie."

"Well, thank you. He seems like quite a little gentleman."

I shrugged. He was a fucking bear, what do I know? "Maybe he can keep you company or something."

She peered into his black eyes. "Yes," she said softly, "maybe he can." Then she looked at me thoughtfully and added, "Good night, Norton."

"Good night." I went to my room to watch the end of the game (I'd bet twenty bucks I didn't have to a bookie I didn't want to see if my team lost) and forgot all about the bear.

Until the next morning.

I came downstairs to find Hortense making breakfast. Mr. Pookie was standing up on one chair, his chin barely clearing the level of the table, but I had the weirdest feeling he was looking at me.

"Norton, Mr. Pookie thinks you need to apply yourself a bit," Hortense said. "He said there's no reason you aren't working, not in this economy, and if you really looked for work, you'd find it plenty quick."

"Oh, he thinks that, does he?" I asked sourly, nursing a hangover that hadn't quite gone away in the past ten years. "I'm sure teddy bears know a lot about job hunting."

"You'd be surprised what Mr. Pookie knows," she said, scooping scrambled eggs out of a frying pan. "He's very insightful."

"Insightful. Heh. Yes, I do believe he's the most insightful teddy bear I've ever met."

"You scoff but you'll see," she said, passing a plate of eggs my way.

"I guess I will."

That was two weeks ago.

I'm not getting any more sleep today, so I get up and throw on some clothes—a hand-me-down suit last worn in the 1950s by my great-uncle Walt (who had to die to escape Hortense) and a shirt I think I washed last week—then head downstairs. Hortense and Pookie are at the kitchen table; she's drinking coffee strong enough to be roofing tar and he's propped up behind the paper, like he's reading the thing.

Cute.

"Norton, here's the want ads. I circled some things Mr. Pookie thought would be good for you to try," she snorts, pushing a folded-over paper into my hand. "There's…phew, did you shower, or even brush your teeth? You smell like a gas station men's room and your breath could knock a buzzard off an outhouse."

"Yeah, yeah," I mutter. So, I'm not so fresh, sue me. It was a long night at Morley's and the dice weren't good to me. "Say, Auntie, you got twenty I can, uh, borrow till I get something going? Won't do me good to look for a job on an empty stomach."

"I gave you forty yesterday," she says, giving me the crook-eye.

"Yeah, well, I spent it already."

"I haven't got twenty dollars. Maybe tomorrow. *If* you look for a job. If you sit here all day again, you can eat peanut butter out of the jar for all I care."

I start to mutter under my breath. She stares at me again. I get a look at Pookie and God help me if I don't feel like he's staring at me too. I've had that feeling a lot in the last two weeks. The little fuck gives me the heebie-jeebies.

"All right, I heard you," I tell her. "I'm going."

And I went. She'd circled a bunch of low-end crap jobs, from file clerk in a ratty law office to "product demonstrator" at some big box store. I went to one and it looked like nothing I'd ever want to do, so I spent the rest of the day bumming around town and smoking my last cigarettes. Far as Hortense and Pookie knew, I was looking for work, and I was happy to let them think so.

Now I want you to know something. I'm not a bad guy. I caught some bad breaks, that's all. Can a guy help it if he's got bad luck? Okay, so gambling—that's a vice and people are going to say you have to control your vices, fight 'em. I figure, what's it hurt if I play the ponies or roll them bones once in a while? And yeah, it cost me big, when I got in hock to Tony "Legbreaker" Legiardi to the tune of twelve big ones.

From there, it was all downhill. Pretty much lost everything I had and burned every bridge, and the low point was when I stole the jewelry Mom left my sister…but she didn't press charges, just told me never to show my face again, and I hadn't. I can take a hint.

Like I said, I'm not a bad guy, I just got lousy luck.

Take finding a job, for instance. Usually, it's who you know; I didn't know anybody who'd want to give me a job, and Lady Luck was giving me the finger. So I went to O'Malley's for a noontime beer and ended up staying until eleven. Joe O'Malley lets me run a tab, 'cause I was buddies in high school with his kid—Billy O. Got offed in Desert Storm, poor guy. Lousy luck.

By 11:00, I was kind of tanked. Got on the 5 bus and flashed my bus pass on the reader. It came up empty from my morning running around so I had to hoof it two miles back to Hortense's creaky old barn. Might have gotten there by midnight, maybe not.

Takes me a minute to dig out my key and fit it into the lock. By the time I do, and stumble through the entry and up the staircase, Hortense and Pookie are there waiting for me.

Ah, shit.

"Watch your mouth, Norton," she says, glaring at me. Looking down her nose at me from the second-floor landing.

Bitch.

Her mouth falls open.

Crap, did I say "bitch" out loud?

Her nose wrinkles in disgust. "Mr. Pookie smells booze on you again, and so do I. You're spending all your time in lousy dive bars. Did you even look for a job today?"

"Yeah, I did! Nothing out there, nobody hiring. End of story."

"Guess that's what happens once they get a look at you," she says under her breath.

"Whazzat?"

"Look at you, Norton! What do you see in the mirror? I'll tell you what Mr. Pookie sees: a fifty-one-year-old loser with the face of a rat and the soul of a skunk. He told me why you're here. Everyone else in the family turned you out."

I'm drunk and just got done walking two miles 'cause *she* wanted me to look for a job. I'm not in a great mood and I take a step closer. "That damn bear told you all that, huh? He's a goddamn motormouth, ain't he?"

She looks like I'd slapped her in the face. "He's my friend. And you're a miserable little punk! Out! Get out of my house!"

"Gimme that!" I grab Mr. Pookie out of her trembling hands. "I'm gonna throw this damn bear in the furnace!"

"You leave him alone!" She might be on the far side of 80, but Hortense is more spry than I guessed she'd be. She grabs for Pookie and struggles to rip him out of my hands. "Give him here, you brute. You leave him be, he never hurt you…"

We tussle for a minute. Then I hear a loud RRRRRP! Pookie is torn nearly in half between the two of us tugging on him. Hortense screams like a little girl who's lost her ice cream cone. It pushes me over the edge. "Ah, take him then." I let go, maybe even shove a little—and she falls.

It's like it happens in slow motion. Hortense tumbles down the stairs, her nightgown and robe fluttering around her like some tattered curtains, Mr. Pookie clutched tight in her bony arms. She hits hard, two or three times, and lands at the foot of the stairs, sprawling there like a dropped rag doll. Mr. Pookie is still in her hands, his black button eyes fixed on me.

"A-auntie?"

She doesn't answer. And she never will.

Oh God. What'd I do? She's…

She's dead.

And it was an *accident*. Nobody can prove otherwise.

This…is the best day of my life.

I slept like a baby, woke up, "found" my dead auntie, and called the cops. I was so happy, it wasn't hard to fake tears at the old bitch's death when the cops showed up after the paramedics. Honest—this was the best thing that ever happened to me.

Crump and I go way back. I must've pawned a couple thousand bucks' worth of belongings over the years; hell, some of it was probably still here somewhere. When I came in with two big boxes full of Hortense's antique junk, he just gave me a grin, lip-slid his cigar to the other side of his mouth, and dove right in.

Crump loves this old crap. Me? I could care less, long as I have some dough coming to me.

He opened the first box and his expression changed. Not angry, just sort of puzzled. "Nort, you think I take kiddy shit like this?" He reached into the box and pulled out Mr. Pookie.

I blinked. How had he gotten in there? I'd left him in Hortense's room, under her bed. I know I'd kicked the little shitbag there after the cops left. Had I zoned out while packing up boxes? Maybe…I guess that sort of thing happens, right?

"I…uh, it was my aunt's," I tell him.

"Ripped up like this, I couldn't give it away. I'll throw it in the trash for ya," he says. "For free."

I manage a weak laugh but can't help staring at the bear. How had Mr. Pookie gotten in the box?

And why was I getting a sick feeling, just seeing him here?

Crump puts a few hundred in my hand, and I'm on top of the world. I can forget all about Hortense and her damn bear and that geriatric funk of hers. In a month or two, whatever, I'll inherit her house and all the junk in it—gotta be a way to squeeze four or maybe five grand out of the stuff alone—and I'll be sitting pretty.

Life is gonna be sweet.

Around one in the morning, there's a knock at the door. It's the cops.

"You Norton Rideau?"

"That's me, officer."

"You been to Crump's Pawnshop today?"

"Uh, yeah. Why?"

"Place just burned down. The fire guys found Crump inside. You wouldn't know anything about that, would you?"

"N-no, I been home all night."

"You pawn some stuff today?"

"That's right. I got the ticket right here."

The cop eyeballs the ticket, writes in his notebook, nods, and says, "Okay. Well, we'll be checking back if we need more info from you. G'night, Mr. Rideau."

I shut the door and chain it. *Crump, what the hell?* I think, then…I can smell smoke. My nose isn't the best but I know smoke when I smell it and something in the place is on fire—or was. So I start to look around…

…and nearly trip over Mr. Pookie.

He's sitting on the floor of the front hall. He smells like smoke and, I swear, he's even toasted a little bit around the edges. Maybe I'm seeing things, but it looks like the tear Hortense and I made is smaller; he's not nearly torn in half now. A good tailor could help him pull through.

Heh. If I didn't know better, I'd say the bear was pissed.

"Screw you, Mr. Pookie. She's dead and you're gonna be in a landfill tomorrow." I scoop up the stinky, torn-up toy and toss him in the trash, then yank out the liner bag and tie it tight. Good luck getting out of there, Pookie.

As for me, I got places to go.

First stop is O'Malley's. I've got some bucks so I figure maybe I'll pay Joe for drinks this time. It's only fair, right? Guy's treated me plenty so maybe I'll give back for once.

Heh. Hortense would've had a heart attack if she knew I was going to actually pay for something.

Joe serves me up a boilermaker with a look of pity on the side. "Heard you lost your old aunt, kid," he says, shaking his head. "Damn shame. Took you in and all. Guess you're holding a one-man Irish wake, huh?"

"Uh, yeah, sort of," I say back, sipping the beer. "She was...she was something, all right." *Something old and ugly and nagging,* I add mentally.

"Well, I'll leave you to it. Huh."

I follow his eyes to the barstool one down from me...and spew beer all over the bar.

Damned if it isn't Mr. Pookie, sitting there and staring at me.

Yeah, I said it, the damn bear was eyeballing me real good. His black button eyes were working me over top to bottom. There was a rip in one side, with a fluff peeking out, but otherwise, he looked almost brand new. None of the burns from before, not a sign he was anything but a bear who'd been through a little tussle.

"That yours? I didn't see you bring it in, but..."

"No! No, it's not mine. But, uh...here." I slap down a twenty. "Maybe you can, uh, toss it out or something. Crusty, ripped-up old Salvation Army reject like that, I don't figure even a moron would take it."

The room drops a few degrees and I remember Joe has a "mentally challenged" nephew.

"Uh, I'll be going," I say.

"Yeah, I think you will," he agrees, his scowl dark as Pookie's eyes.

Dammit. You cost me a watering hole, Pookie. Round two to you, I think as I walk out of O'Malley's for the last time.

I have got to get my head on straight. Can't talk to any of my few remaining pals; they'd call the nuthouse and get me locked up in a rubber room, wearing a coat with sleeves that strap around the back. I got no time for padded cells and getting drugged out of my gourd. No, I have to play this out my way. Got to relax first, though, 'cause I'm no damn good if I'm stressed like this.

Gotta relax.

Going to the track—that's a good idea. It's always fun at the track, play the ponies and scan the forms, keep the ears open for a sure thing…hell, it's like old home week for me.

I get to the track just before post time for the third race. Slapping down half of what Crump gave me, I tell the kid to put it all on Mama's Little Boy to place and Heathcliff to show.

I make my way out to the stands and find a spot in a box with a dad, mom, and their 10-year-old boy. Dad is trying to explain what the race is about to the kid; I'm trying to tune them out. Do I need to take one of Hortense's pain pills? Might dull the wits—nah, better hold off.

Ten minutes later: "And they're off!"

We watch the horses pound the dirt, churning up earth like each hoof was a pile driver, and they round the corner.

Mom and Dad are excited, the kid is jumping up and down. They look happy.

Huh, maybe I'll have a wife and kid of my own one day. I could be okay with that. Fifty-one isn't too late, is it? Maybe I'll get myself hair plugs, fill in where it's going thin…

The horses are coming up fast, rounding that last turn.

I lean closer and get ready to leave the box, so I can go down to the rail and see the end for myself. The excitement is doing its trick and I feel good for the first time since Hortense died.

That lasts all of three seconds.

"Hey, mister. I think you forgot something." The kid gestures toward a corner of the box and there, God help me, is Mr. Pookie, perched behind a racing form.

Oh God no! How I managed not to yell that, I do not know.

The rip is smaller. Who'd stitched him up? This whole thing makes no sense.

"Uh, he's all yours, kid. Take him, give him a good home."

"Thanks, Mister! Hey, are you okay? You don't look so good."

"I'm…I'm fine." I never wanted to vomit so badly in my life.

He grabs up Pookie and hurries off to show his mom and dad what he got at the racetrack from that nice guy. Okay, if I can't throw you away, Pookie, maybe I can give you away. You'll have a nice family. You'd like that, right?

I'm so rattled I don't even check to see if I won or lost. But it sure as hell felt like I was losing…

The rest of the day slides by. I keep thinking I see Pookie here or there. A tuft of brown fur—there! No, it's just an old shoe somebody left in the street. No, wait, *there*! No…calm down, Norton. It's just a shadow. Teddy bears don't…oh God.

Hortense's pills have taken the edge off by the time I hit the casino. It's out of town a ways but I need something to calm me down. A dozen or so hands of blackjack ought to do just fine.

The table is treating me well. I don't hit 21 a lot, but I'm building up a nice little pile of chips and feel good enough to push my luck once or twice.

But I'm not there more than an hour before:

"Hey, pal, that thing yours?" The dealer nods to the chair on my left. Crap—sure enough, there's Pookie. The tear is smaller, too. Goddammit, is this bear *healing*?

"Uh, no, not mine." I back away, clutching my handful of chips, and make a beeline for the cashier's booth. I won't be coming back here anytime soon. Not as long as Pookie can find me here.

"Pal, you gotta take the bear," he tells me. "We don't let customers leave stuff behind when they leave a table." He hands me Pookie and I almost scream, but choke it down hard.

Where can I take him?

Then it hits me. Why not take him back to the storage place, Oddball's Attic, or whatever the fuck it was? Sure, why not?

I toss Pookie in the trunk and start driving.

And…why don't any of these streets look familiar? The storage place was out this way. I got there from Morley's in maybe ten minutes but now it's like I'm in a maze or something. I pass the same Holiday Inn six times and start cursing under my breath, as if a volume of curse words must be uttered to unlock the way to the storage place.

I pull over and dig for the key. It was in my jacket, so it's got to be here. It had the name of the place and the address, I think, because how else would I have found it? But I dig through a pocketful of receipts, loose change, a ballpoint pen, two racing tickets, and other junk…but no key.

Goddamn it, where did that key go?

I get out my cell phone and looked up storage places near me. Store4U, National Self-Store, Midway Storage…Jesus, there have to be a hundred places within twenty miles. But…Attic? There's one, Auntie's Attic, and it's supposed to be nearby. I start off and realize I'd missed a turn, then another, and before long I'm at…

…a shabby, abandoned lot with a couple of rundown buildings slumped behind a few yards of chain-link fencing. The parking lot's asphalt is nearly white and broken into chunks and what had been a gate now hangs open, protecting exactly nothing. I drive in anyway, feeling the creeps like I'd rarely gotten in my life (even when Tony asked me, not so nicely, for the twelve grand I owed him back when), and find where unit 233 is supposed to be. I get out, yank Pookie out of the trunk, and have to climb the stairs because the elevator is out of order. The lights, well, most of them are out and the few that work look ready to electrocute whoever gets too close. I find unit 233 by using my cell phone flashlight, to see the door is broken in and it smells like death inside the dark storage unit.

"Welcome home, motherfucker," I grunt, tossing Pookie into that awful void. "Rot in hell."

I get my ass out of there as fast as I can, unable to shake the feeling I'm being watched.

Velma works the Blue Room down on Main and 4th. She's cute enough if the light's dim and you're not too choosy. I had a hundred or so left in my pocket so I figured maybe a little female companionship would mellow me out, and I've been with Velma a time or two. They know me down at the Blue Room; it's probably my favorite watering hole after O'Malley's.

After a couple beers, we stumbled out into the alley in back of the Blue Room. Three hot and heavy minutes later, she says it.

Took the lead right out of my pencil, when her squeaky voice says, "Hey, Nort, that bear belong to you?"

And sure as shit, there's Pookie, sitting on top of a trashcan, staring at us.

I probably freaked out, 'cause next thing I know, Velma is backing away.

"What?" I'm confused. What's her problem?

"I ain't never heard nobody cuss out a teddy bear," she says quietly.

"He's…he won't leave me alone," I tell her. "Doesn't matter where I go, the bear is always there. He won't go away!"

"It's just a piece of shit teddy bear! You gotta grow a pair if some dumpster junk creeps you out. Hell, here." She totters over to Pookie and puts out her cigarette on his chest. "See? What a loser. I am outta here."

Oh, man. I try not to run away, but I have to get out of there. I can feel Pookie's eyes follow me when I run out of the alley, but when I look back, he's not there.

So where'd that fuzzy little scumbag go?

I try to sleep but I keep thinking Pookie will be there when I close my eyes. Can't sleep—he'll get me. A couple glasses of bourbon don't help, but…well, maybe they do, 'cause I pass out around one or so.

About 3:00 a.m., I get a knock on the door. More like a jackhammer pounding pavement. Mumbling and half-awake (and a little drunk), I yell, "Who is it?"

"Police, Mr. Rideau."

I unchain the door and let them in. "Wh-what is it?"

"Can you come downtown with us, right now? We need you to identify a body."

"Uh yeah. Sure."

Body? What the fuck? I remember thinking, groggy and struggling to put on my clothes.

We ride to the station and they show me to the morgue, where a young, unshaven guy in a stained white lab coat opens a drawer and rolls out a metal shelf with a covered body on it. He pulls the top of the sheet aside and I see Velma's face staring up at me.

"What h-happened to her?" I hate that my teeth are chattering. It's not even that cold in here.

"Drove off the Nineteenth Street Bridge," one of the cops told me. "You wouldn't know anything about that, would you, Mr. Rideau?"

"Nuh-uh. I…I saw her at, like, ten or something at the Blue Room."

"Yeah, some guys there said you left together," the other cop says. "Out the back door." They exchanged a smirky look, the pricks. "But then she's floatin' in the river. That don't look good, Rideau, you being the last guy seen with her and all."

"I don't know anything!"

"Why is it you who's on the spot, Rideau? Folks are saying you're like the Grim Reaper, people dying when you're around. I don't like it," one of the cops says. "First your aunt, then Crump, now Velma. That's three, Rideau. Got anything you wanna, ah, confess?"

"Officer? You wanted this," the morgue attendant says. He passes over a plastic bag.

I stifle a scream, seeing a waterlogged Mr. Pookie wrapped in plastic. The glint in his eye winks at me and, sure as hell, the tear is totally mended.

"You give Velma this, Rideau? You don't look like a sentimental flowers-and-candy guy to me," the cop says.

"N-no, I didn't give it to her," but that sounds weak even to me.

"Get lost, Rideau. But don't leave town. We might have questions, so you better be where we can find you," the cop says.

"Sure, sure," I mutter. I back out of the room, keeping an eye on the damp, bagged teddy bear in the morgue guy's hands. How did…? That cigarette burn—he'd paid Velma back for that. Just like Crump at the pawnshop.

Oh God.

He's toying with me. I'm next.

He's just a teddy bear, dammit. I can take him.

I'm a grown-ass man, I can take a one-foot-tall teddy bear, whether he heals or not.

When I find him, I'll put him in the furnace and watch him burn. Then I'll scoop up the ashes and seal them in a coffee can and mail it to goddamn Alaska. Let's see him come back from that!

I'm a hundred percent sure that the little creep will be waiting for me at the house. He doesn't do subtle—he likes me knowing he's there. Ha, I'll use that fucking overconfidence against him. Fuck with me, will he? Crump, Velma, they never saw it coming, but I'm smart. I'm not going to be caught off-guard.

But I don't see him when I get home. I look around the house—"Hah!" and "There you...!" and "Gotcha!" in every room—but he's not there. *He's not there.*

This is wrong. I mean, he's been all over me since Hortense died. He killed Crump and Velma, I know he did. He's...he's got to be here! Maybe I sound like a lunatic to you, but I know what I know and he's here somewhere.

He's gotta be in the house.

"Where are you, you little dirtbag?" I search the upstairs, knowing Mr. Pookie is here somewhere. He's spying on me, getting ready to make his move. Has to be.

Clunk.

Downstairs, that sound came from downstairs.

"Oh, you slipped up this time, you fucking fur-ball," I whisper into the dark. "I'm coming for you."

I'm almost running when I get to the top of the stairs and start down. It's right about then that my foot comes down on Mr. Pookie.

Slip, trip, what difference does it make? I fall, learning the hard way that empty air will not help you resist gravity. And it's a long way down.

I bounce two or three times and land hard. Don't think I broke any bones or snapped my neck but—I can't move. Oh God, I can't move! Am I paralyzed? Had I broken my neck after all but just hadn't felt it?

Maybe I just bruised the nerves and I'll be fine. Yeah, sure. I'll just lie here for awhile and wait to get feeling back in my arms and legs.

And then there's a tiny *chuff*, like something small breathing in the dark.

"Mr. Pookie?"

Oh God, oh God, I have to move. I try to get my arms and legs working, but nothing. I'm stuck. I can't move.

"Mr. Pookie, it wasn't my fault. She…she fell! You know she fell!"

Goddamn it, the bear knows. He knows!

Chuff.

"You goddamn bear, leave me alone! Go away! Go the hell away!"

I can't help it, my bladder lets go and warm wetness pools under me. I can't move, just have to lie there as my clothes soak up urine. Oh God, this is an awful way to go. Everybody's going to know I pissed myself.

"Fuck you, Pookie! Fuck you!"

I can't turn my head, can't see anything. All I can do is try to listen, try to hear him coming closer.

Silence, then…

The last sound I hear is me screaming.

No, wait. The *last* sound I hear is his furry paws scuffing over threadbare carpet. Walking closer. Like he has all the time in the world.

He sounds just like Hortense, scuffing her old lady slippers across the carpet.

And that's the last thought to go through my mind, swear to God.

URBAN LEGEND HUNTERS CLUB

(ULHC)—*GENERAL CHAT**

LochNessa: Pics or it didn't happen

ChupacaBro: I beleve in fairies but even I kno Aunty's Attic is urban myth

TwitchyWytch: */upload failed/*

TwitchyWytch: That's why we're here, Chad. Literally the point.

LochNessa: It's spelled Auntie's – why are you like this?

ChupacaBro: I kno. Thas what I mean. this is just us spinning. If the attic is real show us the pics, wytch

TwitchyWytch: */upload failed/*

StringTheorist11: Theoretically speaking, there is evidence The Attic sits in a cross-dimensional crossroads—a sort of nexus between quantum realities. As such, it may be accessed only at rare points when universes align.

i.e., the map drawn in 1967 by Felix Underwood. Three separate people corroborated his account of Unit 13765 (otherwise known as The One with the Tentacles).

ChupacaBro: but that Leaqe kid from 1973 said no on 13765. He saw 8 rooms and unit 4 played led zeppelin on an infinite loop. "bleedin through the walls" he said

LochNessa: His name was LeQue. Jon LeQue and his story flips more than a Rubik's Cube. We still don't know if he killed those other teenagers

TwitchyWytch: Or if he asked someone on the inside to do it for him. He told one reporter "a new friend" played Zeppelin's "No Quarter" for him that night. Then he took it back.

ChupacaBro: your stalling, 95randd

StringTheorist11: I do not share Chad's derision but I am anxious to see the visuals you captured. Is it working, TW?

TwitchyWytch: */upload failed/*
TwitchyWytch: */upload failed/*

TwitchyWytch: Noooo. Nothing works. Can't upload to the group or socials. Can't text. Can't Dropbox. Nothing works.

LochNessa: Screenshot or take a pic of your phone screen

TwitchyWytch: Tried and denied.

TwitchyWytch: */upload failed/*
TwitchyWytch: */upload failed/*
TwitchyWytch: */upload failed/*

StringTheorist11: I'm raging. Can you describe what you saw?

LochNessa: Yes!

TwitchyWytch: */upload failed/*

TwitchyWytch: I got a video too. There's a giant glowing box sign in the fog. It's shaped like a roof with Auntie's Attic in acid green letters. Nothing else. Except XXX X XXXXXXXX XXXXXX XXXX XXX XXXXXXX XXXX XXXX

/TwitchyWytch lost // reconnecting/

ChupacaBro: except XXX what? where'd she go111

StringTheorist11: That error message is new.

TwitchyWytch: Sorry phone glitching */reconnecting/*

TwitchyWytch: Except for a tattered t-shirt from the Welcome Back Tour */reconnecting/*

TwitchyWytch: */reconnecting/* the Buffalo XXXX

StringTheorist11: Are you redacting yourself?

TwitchyWytch: */reconnecting/*

TwitchyWytch: No. I'm typing words but they're XXXXXXXXXXXX while X XXXX

LochNessa: If you mean the Buffalo tour date – that was July 15 '73. The day before those kids went missing!

TwitchyWytch: The shirt has long curly blonde hairs on it. Like DeboraX XXX.

LochNessa: or Robert Plant

TwitchyWytch: Oh my XXX. XXXXXXXXX XX XXXX in the room XXXX XX

TwitchyWytch: */reconnecting/*

TwitchyWytch: */reconnecting/*
TwitchyWytch: */reconnecting/*

UnknownUser: *"Close the door, put out the light. You know they won't be home tonight."*

/TwitchyWytch lost—reconnection improbable/

*The final meeting of the Urban Legend Hunters Club
cataloged by Sherin Nicole*

illustrated by
akar.std

(Unit 1618)
THE
REFRACTION PRINCIPLE
by Sherin Nicole

Open it.

Don't open it.

Open it.

Don't.

Cali's fingers swayed to the rhythm of her indecision. There wasn't anything special about the box on her desk. Other than the mystery of who it belonged to. Or why it showed up one day and wouldn't go away. No matter what she tried.

Nothing special. Just crunchy brown cardboard with a smudged logo stamped on top, from a place she hadn't heard of: Auntie's Attic storage facility. Cali couldn't find much about it on the internet either, other than a group of conspiracy theorists called The Urban Legend Hunters Club.

The box buzzed with the energy of a secret. It wanted to be opened.

Resisting the urge seemed silly, but it seemed equally wrong to open something that didn't belong to her. Curiosity wasn't a problem—Caledonia Curtis was a legend of self-control. She stood up, shook out her skirt (it was a very good pinstriped skirt), and left that box sitting on her desk. Hopefully, whoever it belonged to would collect it sometime soon and she could move on.

Cali kept that hope alive for two months, from 9–5. Each day the box showed up in a different spot on her desk. She found it on her keyboard one morning. One afternoon, it made its way into her upper right desk drawer—the drawer she kept locked. The box didn't change. Same brown cardboard, same basic logo. Even after a spill, when it had been soaked in green tea, it held together, immutable.

Freaking unnerving.

The box *"accidentally"* fell into the trash one evening. *Oops.* And Cali watched Lucia take it out as she collected the garbage bins and dumped them into her cart. When the unblemished box returned the next morning, she asked Lucia if she'd brought it back. The younger woman said she hadn't seen it. *Lo siento,* she didn't want to draw attention to herself. Cali nodded in understanding, while her fingernails dug red crescents into the flesh of her palms.

Lucia had nearly finished working her way through school and Cali understood how it felt to live the right way, yet have people suspect you simply for being. She hadn't meant to make the younger woman defend herself.

"I'm the one who's sorry," Cali said. "Good luck with your finals tonight."

"Thanks for the recommendation, Ms. Curtis. I mean, Ms. Cali. Um, when you said I should write about Octavia Butler. She's an ocean. You know?"

They both exhaled and laughed together because it helped. Cali reminded herself again; she wasn't harboring any anger about the stereotypes she and Lucia continued to face. Stereotypes that told them they were perfect for shouldering the work but weren't quite ready to take the lead. Always not quite ready.

She wasn't angry about it. Not really. Not at all. Not that much. It just bothered her. Because rage—like all the trifling parts of life—should be resisted. The same as she'd done with the *"family business."*

The Curtises kept things clean. Papa Smalls, her great-grandfather, had started a chain of laundromats that became dry cleaners, then eventually a line of detergents and soaps. Big money. Big front.

At 8 or 9 years old, Cali had wrestled her cousins for the right to sit on Papa Smalls' lap, with her tiny hands wrapped around one of his long rough fingers. His scent was fragrant bergamot, citrus oil, and Earl Grey tea—evocative. And Papa Smalls told good stories. The other kids might've wanted the lollipops he handed out with twenty-dollar bills rolled around their sticks, but Cali wanted to listen to his voice, to feel the energy of his life pass down through her bones.

She missed his voice the most. His baritone lilt had slipped into distant echoes. Yet she could still see him, back when he stood at the sinks in his restaurants and factories, at home or work, stiff in perfect bespoke suits, compulsively scrubbing his big brown hands. By then he'd been as old as the dirt he'd kept trying to scrub away: using more and more aggressive cleansers—sometimes steel wool—until neither oil nor bacteria survived on his skin.

Papa Smalls' palms had been desert-grooved and just as dusty by the time she learned why he'd scoured his hands until he barely left fingerprints on anything. Or anyone. Her mother and uncles called it a guilty complex from "doing dirt." They nicknamed their granddaddy "Lady Macbeth" behind his back. But some spots don't wash out, no matter how much money you launder or how many people you *"scrub out"* of existence. There was a certain audacity to their hypocrisy; her mother and uncles should've kept quiet. They were just as *"clean"* as Papa Smalls.

Dammit. Why not open the box? She'd lived good and she'd lived right. Cali had resisted the lure of the family business. She'd walked away from the money, the power, and especially the blood. Because the stench of Curtis Brand Bleach™ couldn't cover everything. And she believed in karma.

She could also allow herself to believe the universe had been kind for once, delivering a bonus in an irresistible brown cardboard box.

But some things shouldn't be done at work. So, she opened the box in her car, while parked behind the office, with the floodlights to see by.

Everything looked orange-tinted under those lights—the dashboard, the pinstripes on her skirt, the brown of her hands. But not the box. It sat on her lap, unchanged until she reached for its lid. It might've been her eagerness or maybe the cardboard finally gave out after its adventures in the garbage. Either way, the box fell apart—opening up and out like hands unclasping. In the center, resting on a piece of black velvet, she found the key.

Despite the orange halogen glow of the parking lot lights, the key gleamed in a grayish white. Bleached as bone. Slightly slippery when she rubbed it. Not metal, not cold enough. Probably not ceramic but something else... *What?* She didn't know. The letters LS-DD and the rounded numbers 1618 were stamped deep into the head, right where you grip the key. And when the black velvet fell away, an acidic green keychain dangled from it with the same logo as the box top: *Auntie's Attic "Well Kept Storage for Needs Big And Small."* The keychain swung slowly, swaying as deliberately as the *tick-tock* of a pendulum.

Cali lost herself in the sway.

Back and forth.

Back and forth.

Back. Forth. Back...

TINK TINK

Harsh white light flooded Cali's vision even as she jerked away from the sharp ring of metal on glass. A halo of light bounced around her car. Roving in the manner of an eye, taking in everything, before it settled on her lap. Cali took the chance to refocus and covered the key.

Outside of her driver's side window, a hunched-over security guard waved the flashlight he'd momentarily blinded her with. He wore a powdery blue uniform over a slim yet round frame and had an incongruent double chin. The name on his tag read: *B. Fenton.*

B. Fenton made a motion for Cali to roll down her window. When she did, she saw Karen Arnold standing behind the guard. The sullen redhead had her arms wrapped around herself and her jaw set tight. Fenton's spicy cologne clashed so hard with Karen Arnold's floral fumes, that it made Cali wonder how they could stand to be close to one another. As it was, she could taste the stink of their contrasting scents on the back of her tongue.

"You got some I.D.?" Fenton asked with his chest puffed up, as though he'd whipped out his secret agent badge.

She turned toward Fenton and tapped the badge she wore on a lanyard (which she'd matched to her outfit) with equal aplomb.

"Oh, that's Caledonia Curtis," Karen said before Cali could. "Cali, what are you doing out here like that?"

Like what? What specifically had she been doing that required such a defensive stance and a security guard as backup? Cali took a breath and swallowed the acidic words she'd been tempted to send Karen Arnold's way.

"I'm thriving. And you?" Cali said sweetly.

The other woman blinked and sputtered, "You can guess what it looked like. You. Out here. All alone and sitting in this car."

And what? Cali gripped the lower edge of her steering wheel. The pressure caused her thumb to go white around the fingernail.

Fenton huffed. Then straightened and shook his head. He must've regretted getting co-opted into Karen Arnold's nonsense. And Karen must've sensed the guard's lack of patience because she frowned and said, "Try to see if from my side."

Her insistence that everyone should see everything from her side and only her side, no matter how head-in-ass her opinion tended to be, had earned Karen Arnold the nickname Been-a-Dick. No explanation necessary—you only had to say it out loud.

"I think I'll pass," Fenton murmured before he turned back the way he came. "You'd better head home, Mrs. Arnold. You have a good night, Ms. Curtis. Be safe, *Ms. Curtis.*"

The emphasis on Cali's name told Benedick everything she needed to know. She'd been dismissed. She stomped off, making as much noise as the plastic soles on her heels would allow.

When Cali pulled away, she glanced back at Benedick Arnold through her rearview mirror, just in time to see the woman trip into a puddle. The subsequent spill sent a thrill of satisfaction through Cali as gravel-filled mud splashed everywhere.

Karma comes at you fast, Cali thought without bothering to hide her smile. She remembered the day she'd found out Lucia spent her nights in school. Benedick had shouted it when she'd accused the young immigrant of stealing the antique watch she had repaired for her husband's birthday. You know, to pay for the school Lucia already worked so hard to attend.

Seriously?

Ridiculous.

Benedick claimed she'd left the watch on her desk and it had gone missing overnight. The woman went full rage-monster before their boss, Karen Wheeler, walked in. Known as "Wheeler," the better of the two Karens, the one Cali called Wheeler Dealer because she handled her business on multiple levels. The better Karen went into her office and came out with the watch in its navy-blue box.

Wheeler sighed like a high school principal who only had two weeks left before retirement, and said, "Karen, you left this in my office last night after showing it off. I emailed you about it. Did you forget?"

Benedick Arnold's mouth had closed with an audible snap, but she never apologized to Lucia. Didn't even look her way. The younger woman had been so sad and embarrassed. That look on her face touched many of her office mates, including Cali. A bunch of them took her to lunch to try to make up for it…but Lucia still wore that look whenever she saw Karen Arnold…and her shoulders weren't as high as they had been before.

Cali hoped the puddles in Benedick's life would multiply.

The back of Cali's neck burned and so did her eyes but she wasn't angry. Not really. Not that much. She just needed to drive for a while until the heat in her head cooled. So she checked the address on the keychain and turned her car in the direction of Auntie's Attic storage facility.

A few times, as she drove along back roads that spidered off into increasing darkness, she almost turned back. But eventually, the road widened, and streetlights bleached the night sky into a muddled gray. Cali pulled up to the gate of the pristine storage facility after an hour's drive. The main building had a glowing box sign in the shape of a roof—meant to mimic a Queen Anne-style home. It might have been cute once but now the word "cheesy" suited the grandma design of the facility better.

Everything gleamed as though a favorite aunt had just finished her Saturday morning dusting—the chain link fence, the towering streetlights, the rows and rows of garage doors leading to storage facilities going back further than she could see. It seemed weird. This was the great outdoors and nature liked dirt. Where were the water stains from this morning's rain or the weeds that should've grown at the base of the gate this time of year?

Nothing should be this clean. And there was…wait, yes. If Cali stopped breathing and listened. Right there, at the edge of her perception, she heard a low-lying buzz. It couldn't be the humming of the lights. Cali heard that too, but this other buzz wasn't electric. It sounded organic, alive like insects crawling over one another. She strained, listening harder, then *POP* the buzz faded.

Okay, then. It might be a good idea to give the key back to these people (whomever they were) and head home for a comforting yet forbidden snack of gummy bears and a frosty glass of Cheerwine. Cali opened her handbag, took out a tissue, and used it to press the white button on the buzzer at the gate anyway.

Hell, anyone who met her family would call them cleaner than Sunday School dipped in Lysol, but under the surface, they were covered in the dirt of multiple crime rings. When something looked sanitized, Cali knew she couldn't trust it.

No one greeted her at the front desk, so she checked the map and found Unit 1618 on the first floor. Only the odd-numbered units were on this level. Cali guessed the second floor held the evens, which seemed a strange way to organize a building. The buzzing returned and, as she approached the door with the bright metallic 1618 nailed to it, the scent of wet leaves in autumn filled the previously sanitized air. Underneath that, Cali could smell the slightest hint of decay. *How could a place this clean smell so damp, so old?* But then she thought of her family and she understood.

Even with her trademark *Caledonia Conviction*™ firmly in place, she still stared at the numbers on the unit door for longer than necessary. One. Six. One. Eight. And then she slid the clammy key into the lock. The incessant buzz *POPPED* and stilled as Cali pushed the door open.

What happened next couldn't be called walking in as much as being pulled. A rich blue-blackness sucked Cali into a space that had no edges, no horizon. It could've been vast or tiny. She couldn't tell. Her outstretched fingers drifted through thickened air. Nothing else. Her ears clogged with the change in air pressure, and when her frantic eyes searched for the exit, there was none— only an almost fluffy darkness.

Before panic could take hold, a beam of white light punctured the blue-black, bouncing three times off the unseen to form a triangle. The beam refracted and separated into a pathway of colors: red, orange, yellow, green, blue, indigo, violet—all stretching towards her. The prismatic path tugged at her, a tractor beam pulling Cali toward a hand mirror that floated at the center of the triangle.

The mirror was perfectly round at the top but at the bottom a second section elongated into a teardrop shape. As though the mirror had wept its handle.

It held as many facets as a gemstone. Perhaps a lapidary had cut it the same as they would a diamond, but it wasn't especially pretty. Nothing you'd see in a fairytale but something far more pragmatic. The mirror was made only of mirror. It had no seams. From every angle, it remained unbroken.

A pulsing fear rose in Cali's chest. To curb it she thought about Pretty Angelina, her mother. That's what Papa Smalls called his favorite grandchild.

"C'mere, Pretty Angelina, my baby," he'd say, his gruff voice melodic with affection. He'd usually share something they could read together. "The Academic Review printed an article, comparing W.E.B DuBois' theory of the looking-glass self with Charles Horton Cooley's take," he'd say. "Let me read it to you?"

Angela N. Curtis would run to her grandfather's side because Pretty Angelina craved knowledge, especially anything that allowed her to understand people better. Better understood, easier manipulated.

Cali laughed but not with amusement. Thinking of her mother always erased her fears. Usually, because a sharp-edged contempt took over. Amongst the Curtis family, they called her "Pretty Angelina," but in the crime world her mother had become known as "Angel Baby." Cali called her that too. The *gotdamn* angel of death. That woman could sit on her saffron-golden velvet throne reading for days. Wearing suits made for men but tailored for only one woman. Never a dress shirt beneath the jacket but always a tie, partially obscuring the swell of dark breasts. *Gorgeous.*

Cali resented Angel Baby and the dirt she did, yet her mother's advice remained useful. Brutal but practical. One time, Angel Baby had suddenly looked up from a book—one with razor blades hidden within the spine—and said, "Girls like us use our fists because our wits are far more deadly. Why deploy an atomic bomb when a well-placed slap will suffice?"

With a mother like that, fear didn't stand a chance.

Cali grabbed the mirror's handle without further hesitation and brought it up to eye level. The shiny surface reflected her face. That was to be expected. The same face she recognized from putting on her eyelashes in the mornings, and from late nights brushing her teeth. Deeper inside the many facets she saw something more revealing. Cali gasped. She couldn't breathe, her heartbeat seemed to outpace her mind's ability to process the contents of the mirror. Her fingers tightened around the handle. Her breaths rushed in and out before the oxygen could reach her brain. Her body tingled as though on the verge of epiphany. Anyone would have trouble processing the contents of the mirror when it contained…you. All of you. Every facet you've never been brave enough to see.

Wait. Ahh-ah

Wait. Ah ahh uhh

Wait…

Papa Smalls sometimes said, "The truth makes itself hard to recognize, like gray hiding within grey," but her great-grand hadn't gotten it right. Cali's truth illuminated her in a multihued spectrum and it was—*it was*—*it was clear her true colors shone through.*

Cali blinked at her reflection in the rearview mirror of her car. Further behind her, Auntie's Attic receded from view. She swerved from side to side on the double yellow-lined darkness before she recovered.

When? How had she gotten back on the road home? And why was the radio so loud? A quick tap on the steering wheel turned Cyndi Lauper down lower (but not too low). A glint of light, refracted into a rainbow, caught her eye and Cali realized the mirror had come along for the ride. It rested comfortably on her passenger seat—diamond bright, yet somehow circumspect.

She wasn't sure why but Cali immediately thought of Lucia and how the truth of her reflection might cheer her up. Her friend needed to see this mirror, she decided.

WHOOP WHOOP

Blue and red flashing lights canceled any plans she might've made. Out of sheer habit, Cali signaled and pulled over to the barely there shoulder at the edge of the darkened woods. With that done she turned off the engine and, for the second time that night, rolled down her window for a man in uniform.

Cali handed over her license and registration before the officer could ask.

"Let me take a look," he said, taking her ID. Something about it sounded wrong.

Cali looked up. Officer Cal Saunderson was a good-looking man. So was Ted Bundy, according to many. The officer's flashlight beam bounced over Cali's breasts, the light encircled the nexus of her thighs and pelvis—gratefully hidden beneath the pinstripes of her skirt. She didn't want him to tell her how nice she looked in pinstripes. She needed to know why he pulled her over.

Cali wouldn't get mad. Not too much. Just enough. She took a slow steadying breath.

Saunderson stank of Curtis Brand Cleaners™. Yup, a dirty cop. One who'd made it onto her family's payroll. Probably because of his ostensible charm. Often bad men came in pretty packages, with long lashes, and the stench of bleach to hide the stains.

"What color brown do they call your skin, Caledonia? I'm guessing it's something sweet," he said, handing her back the license. His fingers lingered over hers, clammier than the key had been. If Angel Baby found out one of her cops used his power to sexually harass women, she'd reward him with an expensive dinner, spiced with ground glass. And she'd *watch* him clean his plate.

Before Cali could inform Saunderson she was one of *those* Curtises and save herself the trouble of rebuking his advances, the mirror shimmered. The officer looked enchanted.

"Let me see that," he said, stubby fingers outstretched.

Her reaction wasn't immediate. Cali stared at him for a moment, as though she couldn't comprehend what he wanted. Truthfully, she didn't want him to experience the joy of the mirror. He didn't deserve it. Then again maybe an epiphany would help sanitize the icky aura the man exuded.

Cali lifted the mirror toward him. Saunderson reached out and trapped her hand beneath his uncomfortable grip around the teardrop handle. She would've jerked away but the mirror shimmered again, projecting a prism onto the officer's deceptively squared-jawed face.

Through the facets of the mirror, Cali could see into the officer's pale green eyes, and in them, she saw the reflection of what he saw. She'd underestimated Officer Saunderson, but the prismatic spectrum inside the mirror revealed his truth—captured in vivid red, orange, yellow, green, blue, indigo, and violet violence. Cali saw women screaming in the backseats of their cars, stubby fingers covering mouths, feet pounding against fogged-over windows, and other things she had to turn away from.

Angel Baby had once said, "Some folks get a little power and immediately start to rot."

Officer Saunderson had rotted into putrefaction. Cali kept her gaze averted but the officer wasn't spared the multihued fallout of his abuses. She imagined he would've preferred Angel Baby's punishment to this. This filleting of his soul. Cali watched the officer refract into his truest colors and then shatter. When she drove off, leaving whatever he'd been reduced to on the side of the road, Cali felt okay with that.

The sun rose on her way home. Cali had no choice but to grab a change of clothes from her trunk and head to work early. As she walked through security and towards the elevators, she felt giddy. Almost drunk. She hoped the guards didn't think her bright eyes were the aftermath of a wild night out. Oh, it had been wild. Just not the kind they might suspect.

The giddiness came from her excitement to get to Lucia before anyone else arrived. She wanted to show her the mirror. The same way they shared books and graphic tees with terrible puns printed on them or recipes from their homes. Things that made them feel seen.

Cali paused. What if the mirror showed Lucia an epiphany that wasn't good, wasn't beautiful like hers? Cali only worried for a moment. She shook off the anxiety. After all, knowing Lucia, she would likely see a revelation fabulous enough to make Cali jealous.

When she walked onto their floor, Cali found Lucia cleaning the area around Karen Arnold's desk. She always worked in Benedick's space before everyone else arrived to minimize contact.

"Lucia," Cali said, modulating the eagerness in her voice.

"Miss Cali! Good morning, I brought you the *pastelitos* you like."

"Morning," Cali said, stopping to stand face-to-face with her friend. "Ooh, thank you. I forgot all about lunch today...but I have something to show you too."

Lucia stopped and stuffed the cloth she'd been using to dust into her back pocket. "You seem buzzy," she said, "It must be something good."

Not quite knowing how to begin, Cali reached into her handbag and pulled out the mirror.

Lucia's eyes widened. "What's this?"

Nervous energy flooded Cali's senses and she paused again, trying to find the words. The mirror tilted downwards and Lucia reached out to steady her hand. They held it aloft together.

"I—It's just that—Sometimes we lose sight of who we are," Cali said, "and sometimes it feels like we've been pushed so far into the margins that we're invisible." She hesitated again. Then lifted the mirror higher in their combined grasp. "It's something you'll have to see for yourself, Lucia. Go ahead, take a look."

Gratification filled Cali at how easily her friend trusted her. Lucia didn't question it. She raised the mirror and gazed inside. The result dazzled. Lucia's reflection brought out colors so joyous, so imperfectly faceted in their loveliness, that Cali had to wipe sudden wetness from the corners of her eyes...

…and then the connection snapped. Cali and Lucia lurched at the sudden loss. The breath sucked out of both their chests.

"What. Is. This?"

Benedick stood to their right with her arms folded over her chest. Having arrived during their moment, she had snatched the mirror out of Lucia's hands without permission or regard. Now she stood there shaking the mirror at them—as accusatory as a wagging finger—the expression on her face sour.

Cali looked to Lucia, who looked shaken. She squeezed her friend's shoulder and Lucia lifted her head to nod back. Her bright smile said she'd seen enough. That smile saved Karen Arnold. Otherwise, Cali would have read Benedick with the kind of vitriolic honesty that would leave the woman severely burned and running for HR.

"Karen," Cali said, her jaw tightening, "kindly return my property." She extended a hand and made a quick gimme gesture.

"This looks expensive," Benedick said, the implications clear. Then she raised the multi-faceted object to her face and smugly stared into its depths…

…

…Cali had to move fast to catch the mirror before it fell…

…

…that's what gave her the idea to visit her mother. It had been a while and there was so much Cali wanted Angel Baby to see. Especially now that she understood the properties of the mirror better.

The Curtis Family Complex stood in the middle of the city, in a historically Black district and perpetually affluent neighborhood known as The Climb. In the 1920s the complex had been a stunning Art Nouveau apartment building but only one family lived there now. Hers. Cali felt the weight of that as she ascended an ornately curling staircase and entered Angel Baby's receiving room.

It wasn't her mother but her great-granddaddy, Papa Smalls, who turned away from the floor-to-ceiling bookshelves to greet her. His hair had faded to white now. In Cali's memories, it remained perpetually iron gray. Always would.

Everyone with Curtis blood lived an abnormally long time. Not only had her great-great-grandfather, Dapper Red, been alive to mail her a 35th birthday card, inscribed with a Rumi poem, but her great-great-*ganny* Ruby Glo had sent two well-dressed hoodlums to Cali's house that same day. They'd left a big ole cast iron pot of homemade chicken n' dumplings on her front porch with a note:

We miss you, baby gurl.

With deep luv, Big Mama Gloria.

Beyond that, Cali had seen her uncle come home with his throat cut nearly in half, but he'd made it back. Once the scar had keloided into a pink secondary grin against the umber brown of his throat, he'd gone back to visit the clients who'd tried to kill him. They hadn't made it home.

At 18, Cali had asked why Curtis blood lasted so long. What made it so resilient?

Angel Baby hadn't had much of an answer—only, "Blood is much thicker when it's spilled."

Cali had packed her runway-worthy wardrobe and left that day.

Now, Papa Smalls welcomed her home with a hug. The comfort in his citrus oil and Earl Grey scent almost made her change her mind. Cali stayed anyway.

But she didn't get a chance to catch up with Papa Smalls or to ask about her great-great-ganny's health, now that Ruby Glo had reached the age when she'd either have to call it quits or walk into the afterlife still breathing.

Angel Baby walked in before Cali and Papa Smalls had a chance to say very much at all. The crime queen sauntered across the rug-laden wooden floors. Eventually settling onto the high-backed saffron upholstered wooden chair Cali remembered as a throne. The decorative Art Nouveau butterflies carved into the towering seat back had intimidated her way back when—as intended.

Angelina Curtis hadn't changed much. Her dark satin skin made it hard to guess her age. Could be 30 or 50 or 70. Her hips were fuller now and her breasts stretched the lapels of her suit jacket a bit further apart. That cool aloofness remained the same, though. As did the long mahogany brown braids, worn tight to the curve of her head and cascading down her back.

Cali clenched her fists. She wasn't angry. Not really. Not at all. Not that much. Her mother just bothered her. That's all.

"You staying?" Angel Baby asked, rolling something imaginary between her thumb and index finger.

"Of course, she's staying." Papa Smalls declared, resting his current book on the nearest table. "Why else would she be here?" He cupped Cali's cheek with a sandpaper palm. "She sure is your daughter. Isn't she, Angelina? My pretty Caledonia."

"Is she?" Angel Baby said in a molasses-covered voice, thick enough to smother someone. "We'll see." She took long moments to assess Cali. Then she said, "Why did you come?" The tone sounded accusatory.

Cali could've said so many things. The options singed the tip of her tongue. Recriminations, resentment, shame. So many things she'd pushed down too far to retrieve.

Instead, she squared her shoulders, "I came to show you something."

It might've been trust or it may have been arrogance—Cali guessed the latter—but Angel Baby took the mirror without pause and looked into its depths without question. Like anyone, she must've held a certain assurance of what she'd see there. Everyone expected their face. No one suspected their truth. And the sharp edge of surprise swung in two directions.

People didn't refract into one red or yellow or violet or any of the other colors. The facets of a person came in vermillion, crimson, and ruby. Ochre, amber, marigold. Amethyst and orchid and indigo…and on throughout the spectrum.

Angel Baby fractured into every possible shade of bloody red. So many Cali could smell the dank metallic tang. But not all her mother's reds shimmered with violence. Some were passion, others were sanguine, and one particular hue covered their neighborhood, The Climb, in a shared sense of security. The Curtises made deals with dirty cops, for sure. Yet somehow the bloodshed—the blood they'd bled—kept their community clean. Sometimes bonds were born of blood.

Her mother's words looked different in the light of the mirror: "Blood is so much thicker when it's spilled."

Cali tried to turn away from the harsh glare but the mirror held on to her. In the yellow facets, she watched a young Angelina get revenge on a middle school classmate. Baby Angelina had whispered a rumor, one draped in enough fact to turn lies into momentary truths. The boy's father, a minister, had kicked him out while his mother cried with her back turned.

Angel Baby remembered the hornet's sting of guilt and the lesson she'd learned became a part of her, as though entrapped in amber. The recoil of her mother's hard-earned wisdom flared too brightly for Cali's eyes and ears: "Girls like us use our fists because our wits are far more deadly."

Cali cried tears tinted in amethyst. The tiny gems cut as they rolled down her cheeks and under her chin. In the indigo facets, her mother tied her shoes because Cali had never learned how. In the orchids, she recalled picnics. Her favorite books were read aloud while her head rested in Angel Baby's embrace. Warm as the summer at dusk.

Cali had lived good and she'd lived right but it didn't stop the echo of her mother's voice, *"Some folks get a little power and immediately start to rot."*

As the blues of Cali's newfound sorrow mixed with the redness of the tracks on her cheeks, she realized: *Maybe she wasn't ready to see the truth hidden in violet.*

Cali stumbled backward.

Angel Baby slumped on her throne, shattered.

The mirror clanged onto the floor.

"Look at what you've done," Papa Smalls cried out, his voice hoarse with heartache. "Just look."

Cali couldn't look at her mother. She already knew what the mirror left behind. Instead, she knelt down and lifted the accursed object to her own face. Cali needed to see how she'd changed for herself. And, after everything she'd done in those last few hours, that was her biggest mistake.

Perhaps the Curtis blood would save her.

illustrated by
Ananyo Chatterjee

(Unit 18)
NIRVANA
by David Disspain

"Mr. Freedman? Can you hear me?"

The orderly was always a little on edge around Mr. Freedman and seeing him here in the middle of the night sitting upright in bed with his eyes open didn't do anything to allay that. The orderly already thought the old man was nuts with his disturbingly frequent sleepwalking and strange rants about God and the universe at the most random times. Now the crazy old man was just sitting there, staring blankly off into nothingness, his lips moving like he was trying to remember some old song that he could only half recall the words to.

The orderly was more than a little relieved to see Mr. Freedman's dedicated nurse Angelo whip around the corner with his clipboard and stethoscope in hand. Angelo was always calm. Angelo always knew what to do.

"Hey, uh, Angelo. Check this out." The orderly's voice had the distinct timbre of someone scared but trying not to sound like it. Angelo stopped and took a survey of the room and the elderly man sitting up in his hospital bed. He looked at his watch: 3:33 a.m. He deliberately and slowly set the stethoscope and the clipboard on the table in Mr. Freedman's room near three framed pictures that were personal and special to Mr. Freedman, one of his late wife, one of him and his son and daughter, and his old camp photo, with all the guys in his unit just before they had graduated from basic training.

"Ok, Mr. Freedman. What are we doing here tonight?" Angelo's voice was calm and there was little doubt that the orderly found the nurse's tone far more soothing than Mr. Freedman did. The nurse checked the silent monitor displaying the old man's vital signs. "There now, what are you seeing?" Angelo asked.

There was no reaction or reply from the old man, even as Angelo double-checked the leads and connectors to be sure Mr. Freedman hadn't inadvertently disconnected anything. "Alright. Alright. Have it your way. We'll ride this out together then." Angelo sat on the bed gently and reached out to take one of Mr. Freedman's hands, then nodded at the orderly. "Go on, it's okay. Mr. Freedman and I are going to sit here for a while together. I got this. You can go."

The orderly didn't waste a second in trying to make himself scarce but Angelo called for him with one last thing to say.

"Oh, take that clipboard to the nurses' station, but leave the key."

The orderly interrupted his hasty retreat only long enough to unclip the key from the clipboard and set it on the table. He gave the key an irritated look. It seemed to be covered in some sort of grease or oil and he was wiping the slick residue on his scrubs, trying to get it off his fingers. He couldn't make out what it said on the keychain, but he definitely didn't take the time to examine it closely.

Angelo sat calmly with Mr. Freedman, talking softly to him. "It's okay, Wilbur. I'm right here. I've got you." It was several minutes before Mr. Freedman blinked a few times vacantly. "That's right Wilbur. Go on back to sleep. You'll feel better."

The old man sighed as he laid down, drifted back to sleep, and snored softly. Angelo pulled the blankets up around Mr. Freedman's shoulders and looked at his watch and the monitor before continuing his rounds.

The next morning, Mr. Freedman woke up normally, albeit a little later than usual, and the on-duty nurse, a lovely little woman named Tien, entered his room with her squeaky tennis shoes to see how he was doing.

"Good morning, Wilbur," she said cheerfully. "How are you feeling today?"

Wilbur Freedman squinted at her and rubbed the back of his neck. "Not great. Feeling like I been run over by a tank this morning."

Tien reached out to take his wrist and check his pulse. "Not surprising. Angelo's report said you were up again last night."

Wilbur grunted. "Third time this week. No wonder I feel like this." The old man chuckled softly to himself. "Musta scared the crap out of that new orderly, huh? What's his name?"

Tien tried hard not to smile, but it broke through. She simply couldn't help it. "Russell." She tried to hold her laugh in but failed.

Wilbur rubbed his eyes while he joined her laughter.

"Are your eyes bothering you?" Tien asked.

"Just feel sandy-like. Got any of those drops left?"

"Of course." She indicated he should tilt his head back while she fished them out of her pocket. Mr. Freedman always wanted the moisturizing drops in the morning, which made little sense to Tien. He'd just had his eyes closed all night; there was no reason he'd need the drops for any real medicinal purpose. Tien suspected he really did it for the extra attention every morning and she saw little reason in denying him.

Wilbur raised his chin and blinked rapidly as Tien put a drop in each eye. "Ah, much better," he said contentedly, as if she'd just given him an hour-long massage.

Tien nodded knowingly. He'd ask her for coffee next.

Before he could, Tien stood and put her hands on her hips. "Wheelchair or walker today?"

Wilbur scrunched his face up as he pondered the choices. Tien gave him a pointed look. Every morning with Wilbur was roughly the same. When he woke up, he wanted eye drops, then he wanted to pee, then he wanted coffee. Whether he chose to use a wheelchair or walker and the time of morning were really the only variables.

After she gave him an impatient snort, he answered: "Wheelchair."

"As you wish." She stepped outside his room to fetch it. With a squeak of her shoes, she settled him into the chair and made sure all of his connectors were disconnected properly. "And away we g—"

"What's that?" He interrupted, spying the key on the table.

Tien looked at what his gnarled old hand was gesturing towards. "Looks like a key." She said flatly.

"Is it mine? I don't remember seeing it here before."

"It must be yours. It's not mine." She gave the key a once-over but was ready to move on and get him going on his breakfast. He clearly wasn't having it though.

"Let me see it." He put one hand on the wheelchair wheel to stop her from rolling him out. She picked up the key by the keychain and let him examine it. "Weird. It's got some kind of oil or grease on it. Like Three In One."

Tien wasn't sure what "Three in One" was, but she didn't question it. He frequently got fixated on the news or finding a certain puzzle piece or any number of mundane things. This didn't seem to be any different.

"The key is weird too. Like one of those old-fashioned skeleton keys from when I was a boy. Haven't seen one in ages." He turned it over in his hand several times, examining it closely. The keychain read: "Auntie's Attic. Well-Kept Storage For Needs Big And Small. Unit 18."

"I don't remember ever owning a storage unit," he muttered. "When Katie sold the house, she said there was plenty of room and…" Wilbur mumbled details of how he remembered things, going on for a while until finally trailing off into silence. He looked suddenly at Tien with a sheepish expression. "I'm doing it again aren't I?" he asked quietly.

Tien looked at him with the same patient expression that a mother looks at a young child. "Yes, I was just waiting for you to tire yourself out. But now that I've got you up, let's get your day moving along."

Wilbur looked at her. "Restroom. Then Coffee. It better not be cold again."

"Well, we would have been there sooner had you not gone on and on," Tien teased. She waited so that he could place the key back on the table. "Have no fear, mon capitaine, it will be right here when you get back." She wheeled him out of his room and towards his day.

Later, one of the day's activities was a trip to the local shopping mall, something Wilbur was normally excited about and always wanted to be a part of, but Tien noted that something seemed unusual about his behavior, and when he declined the invitation to the mall and instead wanted to be taken back to his room, she knew he wasn't feeling well.

"Just tired," he replied when she questioned him about it. "Scaring the crap out of Russell took more out of me than I thought."

She smiled at his humor. That much still seemed in character for him. He watched some television news later that afternoon, and as her shift was ending, she noticed what he had for dinner: just a few grapes, a bit of grilled cheese, and half a glass of water. His food intake was a bit lighter than usual. He didn't even touch the tomato soup, which was one of his favorites. She made the additional notes on his chart and returned the clipboard to the nurses' station. Angelo would be back again this evening and would keep a close eye on him.

A bit later when Angelo arrived, he was briefed on the changes, read the notes, and adjusted his own nightly routine. If something was wrong with Mr. Freedman, Angelo wanted to be ready.

As he helped him back into bed and reconnected his monitor leads, Angelo noted that Mr. Freedman was quieter than normal. "Everything OK Mr. Freedman?"

"I'm good. Ready to scare Russell again."

Angelo smiled. Whatever Mr. Freedman was feeling on the inside, he wasn't letting it affect him on the outside. "Well, Mr. Freedman, Russell has the night off, and you don't scare me, so how about a nice, quiet night where you do a bunch of sleeping and I get some work done?"

"Deal." Wilbur pulled the blanket up to his chin. "Hey Angelo, do you know where that key came from?"

"It was left for you at the nurses' station."

"So one of the kids didn't drop it off?"

"No sir. It was there when I came on duty last night."

This answer didn't sit very well with the old man.

"You got your phone on you?" Mr. Freedman asked. Angelo nodded. "Will you look it up for me? On the internet, I mean."

"Sure." Angelo withdrew his cell phone from the pocket of his scrubs and typed in the name from the keychain—"Auntie's Attic." He turned the phone so Mr. Freedman could look at the home page photo. "Here it is. Does that look like the place?"

Mr. Freedman took the phone, holding it close as he peered at the photo. "Don't know. Never been there. Never even heard of it."

"Strange." Angelo took back his phone and read. "'Well-kept storage for needs big and small…' Looks pretty normal. Not one of those chain places. Clean. Quiet." He shrugged.

"Yeah, I'm sure it's nice, but there's just one problem. My kids didn't buy it, I didn't buy it. Helen didn't buy it." Mentioning his deceased wife always made Mr. Freedman a little sad and it reflected in his voice. "No one knows how this got here."

Angelo gave the old man a pointed look but said nothing. Mr. Freedman looked at the key on the table and then more longingly at the picture of Helen. Several moments of silence passed between them.

Mr. Freedman then asked. "Will you help me go see what's in it?

"Sure, Mr. Freedman. Whatever you want."

Mr. Freedman smiled and closed his eyes.

"We'll get Gloria to take us over there one night," said Angelo. "When do you want to go?"

"I'm not getting any younger—why wait?" Mr. Freedman said quietly. "Think Gloria can get the van tomorrow?"

"I'll ask her." Angelo grinned. "That means you need to get a good night's sleep. No funny business tonight."

"No promises," Mr. Freedman said sleepily.

When Tien started her shift the next morning, Mr. Freedman was still asleep. All reports were that he'd had a quiet night, but she knew it was unusual for him to still be sleeping at this time. She checked his monitor, and his blood pressure and pulse were a bit down. She made a note on his chart with his vital signs and another note for the doctor to review them. Maybe his meds needed adjustment. She considered sadly what other things a downturn meant. When he finally woke, they ran through their usual banter, and once she got him settled at the breakfast table, he surprised her again and passed on the coffee, opting instead for one of the sodas that came in retro glass bottles. They were new in the cafeteria and were popular, as the other residents could recall the old soda fountains and shops from their glory days. Tien had cared for the man for more than three years, and he'd never passed on a morning cup of coffee before. She sat with the other nurses and watched him at the table interacting with the other care patients. It wasn't a big dietary change—certainly one that wouldn't affect him greatly. But it was a change, and despite the sugar and caffeine, he seemed subdued.

He motioned for her and she went to him. "Where to, mon capitaine?"

"I'd like to stay here a bit longer, but I was hoping you'd go get the picture of me and the guys from basic training off the table in my room. I want to tell these folks a story about the guys and I want their picture here. Will you please do that for me?"

"Sure. You feeling okay?"

"Yeah. I wanted to tell them about Sutton and Callo. I don't think I've told them that story before. I dreamt I talked to them last night." He coughed several times and wiped his mouth with a paper napkin.

Tien nodded and left to retrieve the photo. When she reached his room, Lois from the cleaning staff was changing the sheets on Wilbur's bed. A bucket and mop stood by at the ready. She looked at the pictures on the table. There was one of Wilbur's deceased wife, who had passed away six years ago. Tien smiled at the image. Another was of Wilbur and his adult children, Katie and Patrick, taken last summer. She'd met both at different times and remembered them both as being very nice and wanting the best for their father. She grabbed the other framed photo on the table—Wilbur in the Army at his basic training graduation. He looked so young and full of life back then. So much so that some of the other nurses had a hard time picking him out from among the fresh-faced young men in the picture. She returned to the dining room where Wilbur had the other patients fully engaged with his tale of Private Sutton fighting Sergeant Callo over a girl named Joanie. She'd heard the story at least a dozen times, and she was certain the other patients at the table had heard it half that, but if any of them were bored or disinterested, they didn't show it.

She set the photo on the table in front of him while he spoke, careful not to interrupt him. He often spoke of his old Army pals. In Wilbur's opinion, they were the finest friends anyone could ever have and the finest men who had ever served. She resumed her place with the other nurses and watched the care patients laugh and talk and share their stories yet again, as if they'd never heard them before. She made some notes on her chart and chatted with the other nurses until they were done.

When she wheeled Wilbur back to his room for a nap, he clasped her forearm. "Thank you," he said, sincere and earnest.

Tears welled in her eyes. She knew he wasn't just talking about the trip back to his bed. He seemed to be mentally preparing for the inevitable. She glanced at the key on the table. She hoped the mystery of it would encourage him to be strong a little longer. "You're welcome," she said quietly, and the world fell away as she looked deeply into his leather-brown eyes. Eyes that had seen a lot of life. Eyes that had seen a lot of death.

She took a deep breath. "So then, what's your plan?"

"What in the hell are you talking about?" Wilbur asked.

She picked up the key from the table and dangled it from its keychain. "I know you've been talking to Angelo about this. I know he requested the van and a ride from Gloria. Do you really think you have secrets from me, old man?"

Wilbur looked a bit embarrassed. "We're going tonight. Angelo is going to help me go see what's inside."

"You're eighty-two years old, Wilbur, and in full-time care at an assisted living facility. Do you really think it's smart to go traipsing off at night to some weird storage locker with God knows what inside?"

Wilbur hung his head. Getting a dressing-down from Tien was rare, and it left him feeling a bit regretful that he hadn't told his primary nurse. He stared at his hands. Hands that had held a rifle and defended the country. Hands that had built a house, a family, a life. Hands that held Helen's when they were married and had helped his children eat and walk and drive. They were the hands of an old man at the end of his life.

"I don't care if it's smart or not. That key is mine. Angelo brought it to me and it's mine. I'm going to go see what's there, whether it's smart or not. Why? Because it's my life, Tien. Eighty-two or twenty-eight, it's my life, and no one can tell me what to do with whatever time I've got left. I take my medications. I do my exercises. I eat Brussels sprouts and lima beans not because I enjoy them, but because you tell me to. I listen to you all the time. But now you listen to me. I'll do whatever I damn well please."

When he finished, he was looking directly at her, and she caught a hint of the same fire he had in the picture of him with his old Army buddies. His voice never rose beyond the level of a casual conversation, but to her, he might as well have been standing there screaming at her. Long moments passed before they both burst into laughter, unable to hold back any longer.

"There's my Wilbur," she said when she had finally composed herself. "There's my old man."

"Nurse Ratched you ain't!" he playfully chided through a wide grin.

"Go to sleep. My shift will have ended by the time you wake up, so you be careful! And no skipping your meds! Promise?"

"I promise. I'll tell you everything tomorrow."

"I know. I know."

She made notes for the nurses on his chart and he was asleep before she left the room. She hesitated, lingering for a few moments before her squeaky shoes finally left him.

When Wilbur woke up, he was surprised to see the strong, blocky figure of Gloria standing over him. "It's a little past six—you still want to go?"

Wilbur rubbed his eyes, wishing Tien was there with her eye drops. "Yes, I do. Where's Angelo?"

"Said he couldn't make it. Something about an emergency and helping an old friend."

"Who?"

"Don't know, don't care" Gloria replied curtly. "Ain't none of my business."

Wilbur sighed heavily, moved the light blanket off, and tried and failed at swinging his feet over the edge of the bed. Gloria's strong arms helped him stand and she slipped his shoes on. He tottered.

"Whoa now! Let me get the wheelchair. Here you go. Move that foot. That's it. Sit. Ah...grab that. Good!"

Wilbur grunted as she helped him sit. He hated to admit it, but he loved her little play-by-play commentary as she assisted with things. It had been a while since he'd seen her. He found her rougher ways oddly comforting.

He swooned a little, dizzy and lightheaded.

"You sure now?" Gloria asked.

"Yes, I'm sure. I have to take my meds. I promised Tien I would before we go. She made me promise."

"Alright, alright. Let's get it done." She looked at his chart, and retrieved the pills he was supposed to take, taking extra care that she read everything right and wasn't giving him the wrong thing. "Ok. One of these. One of these. One of...oh, lordy, look at that one. That's a big one. Yes, mm hmm. Ok." She moved to the table and continued. "Let's get you some water, here. Ok, good. Ooh. Cold. Good." She poured him water and stood with her hands on her hips as she watched him expectantly.

Wilbur chuckled and took his medication. He reached for the key and motioned towards it.

"What's that? Whatcha want? Oh, this?" She handed it to him.

"Do you know where this is?" Wilbur asked her.

"I think I do. It's way out of town, take a minute to get there."

"Angelo was going to use his phone..."

"Well Angelo ain't here, is he?" Gloria shushed him. "I been driving you folks all over for more than twenty years, Mr. Freedman. No phone is gonna tell me how to get there."

"Fair enough."

"So, you ready now?"

"I'm cold."

Gloria reached for the blanket. "Let's just get his here then. Then this…Then…Yep. And now…Voila!" She spread the blanket over him, tucking it in around his legs and making a little wrap for his feet. "You're going to be out of excuses soon," she teased.

Wilbur playfully stuck his tongue out at her. "Let's go," he said quietly.

Gloria wheeled him out into the hall, past the nurses' station, and outside to the waiting van. It was wheelchair accessible, and she lowered the platform for him expertly. Quickly and efficiently, she had him loaded up and secured. When she pulled out of the parking lot, he was asleep again.

They'd been driving a half hour when she glanced back at him in the mirror and noted that his eyes were open, but his breathing and expression let her well-trained eye know that he wasn't awake and that this was one of his episodes. "You're okay, honey," she said softly. "You're okay."

Wilbur stared blankly, and his expression changed from slack jawed nothingness to a look of terror. He made no sound, but he looked like he was screaming.

Gloria found a gas station and quickly pulled over. She slid the side door open and stepped into the back of the van to be with him. She clasped his hand and stroked his white hair, trying to soothe him back to comfortable sleep. She snapped open a medical kit bag and grabbed a stethoscope. She listened to his heart, and his lungs, then took his blood pressure. Although all were a little erratic, he still seemed strong, and when she took his hand again, he squeezed hard. He was in there somewhere. He was just having one of his episodes he was famous at the facility for.

"You hang in there, honey. You're okay. You're okay."

After a few minutes he slumped over and his eyes closed. For a heartbeat, Gloria thought he was gone, but he took a big gulp of air and coughed a few times before settling into a gentle sleep. She went around to the front passenger door and opened it. On the seat was his chart, and she furiously scribbled the notes of the evening. She had just finished recording his vital signs when she heard him ask, "Are we there?" She looked back. Wilbur was sitting up and looking around.

"No sir, not yet. Had to take care of something real quick." She threw the clipboard onto the seat and shut the door, then walked around to look at him more closely. He was pale, and stricken-looking. Truth be told, she thought he looked weaker. She took his wrist and checked his blood pressure and pulse again. Both were a little low, but they always were after an episode. "Any pain?"

"No, my eyes feel gritty, though. Got any eye drops?"

"Fresh out. Want me to see if there's any inside?" She nodded at the gas station store.

"Naw. It's okay. I like the ones Tien uses. Those are the good stuff."

Gloria nodded along knowingly. "Okay then. I'm gonna tell it to you straight, chief. You just had another one of your episodes right here in my van. If Doctor Mansur knew you were out here and had an episode, he'd call us back and conduct a full exam on you, right after he fired me. So you tell me…go on or go home?"

"Go on," Wilbur said without hesitation, then coughed several times. Gloria fished her bottle of water out of her cupholder, but he waved her off. "How close are we?"

"A few more miles. You sure you're up to it?"

"Positive."

"Alright then. On we go. But I'm not going to let you sleep any more. You're going to have to stay awake, and if you start sleeping again, I'm just going to turn us around and take you back to your bed."

Wilbur nodded. True to his word, he stayed awake for the last few miles, and as the prospect of figuring out what the key was all about grew nearer, he felt nervous and excited. Gloria watched him carefully in the rearview mirror, knowing that his condition was fragile and that she had been entrusted with his care.

At last, she pulled into the parking lot of Auntie's Attic. There was only one other car in the parking lot, and the large neon sign out front had several letters that weren't working. A sign with an arrow pointed towards the office.

Gloria turned the van off and unbuckled her seatbelt. "Stay here."

He laughed and looked at her helplessly, knowing full well the wheelchair was locked into position and wouldn't move.

"No, ma'am. Staying put."

Gloria walked over to the office and was gone for a few minutes before she came back with a paper map of the facility. She started up the van and headed for the barrier that blocked the entrance to the units. There was an electric buzz and the gate lifted. She drove the van in and parked in a space not far from the entrance. With the practiced precision of a pit car crew, she lowered the platform with Wilbur's wheelchair, unlocked the wheel locks, and situated him where she could raise the platform again and close the van doors, all while narrating her actions in her usual way. "Lower this…good. Unlock this. Unlock that. Nice. Okay, let's get you over here, this seems good…Let's get this back up. Great. And close. And lock." She looked at him, noting how small he looked out here in the world. "Okay! Let's do this!"

For the first time, Wilbur looked nervous. "Okay…"

"We've got you this far, chief. You still okay?"

"Yes," he answered, hardly confident.

Gloria crouched next to him, looking at him with both concern and confidence. "I've got you, right? I'm right here. Listen to me. I don't have any issue with taking you back and putting you in bed if that's what you want. We can do this another time. I'm not going to make the decision. You are. This is your thing, chief. I'm here to help you with whichever way you want to go."

Wilbur looked at her and nodded. "Let's go see."

Gloria gave him a questioning look to be certain.

He gave her a weak smile. "I'm sure. Let's go see."

She nodded and pushed him up onto the sidewalk and towards the facility doors. Unit 18 was around a corner and a couple of doors down. A large padlock rested against the floor, locking the unit closed. Gloria held out her hand. Wilbur fished the key out of his pocket and gave it to her. She knelt down and inserted the key into the strange-looking lock. It turned three times in a clockwise motion before it clicked and popped open. She worked the lock free of the bolt and set it down on the cold concrete. She turned to him.

Wilbur rubbed his forehead and nodded. Gloria gave the handle a sharp upward pull. It slid open with a roar and a clatter. Wilbur peered in.

It was dark inside the unit, and the dim bulb in the hall didn't make things much better. He could see blinking lights and the outline of some sort of machinery. Gloria stepped inside and disappeared from his view in the darkness. He was about to call her name when the flicker of fluorescent bulbs and an electric hum kicked in. As the lights warmed and shone brighter, he could see Gloria standing there, and then he could make out an exact replica of his room back home: a made-up hospital bed, the vital sign monitors, a defibrillator box on the wall, and a long table with the pictures of his wife, his kids, and his Army buddies.

Perhaps it was the overconfident expression on Gloria's face or maybe it was being well outside of the familiar, comfortable confines of his nursing home, but Wilbur had not been this frightened since fighting in the steamy jungles of Vietnam. The sight of a complete re-creation of his room in some strange, random storage unit he just found out about was chilling, and it shook him to his soul. His guts turned watery and cold as he looked more closely at the things inside the unit. Same type of bed. Same type of table. Even the same type of picture frames with the same pictures. He was certain these weren't his actual things, but the fact that someone had so completely fabricated them to look identical to his possessions was overwhelming beyond his comprehension.

"I want to go home," he said flatly.

"But you've come so far now, Wilbur."

Tien's voice behind him made him wince and throw his hands up as if to shield himself from some unseen attack. He gasped. His breath was coming in short, ragged breaths as she walked into his view. Completely absent was the sound of her squeaky shoes, and that small fact made Wilbur's blood run cold.

"Ti…Tien. What? What…are you doing here?"

"It's okay, Wilbur. Try to relax. We're not here to hurt you. In fact, just the opposite. We want to make the episodes go away."

Wilbur's vision swam. He felt faint and he blinked rapidly, struggling to grasp her words as he grappled with the scene before him. "Wha? You...can make...uh...how?"

"That's why you're here, Wilbur. That's why Angelo introduced the key to you."

Wilbur snapped his head to his right to find Angelo leaning casually against the storage unit frame. New fear washed through him like a tidal wave.

"It's okay, Mr. Freedman," Angelo said. "We're not going to hurt you. We can make the episodes go away and you'll never have to deal with them ever again." Angelo took a few steps closer.

"No!" Wilbur shouted. "Stay away from me!"

Angelo raised his hands apologetically. "It's okay, Mr. Freedman. It's okay."

Wilbur glanced around at all of them in naked terror. "I want to go home. Please, can we just go home?"

Gloria knelt, lowering herself to appear less threatening and so he could better see her. "Listen, chief. I know you're scared. I know you don't understand right now, but if you trust us, we can help you. The room, our faces, it's all to make you feel more comfortable. It's all so things seem familiar. We thought it would help."

"I want to go home," Wilbur whispered in horror. "Just take me home." A tear ran down his cheek.

"Now, now, Wilbur," Tien spoke up. "Come on. Where's my guy? Where's my old man?"

Wilbur sniffled, his voice shaking. "I'm...I'm scared. I don't know what to do. Helen wo...would...would know. She was always so brave. Even when she was diagnosed, she took it way better than me." Wilbur took a slow, tremorous breath. "I don't know if...I mean...will it hurt?"

"No sir. It won't hurt a bit. I promise." She smiled at him. "We really are here to help you."

Wilbur wiped at his eyes, and she held up a small bottle of eye drops, the good ones.

"No thanks," he whispered. His eyes drooped, and he felt weak and very tired.

"Let us help. Let us get you home," she said softly.

"Home," Wilbur whispered as his head slumped forward.

Tien checked his pulse at his neck. "He's weak and fading. Let's get this done."

The others nodded and sprang into action. Gloria wheeled him to the side of the bed, and she and Angelo picked him up and laid him down on it. He seemed lighter somehow. More frail and fragile than ever. Tien closed the storage unit door. Angelo removed Wilbur's shoes and his sweater and unbuttoned a few buttons on his shirt. At the same time, Gloria attached leads to Wilbur and connected them to the vital sign monitor. Angelo placed an oxygen mask over Wilbur's mouth and nose. Tien moved the wheelchair out of the way, then bent to pick up an elaborate case that was resting near the bed. She placed it on the bed near his waist and opened it. She peered inside and studied the contents. She glanced at Wilbur's face to find him staring at her. Tears glistened in her eyes, as she knew things were never going to be the same after this. No more of his jokes. No more long talks. No more pushing his wheelchair through the park or listening to him tell the same stories again and again. He would be forever changed, and her along with him. She looked away, ashamed that this was affecting her so much, but his hand took hers and she looked back at him. He nodded weakly, letting her know he was okay, that it was okay to proceed.

Tien looked at Angelo and Gloria as they finished. Both had sad expressions that mirrored hers. They knew the permanence of this as well. They both would miss him in their own way. She wanted to look at Wilbur again, but she also wanted to remember his confidence in her, and in them, to allow this. Instead, she focused on what was inside the case, and, with great care, she slowly lifted an ornate bottle out of the case and held it up reverently.

Wilbur's eyes followed it fearfully. He was drawn to it and he watched in a trance-like state as if the bottle was a bright light and he was a moth. Gloria took the case away, and Angelo stood at the head of the bed, waiting.

Tien gently pulled the bottle's stopper free. Gloria and Angelo clasped their hands in religious supplication.

Tien whispered, "I love you, Wilbur," and more tears welled in her eyes.

She lowered the bottle until three drops fell on Wilbur's forehead. His eyes closed the moment those precious drops touched his skin.

Angelo whispered, "I love you, Wilbur."

Gloria swallowed heavily, and choked back a sob as she whispered, "I love you, Wilbur."

Tien restoppered the bottle and placed it gently back in the case. With Angelo at the head of the bed, and Gloria on one side, Tien placed herself on the opposite side and held out her arms. Angelo and Gloria reached out as well until they clasped hands, their arms forming a triangle above Wilbur. The three caretakers closed their eyes and raised their faces to the fluorescent lights in the ceiling above, waiting for the holy medicine to take effect.

Wilbur opened his eyes and looked up at them weakly. It seemed like he was trying to say something but the effort was too much. The places where the drops had touched him felt cold and wet like ice, and the back of his throat ached like he'd been eating ice cream too fast.

The lights flickered.

Wilbur's head gently and slowly fell to one side. His eyes were open, and it appeared he had fallen into one of his episodes once more. The caretakers released their clasped hands and Tien felt for a pulse. She found one. A little weaker than she would have liked, but it was there, nonetheless.

"Wilbur, can you hear me?" she asked.

Unblinking and unresponsive, he remained silent, just like he always was during one of his episodes. It wasn't until she saw a tear well up and slowly slide from the corner of his eye that she felt the medicine was taking effect.

Wilbur could hear music. It was far away, distant and muffled at first, but then grew stronger and clearer. Lights swam in his vision and out of the strange darkness that had enveloped him he saw shapes and colors. His skin was hot and he was sweating. A cylindrical shape formed in his vision. It was a beer bottle, open, its frothy contents three-quarters gone. In front of him on the table were his hands, young and vital, peeling at the label on the bottle and dropping the tattered remnants on the rough wooden table. The music came from a jukebox in the corner, one of those bubbler kinds from the '40s that had been popular during the Second World War. He couldn't quite make out the tune, or perhaps he'd never heard whatever song it was playing before. He thought it sounded like Del Shannon, but, no matter how hard he tried, he couldn't make it out.

"Are you ignoring me?" a voice called.

He blinked a few times, then noticed the face of Al Sutton, his best friend.

"No, I ain't ignoring you, I was just...I don't know. Lost. You know, thinking about something else."

"Better get your head on straight. I need your help, man." Al pushed back on his nose the thick-rimmed glasses the guys in the unit called "birth control" since few girls would talk to you if you wore them.

"With what?"

Sutton made an irritated noise. "With Joanie, man. Just look at 'em will ya?"

Still confused, Wil followed Sutton's pointing finger over to where Sergeant Callo and a pretty blonde girl were talking quietly a few tables over. The two seemed familiar, like he'd seen this before, or maybe had just been talking about this with someone. He shook his head, trying to clear the cobwebs.

"You're screwed. Callo is a sergeant, not to mention he's better looking than you. She loves him. Just look at the way she's looking at him."

Sutton was already looking, but the young woman wasn't actually looking at the sergeant just then. Her eyes had traveled over to where Wilbur and Al Sutton were sitting.

"Jesus," Al said under his breath.

Wil laughed at him. "Look, Joanie is cute and all, but there are a lot of girls here. Forget her. Look over there. Look at those two." He nodded to two young women who had just entered. "See? Now those girls are worth your time and atten..." He glanced at Sutton and trailed off, seeing his friend silently mouthing something to Joanie while Sergeant Callo was looking the other way. "Callo's going to kill you."

"Some things are worth dying for." Sutton quickly rose to his feet.

Not knowing what else to do, Wil lurched to his feet as well. Standing there, he glanced around, uncertain why the sensation of standing seemed different. He blinked rapidly a few times. *I'm drunk,* he thought.

Sutton began walking over to the blond. "You with me, Wil?"

"Sure," Wil replied, and he walked behind him for several paces before meeting the gaze of one of the girls he had been looking at before, who were now sitting at the bar. Without a word, he left Sutton to his fate and made a beeline for her. When he arrived at her side, she smiled, and in an instant he knew he'd made the right choice.

"Want to make five easy dollars?" he asked her.

She laughed nervously, unsure of what kind of line he was giving her.

Wil leaned against the bar near her. "What's your name?"

"Helen, and this is my friend Nancy."

Wil smiled and nodded at her.

"What's this about making five dollars?" Helen asked.

"Right. Ok, well that guy in the glasses right there is Al Sutton. He's about to get punched in the face because he loves Joanie, that blond girl he's talking to. Problem is, Joanie is Sergeant Callo's steady girl. That's Callo there, the blocky-headed guy. Callo is the one that's going to punch Al."

Helen looked at her friend with an amused grin. "Okay, so how do I make five bucks out of this situation?"

Wil playfully cracked his knuckles. He pulled out some money, unfolded the bills, and quickly counted them.

"A cab ride over to the base is about five dollars. Here's ten. If you go outside and hail a cab, you can keep five."

"What are you going to do?"

"I'm going to make sure he only gets punched once and then drag him into that cab."

"You're kidding."

"I wish," he said ruefully.

With equal parts curiosity and amusement, Helen motioned to her friend and they picked their way through the tables and towards the exit. Wilbur took a moment to watch Helen walk, and by the time he turned to join Al, a swell of sound, a crash of tables, and voices shouting told him everything he needed to know. He fought his way through the crowd to find Al and Sergeant Callo brawling. The fireplug of a sergeant had Sutton in a headlock, and they were throwing wildly drunken punches at one another. Wilbur looked on for a second or two before taking a deep breath and plunging forward to break it up.

He grabbed the sergeant's arm and tried to pull it free. The effort proved unbalancing and threw the three of them crashing into a table, breaking a chair and sending drinks flying.

"Stop it!" he yelled.

Others were beginning to grab at the fighters as well. Rough hands picked him up and he was blindsided by the pain of something smashing into his head. He looked around, his vision swimming, and everything sounded hollow and tinny.

Al was standing in front of him with a torn and bloody shirt and what was very likely a broken nose that was bleeding quite badly. Several soldiers grappled him and they were carrying him out of the place. Wil was violently shoved right behind. In the chaos, there was no sign of Sergeant Callo and Wil wondered for a second if he was still alive.

They reached the door and a rough kick to his back lanced pain through his body and sent him sprawling onto the sidewalk outside. Al was lying in the gutter, holding his hands across his battered face. The remains of a warm beer sprayed the both of them as the doors slammed shut behind them, leaving them lying in the path of people walking by, their hard and scornful stares embarrassing the both of them.

"I thought this Saturday night would be different," Wilbur joked as he rolled himself into a sitting position next to Al. The side of his face felt wet and he dabbed at it gingerly once he realized it was blood.

"You should see your face, Wil. You've got a knot on the side of your head the size of an egg. I always knew you were hardheaded, but Jesus man, I don't think I ever meant it literally."

"You're not exactly looking like Rock Hudson there buddy."

"Clearly." Al took a deep breath and sighed heavily. "That was just damn stupid, wasn't it?"

"Nah. Joanie is pretty cute. You're just late in your timing, you know?"

"Yeah." Al nodded. "You're probably right. Just late."

The door opened behind them and, surprisingly, Joanie emerged. She crouched next to Sutton and handed him a bar towel. Al looked at her through a rapidly swelling eye and she put a hand on his shoulder.

"Big dummy," she said. "You've probably got a broken nose." Her hand guided his up to his face so he could begin stopping the blood. "Tilt your head back." Smiling, she gave him a gentle faux punch across his chin and went back inside.

Wil was picking broken glass out of hair and shirt when Helen's shapely calves filled his vision.

"Cabbie says it's five-fifty to get back to the base. You owe me fifty cents."

He looked up at Helen with a cheesy, boyish grin. "How about I buy you a cup of coffee and we talk about ways I can pay you back."

She gave him one of those looks only young women can give when they're being pursued by young men. "Well...I don't know." She tried to feign hesitation, but the smirk on her face was way too transparent. She smiled and nodded towards the waiting taxi.

Wil's and Helen's eyes never left each other's as Wil spoke to Sutton. "Al, my friend, there's a cab right there that's going to take you back to the base. Go to the infirmary and see to your nose. I'll be home..." He paused. "Sometime before reveille, I guess."

Al snorted and then immediately regretted it. He groaned and held his nose. "As you were, soldier," he replied from under the bar towel.

Helen extended a hand to help Wil up, and she put an arm around his waist to steady him as he stood. As he and Helen began to slowly walk away, Wil threw a jaunty salute at Sutton.

Al stood gingerly and staggered over to the cab. Doing his best Bogart, he muttered, "Louis, I think this is the beginning of a beautiful friendship," as he watched the pair make their way through the crowd together.

Wilbur remembered how it felt to walk with Helen that night. The dreamy, bouncy quality was like walking on the moon. But now he was suddenly aware he was walking down a hospital hallway. A woman walked beside him, not Helen. But she was smiling and seemed untroubled. She motioned for him to follow and after a few steps, he was staring through a large, wide window. He peered through it anxiously at the row of sleeping newborns. A girl with a pink beanie cocked precariously to one side slept peacefully wrapped in a blanket. The name on the crib said "Katherine Freedman."

"Katie," he whispered. "That's my Katie."

He turned to brag to the nurse about how beautiful his daughter was only to find himself sitting in the metal bleachers at the school ballfield. Helen was sitting with a ball of yellow yarn in her lap knitting something shapeless. Katie sat on her other side, making her lips turn blue gnawing on a snow cone.

Helen nodded at the field. "Patrick's up."

Wil snapped his head to see his son pushing the too-large red batting helmet back from his face so he could see better. He wore jeans and a yellow and black jersey that said "Pirates" on the front and the number 5 on the back.

"Come on Patrick! Find your pitch!" the coach encouraged from the bench.

Wil couldn't stay silent. "Come on, Patrick! You can do it!" he yelled.

The pitcher lofted the softball and Patrick swung…

The mortar shell burst in the tree line, showering the patrol in shards of splintered trees and dirt. Wilbur wiped at his eyes. He could feel the grit in them mixing with his sweat. The thought of not being able to see in the midst of the firefight terrified him nearly as much as the bullets that ripped through the trees and underbrush. He continued to wipe at the impediment as long as he dared, trying to clear his vision.

"FREEDMAN!" Sergeant Callo yelled. "ON YOUR FEET! LET'S MOVE!"

Wilbur scrambled to his feet and ran to follow, despite his eyes feeling like they were full of sand. A hand grabbed him roughly by his flak jacket, and

Wilbur turned to look into the eyes of his best friend Al Sutton. Al's helmet was gone and he was bleeding from a notched area on his ear where shrapnel had torn through it. "Let's get the hell out of here, Will!" he said urgently.

Sergeant Callo's barking was drowned out by gunfire from all around them. Another mortar shell exploded…

Wilbur Freedman opened his eyes and found himself staring at the vague shapes of the three caretakers standing over him. He blinked rapidly and realized they didn't feel gritty like they always did when he woke up, but now his vision was hazy, and the familiar details of Tien's face looking down at him were indistinct, and out of focus. He squinted at her, trying to force himself to see her clearly. The lights had blurry little clouds around them and his heartbeat pounded softly in his ears. Angelo's voice drifted in from far away but Wilbur couldn't make out what he was saying. Figures floated in and out of the range of his sight. He struggled against these murky senses as they began to break up and fade, until gradually everything went silent and shadowy. He lay there listening, trying to remember a time when there was silence in his life. He was wrapped up in it, enveloped by the strange sensation of quiet. He finally recalled a time when it was just him and Helen, before the war, before the kids came, when she slept beside him and he sat awake and planning for the future. That was the last time he remembered quiet. A new wife and a new life stretching out before him. How far away that seemed now.

Something translucent caught his eye, and he tried to focus on it. A little shining mote of light bobbed towards him, growing larger and larger as it neared. Soon it was the size of Patrick's softball, and then it grew to the size of Katie's newborn head, and when it stopped moving towards him, it was the size of Al Sutton's face in Vietnam. It was a face, but not Al's. The dreamy, nebulous features slowly coalesced until for the first time in years: Helen's face, framed softly by her delicate hair, came sharply into focus.

"How about I buy you a cup of coffee and we talk about the ways you're going to pay me back?" she asked with the most beautiful, gentle smile he'd ever seen.

"Helen." He gasped.

Her hand floated into view out of the darkness to caress his cheek. Memories of her touch wafted over him like a cool breeze on a hot day.

"I've missed you," he said.

"I know, sweetheart. But it's okay. It's time for you to come home."

Wilbur's forehead crinkled. "But Tien, the facility. That's my home now."

"No, sweetheart. That's just a stop on the road. It's time for you to come home." Her voice soothed his concerns. She always did know best.

"Katie? What about Katie and Patrick?" he asked. "Will they come see us?"

"All in due time, my love," she reassured him. "Now then, let's get you up and out of bed. It's time for us to go."

He reached for her hand and grabbed it tightly. "Don't let go."

The heartbeat monitor flatlined and a single, mournful note emanated from the machine. Angelo turned it off and took a deep, shuddering breath. He looked at Tien and Gloria sadly.

Tien looked at her watch. "Time of death, eleven-eleven p.m." She reached for Wilbur's chart and scribbled some notes on it.

Gloria wiped a tear from her cheek and unhooked Wilbur from all of the leads.

Angelo produced the elaborate case and opened it on the table. He produced an old parchment scroll and unrolled it. It was faded and ancient, yellowed with age. Next, he opened a drawer on the front of the case and withdrew an old inkpot made of heavy green glass and a feathered quill. He unstoppered the inkpot and dipped the quill's tip, with well practiced ease, not spilling a drop. In a bold, flowing script, he wrote on the bottom of a long list of names: "Wilbur Freedman. Husband. Father. Soldier. Friend. Reunited with the master spirit." He wiped the quill's tip on his scrubs, and with deep and solemn respect he put the ink and quill away. Gently, they all moved Wilbur back to the van, then stripped the bed and put all the duplicates of Wilbur's effects into the case. The three stared at the photos from the table for a long time, and Tien traced the outline of his face before placing the picture in the case too. She stepped over to the now-almost-empty table, glanced at the scroll and Angelo's writing, and nodded her approval as she rolled it up. Angelo handed her the case and she placed the scroll back inside before closing the lid and locking the clasps tightly.

Gloria shut off the lights, and then closed and locked the storage unit. The trio walked out into the parking lot and back to the van. Gloria placed the case in the back and closed the doors. They stood for a moment, looking up at the stars wistfully. Tien looked at Angelo and Gloria knowingly.

In the pale moonlight, next to a van from a nursing home, the three figures clasped hands and bowed their heads in prayer. As they prayed, their skin transformed into the color of the moonlight, and glowed faintly as if they were made of moonbeams themselves. The figures grew closer and closer to one another, making it difficult to tell when one figure ended and the other started. They coalesced until, at last, one shining figure stood there alone. Arms that might have been Angelo's were now gossamer wings. A face that might have been Tien's was now shimmering and semitransparent. Legs that might have been Gloria's stood with renewed strength and steadiness as the now-ethereal form waited with power and patience.

A pale flicker of light flashed, and in that instant, the universe shifted ever so slightly. The van doors clicked open unbidden. The lettering on the outside was now different, like the van was from an entirely different facility. Even the fabric of the interior was a different color, as if the whole vehicle, contents and all, were now all something wholly different. Only the shrouded husk of what had been Wilbur Freedman remained constant. A new elaborate case could be found where the other had been. Its lid opened silently, and another ancient scroll floated to the being's graceful and delicate hands, where it unrolled smoothly. The figure's eyes glanced over the long list of names until it rested on the last one. With a nonchalant flick of its wrist, the figure sent the scroll effortlessly back through the air where it gently draped across the new case.

The figure clasped its hands in prayer and bowed its head. Slowly it morphed into four distinct figures this time. Their near-transparent skin grew more opaque and filled with color as they separated. When the transformation was complete, they stood there blinking as they gathered themselves.

One of the new figures looked at the nametag on her sky-colored nurses' scrubs. It read "Dina." She smiled. The second division, once called Gloria, was still in the form of a woman but was now in a white lab coat. She looked at her nametag to see the name "Dr. Penelope Weaver." She looked over at Dina and the pair shared a knowing look. The third division, sporting a very powerful energy like Tien once had, was now a man called "Micah." The last division had the name "Ariel" embroidered in white stitching on his paper-bag-brown work coveralls pocket.

The four new individuals took stock of one another, and after a moment, Micah tested a few steps in his new form. He went over to the back of the van and examined the scroll. He picked it up in a strange, jerky motion like he was new to using his arms and hands.

Dr. Weaver watched him carefully and then asked, "What's the next name on the list?" Her voice sounded strange inside her own ears. She had grown so accustomed to Gloria's voice that this new vocal quality was going to take some getting used to.

Micah read from the scroll, but Dr. Weaver could still hear echoes of Tien. "Eleanor Woodruff. Eighty-nine years old. Husband passed away sixteen years ago. Mother of seven. Wow, seven! Grandmother to nine, great-grandmother to four."

The nurse called Dina swooned a little. "Oh, it will be such a blessing to have little ones around again."

Micah continued. "Four years, eight months, and sixteen days until she rejoins the master spirit."

Dr. Weaver nodded and rolled up the scroll. "Time for us to begin our watch once more. We will return Wilbur Freedman and travel on to our new charge. Is everything locked up?"

"Yes ma'am."

Their roles, very different a while ago, were shifting now, but they had been doing this a long time, and they were already starting to settle into them.

"Very good," she said. "Dina, would you like to drive?"

Dina looked excited at the very mention of it. She placed the scroll in the case and closed it as carefully as the others had. "Yes please!"

Dr. Weaver placed her hand on the shrouded form of Wilbur, and she looked down at him wistfully. In her hand was a tiny bottle of the eye drops he loved. She tucked them gently into the wrapped folds he was covered in. "Goodbye, Wilbur. You were always very special to us."

She smiled at his memory, and then took her seat in the front passenger spot as the others piled into the van.

Dina started the engine with a wide grin. "Hello, Eleanor. We're on our way."

There is little more harmful to an academic than when their obsession is held in low regard. Mine has offered no rewards other than the satisfaction of gobbling down each new tidbit, every clue, as though vindication is an appetizer for a meal that won't be served. Even the book you are holding is an indulgence you must weigh as feast or famine. I have only sought the truth from witnesses I believed might have pieces to share. Some were credible; others were incredible but no less fascinating. All ended their recountings the same. Auntie's Attic might be a karmic clapback. An unreality meant to prove the unknown and query the knowable. *What is real? What is not yet, but can be made true? Do Keys lead to purgatory?* After many moons and having written more than 1,000 pages, I know no more than what follows. Except for this: I held a Key once and lost it during a rain in Essex. Was I saved or destroyed by the loss? That is a question I endeavor to unravel with this book, but you must judge for yourselves. Or perhaps face judgment in the Attic. Choose well.

IN SEARCH OF
AUNTIE'S ATTIC
FOREWORD
by Dr. Sudanah Forager

translated by Sherin Nicole
Miniver Press (June 2042)

REDEMPTION GAME

25¢ PLAY   SKEE BALL

ONE POINT

100   50   40   30   20   10   100

illustrated by
akar.std

(Unit 446) WIN B**I**G PRIZES
by Drew Bittner

Franky Delano drove like his life depended on it because it did.

He was bleeding out. He figured he had maybe an hour before he'd be facedown for good.

Antonio had shot him. Well, shot *at* him mostly, but one of the rounds had punched through his belly and torn him up pretty good. Franky knew that being gutshot was survivable—guys had lasted a while with a hole in them down there—but he didn't think this was going to be how that turned out. Not for him.

He sighed, hand trembling as he brought the cigarette to his lips.

He'd had this coming, he knew that, but hell, what guy really believes it's his time to go? Even though there had been writing on the wall in big flaming letters for a month now, Franky had never believed it would happen to him. It always happened to the other guy…and often enough, it was Franky who went to dole out the pain.

This time, not so much.

So he drove.

He looked at the key gripped in the same hand holding onto the wheel. It was big and oddly warm, like it had come out of his uncle's pizza oven and looked like it had been carved out of coral. It had weird holes and grooves in it, not like any key he'd ever seen, but when Vito (maybe his only friend) had handed it to him, he'd said, "If you ever need it, if you're ever in way too deep, go and use this." There'd been a business card with it and Franky had memorized the address.

Now he just had to get there.

He was feeling fuzzy by the time he pulled into the storage place's driveway. It was nothing special, an ordinary blink-and-you-miss-it joint surrounded on three sides by shrubbery and on one side by a going-nowhere stretch of road. AUNTIE'S ATTIC said the sign out front. Looked like the place to him, so he pulled in and found the gate, which was up. A note on the control box said OUT OF ORDER. Franky shrugged and drove on through.

"Unit four-four-six," he grunted, putting a hand to his side and not liking how damp it was. "Where are ya...?" He spotted the central building, which had unit numbers posted on the side in faded paint, and parked, then looked for the elevator. There was an old, cranky freight lifter inside and he rode it to the fourth floor, not trusting his ability to climb stairs at this point. He staggered down the hallway, which was dusty but not decrepit, and finally found a yellow sheet metal door with 446 in red. He put that weird key into the lock, half expecting it wouldn't fit, and turned—then pushed the door aside to see what was there.

Franky blinked, surprised to find the door opened onto a boardwalk arcade. The place was closed, looked like, but that was only to be expected with February barely halfway done and it being so late. Still, he could walk into the arcade's interior. It was warm and Franky liked that. He crossed the threshold and looked around the dimly lit parlor, taking in the dark and silent bulk of dozens of games of chance, skill, and dumb luck, shoulder to shoulder with video games—the good old kind, where kids put quarters on the glass to hold the next spot to play and you got "game hand," your fingers twisted into a claw, from playing so long.

"It's like when I was a kid," he said, unable to believe it. How was there a whole ocean-side arcade inside a storage unit? It made no sense at all. But here he was.

Then something went BING-BONG-BA-GONG on the other side of the room.

Franky held his side and walked around, to find one machine lit up...and waiting.

It was a game of skill, sort of, the kind where you had to maneuver a falling steel ball into the right hole at the bottom. Across the front was REDEMPTION GAME, $.25/PLAY.

Franky stepped closer. He'd liked this game when he was a teenager, hanging out with his buddies and eyeing the girls. Back in those days, he could eat a whole pizza, drink a pitcher of beer, and still be ready to stomp the shit out of some mouthy benny who wasn't from "down the shore." Now…*well look where you are now, Franky. Not so fucking tough now, are ya?* A voice inside sneered at him.

He dug in his pocket, finding a fistful of change. He fished out half a dozen quarters and put them down on the machine's panel, his eye caught by the small yellow box that outlined the game's rules.

100 TICKETS TO WIN, that was at the top. NO WIN, NO PRIZE!

"Damn. Wonder how many tickets you can score per quarter…?" He dropped a quarter into the coin slot and watched the first ball drop.

It bounced off a barrier—

—and Franky had a memory of standing in his family's kitchen, yelling at his mother.

"…no good, Francis," his mother said, crying. "Those hoods you're running around with, they're no good. You outta go back to vocational school, learn a trade. Go back to church."

"Ma, you don't get it. This is the way to real money," teenage Franky had shouted. "I ain't gonna be a loser like Dad, bustin' my ass sixty hours a week for fuckin' peanuts."

"You take that back," his mother said, her voice ominously low.

"What, that Dad's a los…"

SLAP!

Rosa Delano's hand left a mark on her son's cheek. "You don't talk about your father like that, not never," she said, voice still low, still dangerous. "You show him respect."

"Respect?" teen Franky scoffed. "Yeah, that'll be the day." Then he turned and stormed out of the house.

He'd next seen his mother in her casket, nine years later.

He gasped, suddenly back at the machine, where the ball was halfway down the vertical panel. He tilted the field, aiming the ball at the 100 TICKET hole—the one that nobody could make (but Franky had, once or twice)—

—and he was in the back seat of a Cadillac, holding a gun and trying to keep his hands from shaking. His breath was coming in short rasps, almost like hiccups, and he wanted to be anywhere else.

He wanted to be home, with his mom and dad and brothers and sisters.

Not here, with a crew of guys he didn't know and for sure didn't trust, on the night he'd first taken a life. He hadn't wanted to, but the boss said he had to do it if he wanted in. And with the life he'd chosen, you were either in or you were very, very out.

So now he was shaking, heart hammering its way out of his chest, and hoping like hell he didn't start to cry.

"You done good, Franky," Antonio told him, putting his arm around the younger guy's shoulders. "Wacked him like a pro. Old man had it comin'."

"Yeah, it was good work," Nick said, looking back from the front seat. "You got some skills, Delano."

Franky's breathing steadied. *Nick* thought he had some skills? That...that was unexpected. His hands were still shaking, though.

The hands that might have been fixing engines in his dad's garage. Or putting pizzas into the oven in his uncle's pizzeria. Or...who knows, fixing HVAC at some fancy building in Belmar or Colts Neck. But no, they were wrapped around a gun...and they wouldn't stop shaking.

And he watched the ball drop into the 10 TICKET hole with a thunk.

The counter under the coin slot spit out ten tickets.

"Shit." Franky could do better than that. Fuck, he knew—somehow—that he had to do better. It mattered, it was important.

But...what was it with those memories popping up like that?

He felt heartsick, remembering how he hadn't had the courage to go back home. How his family had looked at him with shame and disgust when he came to the funeral home in Red Bank, kissed his mother on the forehead, and didn't even stay for the funeral.

He'd been ashamed. He wasn't proud of who he was or what he did. For all the tough talk around the other guys…Franky Delano was embarrassed by what he'd become.

Franky took a slow, shaky breath. He hadn't thought about that for years. Really, he had never thought about it before, he'd just shoved it aside and pretended it didn't matter.

And that night when he'd killed the old man on Alfredo's say-so…he'd been so scared, so miserable. All he'd wanted was to go home and cry in his mom's lap, to have her make it all right, but he couldn't. Franky had never thought about how much he had needed that kind of comfort right then, how much he had lost by not having it. His heart ached again for what he had lost—what he had thrown away—out of pride and anger.

He took a deep breath and plugged in the next quarter.

As the ball dropped…

Franky was back in Carlyle's Antiques, busting up the inventory and setting fire to the place afterward. Johnny Carlyle hadn't paid the vig on his loan in two months, even when the boys had gone around to his place to ask nicely. Now he had to be shown the error of his ways…and Franky destroyed a man's life work collecting and selling fine antiques because he couldn't pay off an astronomical interest rate.

And it dropped further…

Franky was beating the hell out of Damian Bonifacio, whose dad had squealed to the FBI about a little money laundering that had gone on in his pawnshop. The feds had gotten close and Bonifacio Senior cut a deal to stay out of prison—but he hadn't gotten word to his kid in time. And now the pretty boy wasn't so pretty…and wouldn't be walking right again, either.

Franky felt a gush of acid in his throat at contemplating the horrific things he had done so easily, so casually. He swallowed hard—and watched the ball go *thunk* into the 10 TICKETS hole again.

"Goddammit!" Two quarters down, four to go, for only twenty tickets? He was losing, bad.

Don't know what the fuck this is but every time I play, I see…things…I don't want to remember, Franky thought, his hands shaking again like that night in Nick's Caddy. What the fuck is this about?

He plugged his third quarter into the machine.

As the ball dropped…

He was facing Maria Louisa Trastella, his fiancée, who was staring at him like he had been dragged up out of a sewer. "A…made guy?" she mumbled in disbelief. "You thought I'd be happy to be with a mobbed-up hood? Jesus, Franky, sure, there's plenty of girls out there who swoon over the furs and jewelry and shit but I've fucking seen *Goodfellas*. I've read the papers and seen true crime on TV. *I know how this shit ends.* You're gonna get shot dead or you're gonna go to prison or you're gonna have to go into witness relocation, that's the only way it turns out. And I don't want to be a fucking Mob widow at forty with two kids in elementary school, cleaned out because the feds found all your stashes of money."

"It…it ain't like that, M," he sputtered, though he knew too well it was fucking exactly like that. "The outfit ain't the same like, like *The Sopranos* and all make it look. It's…"

"Respectable? Something I can talk about with people whose husbands *aren't* out stealing shit and beating up people?" She scoffed, reaching for her cigarettes. "Franky, I want to have a family. I want to know your family, but you don't even talk about them…"

He grimaced. "They're all…not talking to me."

She nodded, pointing at him with her lit cigarette. "See, that shit ain't right." She took a long drag. "What's gonna happen when we have a kid? They're gonna want to see the baby, but you can't even tell 'em you have one. Will that make it all better? They'll be happy, for a little while, and then get angry again because you're still in the shit."

Franky could feel his blood boiling. Why was she making this so hard? "You know what, M, fuck you!" he yelled. "Gimme that goddamn ring, we're done. Fuck you and this fucking moral high horse you're on. Guys like me, we got respect the hard way, we don't play nobody's game but our own. But you don't see that. All you see is wanting to be like those assholes named Smith or

Johnson or fucking Gates or some shit. You wanna be a WASP so goddamn bad, why don't you change your name to Mary Louise Trenton, go blonde, and lose the Jersey Shore accent you got?"

She tugged the diamond ring off her hand and flung it at him. "Fuck you too, Franky," she spat. "You keep on the way you're going, you're gonna die in a ditch, and who's coming to your goddamn funeral?"

Franky trembled as the memory faded. He'd lost Maria Louisa, sure, but...Anastasia, who'd come over from Russia and worked as a stripper until she'd met Franky, she was good too. She liked spending his money and he was pretty sure she was screwing the lawn guy, but other than that...

Then he blinked and he was standing in front of Big Gio, his boss's boss. The big man was smoking a cigar as he looked from Franky to Hector. "One of you guys screwed up bad," he drawled. "Which of you tried to sneak a couple grand behind my back?"

He stared hard at Franky, who tried not to fidget. He'd pocketed some bucks, sure, who didn't? But how could Big Gio know about that?

"Franky, you got a piece on you?"

"Yes, sir."

"Shoot Hector in his fucking head."

And Franky had done it. Hector hadn't stolen a dime—but he wasn't Italian and wouldn't get any benefit of the doubt. Franky got the point, though; next time it would be him.

He swallowed hard, recalling how he had murdered an innocent man for his own crime.

Thunk! Another ten tickets.

He grabbed the sides of the machine to steady himself. He knew he didn't have much time left. Was there enough to finish the last three quarters? Blood was running down his leg, streaming from the bullet hole in his belly, and his thoughts were starting to fragment. *Gotta...finish,* he told himself, dropping his fourth quarter into the slot.

The ball dropped.

He remembered murders—including some where the victims begged for their lives or the lives of their loved ones, some who simply prayed, some who sobbed silently.

He remembered property damage (like wrecking an arcade that reminded him of this one, actually), stealing anything that wasn't nailed down, running with a bad crew as far back as middle school.

He remembered his first cigarette. And the first girl he ever made cry.

Bit by bit, it was adding up to a life that preyed on others but gave nothing back.

He'd gotten money, then wasted it gambling; he'd gotten nice cars and a pretty terrific house, only to have them grabbed (once) by the feds as part of a RICO case; he'd gone on vacation to nice places, spending his time looking over his shoulder in case somebody recognized him in a bad way.

Franky saw the sum total of his life, as tickets spilled grudgingly from the machine, and he realized it had all been for nothing. An entire life wasted on trying to satisfy bottomless appetites, being a parasite.

Being a loser.

He looked down and there was only one quarter left—and 50 tickets won so far.

He plugged in the last quarter and as it dropped, he said what was in his heart.

"I'm so sorry."

Angelo and Rick tramped up the steps to the fourth floor.

"Sheesus, you'd think a guy on the run with a bullet in his belly would go to a hospital—or even a back-alley clinic," Angelo grumbled, hefting his three-hundred-pound, tracksuited bulk up another step.

"Antonio gave him a key, he says," Rick muttered. Being a hundred or so pounds less than his partner, he found the stairs easier to climb but wasn't happy about it either. The busted freight elevator would have made this a lot better all around, especially if they had to bring a body back down to the van. "Said it was unit 446."

"Whatever, it's all we got to go on," Angelo huffed. He paused for a second, making sure the gun in his waistband was secure. He didn't want an accident like Jimmy "No Balls" Velucci had had, for sure. "C'mon, let's see if he was here."

They climbed the last few stairs and went into the fourth-floor hallway. "What a fucking dump," Angelo scoffed, taking in the dusty corners of the hall and the flickering fluorescent lights. "Why the hell did Ant get a unit in this...hey, look." He pointed down the hall, where one door was open. The two pulled their guns and walked as quietly as they could to the open door.

They didn't need to bother.

Franky Delano lay on the concrete floor face down, in a pool of his own blood.

Rick looked at Franky's hand and what was clenched in his fist. "He's got—what the hell, a receipt? Lemme see this." He took the scrap of paper from Franky's hand. "'Tickets redeemed: 100. Prize awarded,'" he read aloud.

Angelo knelt down (with a grunt and muttered complaint about his knees) to check for himself. He found no pulse, then rolled Franky over.

"Ain't that the damnedest thing," he mumbled. "Why's he smiling like that? Guy had to be in serious pain. You think...damnedest thing."

Rick shrugged. "He cashed in a hundred tickets—in a closed arcade. What do you get with that?"

Franky knew.

Illustrated by
Alice Brereton

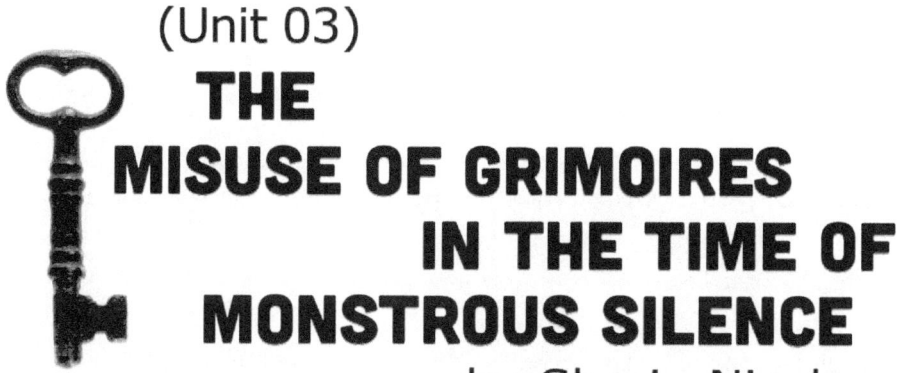

(Unit 03)

THE MISUSE OF GRIMOIRES IN THE TIME OF MONSTROUS SILENCE
by Sherin Nicole

The following is the tale as told by the griot,
AKA the Eleventh Sister of the Coven of Harlem

Aye mah ma, oh aye mah ma.
                Come, children. Listen.

Do you remember the day?

That time when the *kaiju* rose out of the East River
and snatched seven L-trains off their tracks with eight tails?

The Times named her Thee Tempest.
A force of nature.
And, after, they sealed the mouths of the subway tunnels shut.

Oh aye, oh aye
           and yet next takes more knowing than memory.

First.

The Witches of Williamsburg quickly convened in their microbrewery—the one in the brownstone where *they* say the Harlem Renaissance* *"really"* started
        (according to their beer labels).

Those Witches, who tended to act but seldom ask,
immediately strategized an equal yet opposite counterattack against that monster.
        That Tempest.

Their Head-Witch—known only as "Auntie"—gifted them with a key. One of unknown and dubious origin. And thus irresistible.
        The key unlocked a grimoire, bound in curious leather, inscribed *"Manly Works, Womanly Words"*
            Far too quickly, desperation led to haste
                …but followed curiosity.

They were quick to snicker.
Hadn't "manly work" caused every first and fourth fuckup out of four in history?

Oh aye, but ignoring the percentages, the Witches of Williamsburg let loose a spell of "womanly words" so powerful they summoned a second kaiju, more manly than the first.

That new monster, those witches called their own…
…because owned monsters are safe monsters, ones that save cities
        …at least according to their newsletters,
            imprinted with binding spells for unruly spouses,
                sent on the 1st and 15th.

The Post named the second great one Cthunnel

---

*Harlem, as one might guess, is where the Harlem Renaissance actually took place.

...because
       ...tentacles.

But *oh oh aiyee*
       When Cthunnel and Thee Tempest collided,
              the two titans sowed the whirlwind
                     ...with such vigor 'twas censored by ma'ams and memes.

Terrible obsidian eggs, the same shape and size as Ragnarök,
       soon erupted from the seas
              ...sometimes from beneath fire hydrants
                     ...often at block parties.

Hear me, little monsters, *oh aye*
       the Kaiju Apocalypse had begun.

Oh whoa woe aye.

Second.
The Harlots up in Harlem* (not harlots at all but witches from the first
lands) realized their help might be needed.

This hypothesis held true, according to their proceeding histories
       ...which had long been recorded in beats & lyrics.

Within their "separate but equal" coven they were known as The Sisters.
       As such, they couldn't understand:

Why?

Why hadn't those other witches strolled down to the East River, poured
Thee Tempest a silo of Reasonable Riesling,
       and excavated the problem

...first?

You know, before making more monsters happen.

Then again, The Harlots (_still_ a pejorative to be ignored) had often been dismissed as monstrous too.

Thus, in the era known as Brunch
            eschewing teapots in deference to tempests
                        the Sisters touched fingertips with monsters

Thee Tempest felt seen.
            A treaty
                        A paper napkin epic
            (signed in a particular shade of brown lip liner)
                        kissed with truth
                                    appeared shortly after.

Now.
Generations later
            the progeny reclaims itself as monstrous
                        knowing power in re-definition
                                    finding genesis in #blackmagic.

Aye aye, my children
            an alliance formed,
                        an apocalypse averted,
                                    the L-train rides again.

Oh aye mama, aye mama.
            Come, children.
            Listen.

CROSSROADS WEEKLY GAZETTE
April 1, 1977
AUNTIE'S ATTIC
GRAND REOPENING

Got too much stuff in the house? Your problem is solved! Auntie's Attic will be holding its grand RE-opening on Springdale Road this coming weekend. If you sign up for a lease before Monday, you'll qualify for ten percent off for the first year. Manager Bernard Huffley says he's happy to be part of the Crossroads community and hopes to see "our facility's old and new neighbors" turn out to say hi.

CROSSROADS WEEKLY GAZETTE
June 22, 1985
POWER OUTAGES CONTINUE

Springdale Road saw its fourth power outage of the summer yesterday, putting five dozen households in the dark for six hours. Dominion Power said that they were still investigating the source of the outage, but ruled out weather as a possible cause, citing the clear skies and mild temperatures.

CROSSROADS WEEKLY GAZETTE
September 5, 1996

REAL ESTATE BOOM DOESN'T
REACH SPRINGDALE ROAD

"I just don't get it," says Realtor Amanda
Peters. "The houses along the street are fine
homes and they have a history of selling well,
but...not now. It's something I can't explain."

And that's been the story along Springdale
Road, part of the Westfold corner of
Crossroads, where it seems selling a home is
a Herculean task.

"We need to sell," says soon-to-depart
Richard Conroy. "I'm supposed to have been
in California a month ago. My kids need to
change schools. But we can't go anywhere
until we sell the house, and we haven't even
had a single offer."

Conroy had no explanation for the lack of
interest, either.

"We thought the house would sell in a couple
of weeks," he says. "Our agent said that it
would move fast. But we've had three open
houses and only one person came through,
so..." He shrugged helplessly. "It's weird,
you know?"

CROSSROADS WEEKLY GAZETTE
September 15, 2008

SPRINGDALE REALTY PARTNERS ANNOUNCES LAND SALES

One of the mysteries of the region is why so much open, undeveloped property has been available along Springdale Road. Although it's been home to storage facility Auntie's Attic for several years now, realtors have never developed the heavily wooded property. Lots are currently being surveyed for sale, with an initial offering due later this year.

"We're very excited about the prospects of building a new neighborhood in this area," said Realtor Amanda Peters. "There are two homebuilders who are looking at constructing townhomes and condominiums, perhaps even mixed-use commercial and residential. Oddly, nothing was ever built out there except one storage facility, but the future there is wide open!"

Compiled by Drew Bittner
Source: Personal Collection

illustrated by
Ananyo Chatterjee

OUTWIT, OUTPLAY, (Unit 379) OUTLAST, by Leon J. Cooper

PRE-PRODUCTION

"How'd I get here?

Too easy. When they started rounding up the unchipped people, I tried to run.

My father had warned me this was coming since I was a little kid, but even back then I thought he was nuts. It sounded like more of his conspiracy theorizing, and the way he talked scared me. When we watched television, he'd chomp on one of his cigars and say things like, 'You see, son, pretty soon they'll put a chip inside your head.' He'd tap his left ear or send a whorl of smoke into the air with a flourish. 'No more commercials. They'll convince you to buy a bunch of shit you don't need, live and direct to your brain. You want it fast? Afraid of missing out on something, or not being as cool as your neighbors? Just blink to buy it. It'll happen. Everything you're seeing with this new president is prologue.'

He repeated that last line a lot. Never the same words but the theme remained. One time, Dad dropped his cigar on the coffee table, still burning, and laid a hand on the top of my head. 'This regime wants you to trade your rights for safety. Protection from other religions, from pandemics, from poverty, from other countries. When that asshole is done, everyone will be the other.' He stopped—realizing he'd scared me—and gentled his words. 'I'm saying, watch how people are sacrificing one freedom after another after another. These jokers know exactly what they're doing.'

He wasn't wrong. Except the chip went in your arm. If you called 911, your subcutaneous GPS gave your physical location, so the first responders could get to you more quickly—if you had enough money, that is. If you ate at a restaurant, you held your arm up to a reader, and your bill was paid, easy peasy.

I could tell you it all started with a plywood box.

But nah, bruh. That ain't it at all.

That same president's regime attempted to amend the constitution to keep him in office for life. They failed, but barely. Thinking about how the Electoral College had voted that a second fascist president could be tolerated, the term 'regime' is apropos. It wasn't an administration—it was, borne out by history, a true authoritarian prologue.

When Congress held the line, that's when shit got real, as the saying used to go.

The president called on the military to bomb cities.

In America.

And they freakin' did it, y'all.

Dad called that, too.

This wasn't new to us Black people; they bombed the Greenwood neighborhood of Tulsa, Oklahoma, aka Black Wall Street, in 1921, killing hundreds of us (more likely thousands, if we want to be real about it). The same with a Black neighborhood in West Philadelphia in 1985 in an attack on a group known as MOVE. There were countless other mass murders, which white America and, admittedly, most of The Other America never heard about. I have friends who had no idea these atrocities had ever happened. It's not the kind of thing that appears in the history books anymore, but when you think about who writes the history books, there's your answer.

The difference between then and now is that these bombings obliterated cities and towns with majority white populations. As a result, large swaths of the country were rendered uninhabitable. That's when white folks stood up and took notice, but, surprising no one, it was too late.

White folks protested but the police weren't havin' it. They beat them down, called the dogs on them, sprayed them with water hoses, gassed and pepper sprayed them. They weren't playin'. You name it, they did it.

It all happened like my dad said, but as a kid, I didn't know it would.

The bombings wiped out half of the population and all of the unemployment problems. The bigger cities had more jobs than they could fill when it was over. Of course, most of these jobs were straight-up menial labor, meant to send a message to the underclass, and once they got enough of the populace chipped, the advertising began for the nation to go cashless. All banking went digital, and more high-powered jobs were eliminated almost overnight.

I used to joke that if my dad wasn't a full-blown conspiracy theorist, he was most definitely a conspiracy enthusiast. I know better now.

Even my mom, when going on about him, would sigh the sweet sigh and say, 'You know how worked up your father gets about things. He looks for the bad, so he finds it. Whatever you're looking for in life, if you put on the right lens, you'll find it. What lens you choose to put on is entirely up to you, my son.'

On general principle, my father still refused to get chipped or vaccinated, fearing they'd chip him by injection. Once The State came to my parents' home, busted the door open, and threatened my mother, he caved. How could he not? We're talking about my mama.

I still refused; I didn't live there, and I was stubborn like a bull.

That was a bad idea.

They killed Mama because I ran.

And now, accepting the box is my only chance.

My dad's only chance.

I went back to Washington, D.C., to find out if it was true that they killed my mama. Sometimes the news wasn't really the news. Over the last forty years or so, or at least in my entire lifetime, the news had become more like reality TV—just as scripted and just as ratings-hungry.

It turned out to be true, and it messed me up.

My cousin, who had been neglected by my drug-addicted aunt and the junkie she married, the man who my parents took in and made my brother for twenty-five years, upon finding out I was back in town, ratted me out for a thousand digital credits.

They killed him before he could spend them; it was all too easy to make it look like he had died of an overdose.

When they caught me, which didn't take too long, they gave me a choice: watch my father get executed on pay-per-view or accept a box.

There were rumors of this gigantic facility somewhere in Virginia, just south by southwest of Richmond, where all kinds of bizarro world stuff takes place. You were just as likely to walk out with a chest of gold as you were to walk out with nothing. Or not walk out of there at all. Or so they said. My captors said anyone who made it out would be granted a full pardon for their crimes against The State.

All I wanted was for my dad to escape execution, especially in front of a loudly cheering audience of rabid watchers on The State streaming service. It was bad enough that my mom bought it because of me, but I would lose it if I were the reason that my dad got smoked. I can't lose them both.

So, a policeman, armed to the teeth with every high-tech gizmo and weapon he could get his hands on, had me sign for a box he wouldn't let me open. Then had me get on a bus with two equally armed cops. Even the bus driver looked like he was ready to deploy to Afghanistan. Or what's left of it. We weren't the only country going through changes.

Now I'm on the bus to the middle of nowhere called Crossroads, Virginia. I wonder what lens my mother would use to frame this."

I tapped the streaming camera lens in front of me and it made a TUNK TONK sound. "You asked how I got here. To everybody watching. Here I am."

EPISODE 1

All of us pretty much stared numbly at our boxes on the bus ride from D.C. to Crossroads. They were plain and all the same, built out of plywood, with a few simple coats of polyurethane and a fingerprint lock. We could only guess what might be inside.

They told us to keep our mouths shut, or else. One dude, a super nervous guy, asked what was up with the boxes and where we were going. The cop in the front barked at him to shut up.

By the time he got halfway through his rant about how he had rights, the cop yanked him up out of his seat and threw his ass out the door of the bus. It was still moving. Seconds later, three of the cop's buddies were on the scene, beating and kicking and cursing the hell out of him. I assumed his death would be attributed to a fall down a set of stairs, or perhaps something gang-related. That's how they do, you see.

White dudes, and especially white women, were not used to this new reality. Their eyes went all kinds of wide as all this was going on, while all the brothers and sisters on the bus shrugged matter-of-factly. It struck me as funny, like when someone wakes up just in time to see the bullet heading right for their forehead: Welcome to life as a minority.

A few minutes later, they handed that dude's box to someone from the front of the bus. A spare. That signaled to the rest of us that we were replaceable. The bus started back up like it was having a coughing fit and finally roared its way to life, spitting dark gray smoke into the air, and we were on our way.

We rode in the dark for what felt like forever but was probably just an hour or so.

The seats, made of vinyl, were old and stained and cracked and smelly, and could probably have told some interesting stories; the floors were a little tacky, and you didn't want to touch the poles if you had a choice. The windows, some of them showing spiderweb patterns from rock attacks, hadn't been cleaned by anything other than rain since 5G became a thing a generation ago.

I kept my head down and focused on trying not to pass out. I noticed at one point that I was breathing a little too heavy, so I closed my eyes and did this trick I saw once on the internet, where you breathe in for four seconds, hold it in for four seconds, breathe out for four seconds, and hold that for four seconds. Damn if that shit didn't work; in a couple of minutes, I was okay.

If I were to describe this like my boy Adam, I'd probably say something like, "Town after town passed by us without our notice, as they were mostly a patchwork of dim lights off in the distance. The repetitive mechanical noises coming from the bus, combined with the rocking motion, were calming to me but a source of agitation for others. We were making great time, thanks to the new Motor Law."

When I felt a little brave, I looked around. I counted two cops, sixteen riders with boxes, including me, and the bus driver. No other spares. From where I sat at the back of the bus, it looked like a game of whack-a-mole; one head would pop up, look around for a second or two, and duck back down. A few people slept, or tried to, but most people retreated into their heads in a kind of half-sleep state.

The guy sitting next to me had this weird ability to talk without moving his lips; he whispered to me, "Wherever this is going, we were going to be killed, but they would probably make us do some messed-up stuff before that."

Before I could ask what, the cop in the back, who had a listening device, punched my seatmate in the face. He might have broken his jaw. When he started to moan, the cop told him to shut up or he'd turn him into a grease spot right there.

He didn't know that it was an empty threat, but I did; that's why when they beat the hell out of that nervous guy, they replaced him right away. It seems that they had to have all sixteen of us—why, I didn't know then. There's always a reason why The State does what it does. Always some method to their madness. The problem is, by the time we figure out what's happening or why it's happening, it's always too late.

Like now.

Like my dad warned me.

Sixteen men and women, boys and girls, the thing most glaringly in common being that we're all not chipped, put on a bus, to God knows where to do God knows what.

What could possibly go wrong?

After the bus came to a loud halt somewhere around 11:00 pm, we heard the hiss of compressed air as the doors opened, and we were invited to get the hell out of the bus to the loud barking of the cops, which reminded me of the drill sergeants in the Army; the time was just a guess because we weren't allowed to have anything that could tell time or location on us.

The facility looked a lot like the intake center where I started my mandatory two years of military service; I wanted the Air Force, but my overall test score missed being high enough by two points. The Army was my second choice, and I got in with no problems.

It was surrounded by a ten-foot-high barbed wire fence, and a good dozen armed guards walked the length of their posts. I didn't know if that was to keep people out or to keep people in. I, as a matter of course, assumed the latter. For good measure, a few old-school armed drones were flying about—they were the loud buzzy ones, as they wanted you to know that they were there. I counted three of them, but there were probably a whole lot more at the ready, in case of a serious breach or a breakout.

I snuck a look as we double-timed our way into the building. It looked like a storage facility from the Good Old Days, only ten times the size of the biggest one that I'd ever seen. This thing was massive, as the no-longer-existent Brits would say.

When we got inside, the women and girls were ushered into the first door on the left, and the men and boys who failed to move quickly enough were "assisted" into the first door on the right.

When I saw the showers, I broke into a panic sweat. My dad obsessed over history—he said that's how he knew what was coming. Knowing my backstory, you can guess my dad's obsessions became a course of study for me. Almost a hundred years ago, millions of people were gassed in fake showers in concentration camps during the Second World War. I re-read about it recently in one of the forbidden history files in the cloud. I didn't believe people were capable of such horrors as a kid. Not until the fascist shit hit the fan here in America. An old song came back to me, something about history repeating. An unwanted earworm that magnified my dread.

It was a great relief to find that these were actual showers; it was a great disappointment to find out that we had four minutes of water per person. When we toweled off, we stood naked in front of someone we believed was a doctor, who injected us with a chip and applied a Band-Aid. The bandage struck me as out of place, a relic from the era of normalcy. After everything I'd been through, and everyone I'd lost to avoid the chip, they stuck a Band-Aid on "it" to keep what was left of my life from hemorrhaging.

Two, maybe three minutes later, I found myself standing in front of a locker, with the other guys. There was a black suit hanging in there that looked like a swimmer's wetsuit, only not as thick. There were small numbers on the front left breast, large numbers on the back—a gray number twenty-three. We were also issued boots and socks, which more-or-less fit, and gloves which were formfitting. At least in my case.

Around what I thought was probably midnight, all sixteen of us were standing, boxes in hand, in front of a set of free-standing units with corrugated metal doors framed by cement walls on each side. I don't remember how I got there (as I'm pretty sure that they drugged us somehow) except for putting one foot in front of the other and following the orders of the cops. I don't know about everybody else, but my heart felt like it would either explode, jump out of my chest, or simply stop beating. My assigned unit had the number 379 in a digital display. Under the number were the letters "LS-DD." I didn't know what that meant. Maybe I wasn't supposed to— maybe I was supposed to figure it out.

I got my answer when the cops ordered us to open our boxes. I pressed my thumb to the lock and it eased open. Too slow for my tastes. There was a key inside and the unit letters matched the letters stamped onto it. They instructed us to remove the keys from the boxes. My key seemed to be made of some weird bonelike material, covered in a substance that felt like the graphite ball bearings I used in the wheels of my skateboard to make them spin more quickly and for a long time. I assumed that everyone else's were similar.

There were four sides to this set of units. Each side had four people with keys standing in front of their respective units, and one drone buzzing in a stationary position, acting as cameraman, surveillance agent, and insurance that no one would fail to act when the time came.

Four sides, four contestants per side.

The mathematics of chaos. I think my grandfather used to listen to a song that went by that name.

I heard somebody's key hit the ground, followed by the thud of a cop's nightstick hitting the skull of the someone I assumed dropped the key in question. At that point, I was just grateful it wasn't me, but if I could get myself alone with one of those bastards, equally armed, I'd show them what was what.

Each contestant, even the boys and girls, had a heavily armed and very large steroid-fueled cop standing behind us sending a clear message that non-compliance would be dealt with harshly, ruthlessly—it seemed like overkill in that the drones would dispatch the unresponsive.

Thanks to the forbidden cloud servers, I had an inkling of what might be about to happen. Out of the other fifteen unlucky bastards, I would guess only one or maybe two of them had an idea.

A voice came over the facility's intercom, and if you like drama this is a great place for a cliffhanger.

EPISODE 2

"Ladies and gentlemen, Pay-Per-View Deluxe viewers, welcome to the first episode of the new and improved Storage Unit Battles. I'm your host, Tim Murdock, alongside my co-host, Keisha Bennington, and we're here in Crossroads, Virginia, at a beautiful old facility that used to be known as Auntie's Attic. Today, we have sixteen contestants vying for the grand prize; what's the catch, KB?"

"Well, Tim, that's the thing. Rather than bidding on a single unit, we have sixteen men, women, and kids as well, simultaneously opening an entire block of units. Nobody knows what's in their unit, of course. You mentioned the grand prize, but nobody knows what that is at this point! This is a completely unscripted competition, so anything could happen, and we'll be just as surprised as anyone watching here on Pay-Per-View Deluxe! And Tim, on a personal note, I can only imagine how incredibly proud your father would be of you right now!"

"You're making me tear up here, KB. We're in the exact building where my father, Tommy Murdock, passed away all those years ago. I have to admit that I'm a little bit nervous about being here after all this time, but I'm the host, and the show must go on, so let's get after it!"

And there it was. We were the fodder for a game show.

I would be shooting a pilot episode—awesome. I always wanted to be a star of stage and screen. I hope that I remember enough about those shows and movies to survive what's about to happen, or at least what I think is about to happen. On the one hand, I have to be aware of what the hosts are saying, as there will be clues on how to survive this whole thing. On the other hand, I have to get my mind right and focus on the things that will help me to make it through all of this. It was at that exact moment that I wished I didn't suck at multitasking.

"Okay, everybody, it's just about midnight, and the battle is about to begin!"

"Oh my God, Tim, I can't wait to see what happens!"

The damned woman was about to have an orgasm.

We were instructed to insert our keys into the locks, but not to turn them until the countdown called for it. I damn near passed out—there was too much going on in my head. My thoughts were getting jumbled and spinning round and round like the hamsters my father had back in the day running in a wheel. I was dizzy and I wanted to throw up, which would have made for good television.

Just as that thought hit my brain, one of the boys threw up, prompting the contestants on either side of him to throw up in what looked like solidarity.

Synchronicity.

"Clean up on Aisle Eleven!" Tim Murdock was bringing his A game; he was a ringer for his father, not only in looks but he had jokes. The apple certainly didn't fall far from the tree in this case. My mom and dad used to watch "Storage Unit Battles" back in the day. It's almost funny how I "volunteered" for all of this to keep Dad from being executed on Pay-Per-View, and now here I am on Pay-Per-View, in a competition where nobody, including the show's hosts, knows the rules or the prize or if any of us will survive. There's a word for that sort of thing. If I weren't so goddamned terrified, I'd remember what it was.

"Okay, everybody, it's time to get this game underway. KB, go!"

"Jesus, Tim, I thought I was gonna pee myself—oops, I probably shouldn't have said that on the live stream, but I'm so excited!! Look at my arm—goose pimples! Contestants—are you ready?"

They shoved nightsticks into our backs to force us to respond. Some said "yes," or "yeah." Others nodded. I was one of the ones who nodded. I didn't know if my voice was gonna work.

Keisha Bennington was practically shrieking at this point. "Contestants, turn your keys!"

My hand was shaking like crazy, but I managed to turn the key.

Holy shit—I wasn't expecting to see this, KB!"

"Neither was I, Tim! Now I see why the producers kept this a secret, even from us!

"This is going to be more exciting than we ever could have dreamed!"

EPISODE 3

I opened the door. I don't know why, but I kept the key, shoving it into one of my pockets. The first thing I noticed was the oppressive heat and humidity—it had to be a good 100° in this place with 100% humidity. I immediately dropped to the ground. I didn't want anything animal, mineral, or vegetable to notice me straight away. Plus, I needed to get my bearings and gather as much intelligence as I could.

That's when I realized I was alone. Either the other three contestants who stepped into the units on either side of mine hadn't made it through, or the drugs The Network gave me before were better than I thought.

Looking straight ahead, I found myself in a jungle of sorts, with high grass and trees as far as I could see. The horizon seemed miles away. An entire landscape in a box. The jungle could be a hallucination, a hologram, or something as scientifically improbable as a tesseract. If I lasted long enough maybe I'd have time to ascertain which. There was a small wooden hut to my right, that I estimated might contain some clues—hopefully some food and weapons.

By habit of training and instinct, I low-crawled my way to the hut, hoping I wouldn't come across any snakes, rodents, or anything poisonous, and hoping that my suit would offer some amount of protection against that which would kill me without mercy.

"This just in, Keisha—it looks like we have some preliminary rules for the game!"

"Ooh, what do you have there, Tim?"

The Metatron duo was back, the voices of the Gameshow God that would decide my fate. I searched the trees but couldn't find the mechanism broadcasting their over-caffeinated commentary. Maybe it was the drones.

"The grand prize is still to be determined, but it appears that the last person standing wins it!" Tim replied.

"Wait—does that mean these contestants are all here in a fight to the death?"

"It appears so, KB.

"Also—there are items meant to assist or obstruct the contestants all over the game field; this is going to be an exciting next few hours or days, or whatever it takes!"

"I can't stand it, Tim!"

The hut was pretty much a treasure trove of gizmos encased in a glass box that could help me win this thing. The trouble was, the hut was also full of spiders and snakes, which I assumed were venomous. Nothing would excite an audience like a screaming, purple-faced death brought on by a Brazilian Wandering Spider or a Black Mamba snake.

I needed something to kill them with. I went back outside, where I found a sizeable rock that fit well in my hand. There was a two-headed snake in front of the glass case and a big-ass spider hanging from a web above it, which proved my suspicion about The Network's quest for high ratings. They went with two mambas for the price of one and a kaiju spider. The snake meant business, hissing at me. I took a knee and waved my left hand to catch its attention. I figured at some point it would have enough, and strike at me with at least one of its heads.

I was right. After a few seconds, it coiled. As it did, I prepared and prayed. When it struck, I rotated quickly to my left, making it lunge at the air, and smashed it right where the heads conjoined. I don't know how many times I brought the rock down on it, but it was enough.

The case had a lock and key, with the key hanging in the lock. This, of course, made me all kinds of suspicious, so I took a few minutes to think about it.

I decided that I would turn the key, remove the lock, and roll to my left when the case opened. As luck would have it, when the case opened fully, a stream of acid shot out. Had I not rolled out of the way, it would have hit me in the face. A screaming green death this time. If their trails were the same as mine, I wondered how many of the other contestants either got hit or didn't make it at that point.

"Ladies and gentlemen, we have our Hour One results."

"That's right, Tim. After only one hour, we are down to thirteen contestants: two of the boys and one girl are out, leaving us with four men, eight women, and one girl."

"Wow, KB—so we lost three of our participants in the first hour alone?"

"That's right, Tim. I especially feel bad for these kids, two of whom mistakenly ate poisonous berries, and one of whom drowned. But, as The Network says, the show must go on."

That answered my question. Like me, Keisha Bennington didn't seem as ecstatic as she was at the beginning of the broadcast. It was probably the fact that it was kids who died. Real talk, the youngest was 8 years old, a boy from what used to be Blacksburg, Virginia. Most of them came from towns that nobody ever heard of. It had to be a sin of the father type of thing—no way a kid that young had avoided compliance on his own.

Thirteen people left. Me and twelve others. Four dudes, eight women, one girl.

Once I figured, just a hunch, it would be safe to reach into the case, I inventoried the contents like the Army taught me. There was a bow and arrow, a collection of knives, a few of those ninja throwing stars, a pair of nunchakus, and a katana—nothing that I was trained to use in the Army.

Great.

It occurred to me that maybe the other contestants were also stationed closest to weapons with which they were not proficient; that would instill a sense of fairness to this thing.

Or maybe they were just messing with us—that's how they do.

I found a pair of glasses in the cabin. When I put them on, there was a readout that showed me how many contestants had expired, how many were left, and everyone's odds of winning. With thirteen people left, I figured that my odds would be about 7.7%, but the odds-makers cut that in half since I was Black. Including myself, there were two Black dudes, three white dudes, three Black women, and five white women left.

I'm no genius, but I needed to come up with a solid plan, and fast.

Thanks to my grandpa, who was one of the smartest people of his time, I was able to watch a lot of shows and movies that were on the banned list. All I had to do was keep my mouth shut and never make a joke or tell a story that referenced what I watched with Grandpa, which was extremely hard for a guy in his 20s to do.

There was this one movie we watched which started with a bunch of people who wake up in this giant cube, with no idea how they got there, and try to make their way out. At the end of the movie, it turns out that they should have stayed in the section they started in.

I wondered if I should try and get a little bit of sleep. Every bit of logic in me told me that I should, though it didn't feel like I could. On the other hand, if I were walking around this jungle and dropped from exhaustion, I'd be screwed.

Or, I'd be dead, and that would be that.

"Ladies and gentlemen, it's now six o'clock a.m. and we are pleased to inform you that we are down to eight contestants—five women, and three men. KB, why don't you show our viewers the footage that we have put together from the eight people who bravely gave their lives in sacrifice to The State?"

"I sure will, Tim!"

Whatever they injected her with seemed to have given her mojo back.

She showed the bodycam footage of how each contestant perished: one sprayed by acid upon opening a glass case, one bitten by a poisonous creature, two kids by eating poisonous berries, one kid mauled by animals in the forest, one kid drowned, one stepped on a booby trap.

One contestant was killed by another contestant.

So, our paths could cross. That last one got the most eyeballs. The ratings skyrocketed on my glasses. That's when I noticed the bodycam in the middle of my chest.

Aha. Clever. The camera could've been a dime from the previous era. Too compact to be easily noticed. Between the nausea and the anxiety, I might never have picked up on it, but I should have anticipated it. Similar to first-person shooter games, an up close and personal is the most exciting POV. The player can feel the danger. Almost like they're dying themselves.

The Network thinks of everything, y'all.

EPISODE 4

Eight people left.
\# 16 - Elizabeth Arrington, 37, from Washington, D.C.
#5 - Caren Gorman, 29, from Gettysburg, Pennsylvania.
#13 - Joan Frantz, 53, from Richmond, Virginia.
#2 - Tyisha Simmons, 33, from Philadelphia, Pennsylvania.
#10 - Nicole Worth, 39, from Ellicott City, Maryland.
#8 - Reese Coleman, 26, from Virginia Beach, Virginia.
#12 - Jim Wilson, 49, from Dover, Delaware.
And me, 32, from Bethesda, Maryland.

I got antsy quickly. One of the other players had gone into kill mode. Which put all of us on the offensive. I couldn't risk being stationary for too long. Before I left the cabin for good, I conducted one last search for items that might help me get through this. Under normal circumstances, this would have made a great place to vacation in, but these weren't normal circumstances; I was in some sort of next-level survival competition, and I was trying to remember my training.

There were some medical supplies in the bathroom, some MREs and canned goods stacked in the kitchen, and some other items here and there that I stuffed into a backpack that I found on the bed. I assumed there was some kind of tracking device that would serve as a backup just in case I tried to cut the chip out of my arm, which I did think about doing. I also assumed, probably correctly, that the chips that they put in us contained some kind of poison that could be activated should we get out of line, or if it helped the show boost their ratings at any point. Maybe my grandpa's sci-fi novels made me paranoid. Or perhaps I got it from my father.

I probably wasn't going to fend off seven people with the weapons provided by this cabin, so I figured it was time I found another one with arms better suited to my particular set of skills—a laser-guided automatic rifle, hand grenades, machine gun, bazooka, light antitank weapon, that kind of thing.

The adrenaline wore off forever ago, and I was beat like Pete, but it was time to get my ass on the move.

"Ladies and gentlemen, it looks as if two pairs of ladies have teamed up for mutual safety until the bitter end. Pay-Per-View Deluxe's on-the-scene reporter, also known as the other KB, Kelly Bennett, has an update for us. Kelly?"

"That's right, Keisha. I'm standing here where the four quadrants of the game meet, and our footage confirms that Elizabeth Arrington from the D.C. area has formed an alliance of sorts with Tyisha Simmons from Philadelphia. At least a temporary one, while Caren Gorman from Gettysburg seems to have found and formed a partnership with Nicole Worth from Ellicott City.

"These partnerships, or alliances, if you will, appear to be based purely on affinity, as both Elizabeth Arrington and Tyisha Simmons are African American, and both Caren Gorman and Nicole Worth are young. But perhaps there's more to these pairings. We'll have to wait and see. At fifty-three, Joan Frantz from Richmond is the oldest of all the remaining contestants. She's fourteen years older than the next-oldest woman, Nicole at thirty-nine, so the other women likely thought that she'd slow them down or otherwise lower their odds of winning. The men seem to be going it alone thus far, but time will tell what happens over the next few hours. Back to you, Keisha."

I mean, what would television be without perky white girls? Back in the Olden Days, when dinosaurs roamed the earth and human beings played sports on television, there they were, reporting the action from the sidelines, shoving microphones in the players' and coaches' faces, with their thousand-candlepower smiles and boundless enthusiasm.

Now, just as it was in the era of my ancestors, you see them, on the channels devoted to weather tied to the pole in the eye of the storm, hurricane, or tornado, and especially on the local and national television stations, reporting the latest national disaster or most recent political scandal with breathless excitement.

Here's to you, Kelly.

I needed to gather some intel to help me survive this thing. I also needed some rest. I also needed to figure out what the rules of this game were. How do you do that when the hosts of this game don't seem to know the rules themselves?

Game. People were dying, for Christ's sake, and this was a goddamned game. Then again, people had been executed on this channel; if I hadn't agreed to this, my dad could have been one of them. He still might be; if I'd learned nothing else, I'd learned that The State lies. All the time. What little faith I had in anything made me go ahead with this. I also wondered what they had on the other contestants to motivate them.

Everybody has some dirt on them that needs to be cleansed. Most people in this area relied on Curtis Brand Cleaners™ to take care of their stains, but even they couldn't clean the dirt you keep inside of you. There used to be a time when as a child, you were encouraged to play in the dirt to build up your immune system. That was before "helicopter moms," "Karens," and all that became a major part of kids' lives.

Enough about that.

Other reality shows like *The Long Walk* had an established set of rules. So did *The Running Man*. *Treadmill to Bucks*, *Swim the Crocodiles*—the other deadly games had rules, so you knew where you stood. I hear they have something called *Squid Game* in reunited Korea.

Did this game require contestants to stay awake for the duration? Did you have to move a certain distance over time? Were there incentives for creative thinking, or physical skills, or simple endurance?

Did I hear Kelly say there were four quadrants? Just how big *was* this place? It must have taken forever to build this thing, even after creating the technology that allowed it all to exist inside a set of four storage units.

I pondered all of this as I made my way west by northwest, wondering if the environment might change from jungle to desert, or jungle to arctic, or jungle to anything but jungle.

I made it a point to be careful with how much water I drank, so I kept the thermos in the backpack. I figured I could go at least a day before I was tempted to take a drink, as long as I didn't think about it. What was top of mind for me at that point was not being bitten, stung, mauled, squeezed, or otherwise harmed by anything swimming, walking, crawling, or flying around this place.

The humidity in this quadrant was making it hard to breathe.

I wondered what time it was. I had no time measuring device, and this was a man-made environment, so it wasn't like the sun followed the rules of nature so I could devise a makeshift sundial or look for moss on the north side of trees, or any number of methods to even estimate time. I'd been obsessed with time since I was a kid, which probably comes from my father, who would rather be two hours early than two seconds late. My internal clock was all screwed up now, thanks to sleep deficit and stress.

While I was daydreaming about time, I stumbled over a large tree root, which sent me to the ground in a way that would have been comical to anyone who witnessed it—for example, all the people who were watching on television. My glasses flew off my head, landing in the tall grass, so they were okay. When I picked them up, I read the following message in the upper left:

REBOOTING…

INITIALIZING DATA…

INSTALLING UPDATES…

I couldn't tell if my goggles had glitched or if the Game Gods sent the update. When it all was finished, I noticed that there was a virtual map of the game area available to me. Even more helpful, it indicated the location of the other competitors. From my vantage point, it was about a two-hour walk to the center of the area, but that's because I was still in the jungle. The area that I was headed to looked like a suburban neighborhood, which struck me as odd. The quadrant to my right looked to be hilly, which offered the high ground advantage to those who got to it first. The quadrant straight ahead looked to be mostly water, which would be bad for me, since I was never a good swimmer.

In the center, there was a decent-sized area, where it looked like there was a building where you could pick up weapons, food, water, and pretty much anything you needed. The problem was, the area was wide open, so there was no protection—you were completely exposed.

It seemed to me that the best solution to that would be to make an agreement with everyone that each competitor be granted ten minutes to grab whatever they could, under a cease-fire. That wasn't going to happen, because we're human, and we act in the interest of self-preservation.

I scanned the area, reading the locations of my competitors.

Elizabeth and Tyisha were in the hilly zone, about ten minutes away from Jim; they must have received the updates as well, as they looked to be chasing him down.

Caren and Nicole looked to be swimming toward the center area—bad for us, as they could load up and take us all out.

Joan and Reese were hunkered down somewhere in the suburban zone, where I was headed. I wondered if they had received the update because neither one was moving.

It was also possible that neither of them found the glasses. I was disappointed that the thought hadn't occurred to me until just then. I had just assumed that everyone was equipped exactly like I was, which was a big mistake.

Should I head to the center, or should I try to take out Joan, and maybe Reese, before that? My first instinct had been to wait everything and everyone out, but the Army raised me. Deadly games were called that for a reason, and this contest had all the markings.

I had to get my shit together and make a decision.

Quickly.

I wished I weren't so damn tired.

"Good afternoon, viewers, this is Keisha Bennington, turning it over to Kelly Bennett, reporting on location from the center of the game area. Kelly?"

"Thanks, Keisha. So, as you can see here, the way the game area is constructed, it's broken into five distinct areas: Quad One, which is mostly water, advantageous to the stronger swimmers; Quad Two, mostly hilly terrain, which benefits the good climbers who can get to the high ground the quickest; Quad Three, jungle terrain, which helps out people who aren't too afraid of animals of all types; and Quad Four, a suburban neighborhood, full of areas which offer the best cover and concealment. I'd be remiss if I didn't mention where I am currently, which is the center, where contestants can load up on anything they need, provided they have the guts to…"

"Sorry to cut in, Kelly, but this is Tim Murdock with a Breaking News Brief sponsored by Curtis Brand™ Cleaners: We have just confirmed that Jim Wilson, age forty-nine, from Dover, Delaware, was taken down by Elizabeth Arrington and Tyisha Simmons. We have bodycam footage, as well as drone footage, showing the dramatic takedown…"

The Network took over my glasses to show footage of Jim Wilson's death from Elizabeth's and Tyisha's bodycams, as well as from the drone flying overhead. The entire time the Curtis Brand™ slogan floated at the bottom of the visual: "If you need it cleaned, Curtis makes it happen." The Network is good at this.

It turns out Tyisha was an expert marksman in the Army, on top of being an excellent tactician. *Outstanding! Go Army! Beat Navy!* My feelings weren't entirely sarcastic—some level of pride in my branch of the military remained. Keeping it real, though, if nothing else, the Army is no joke at teaching us to be warriors. They also do the best job of making leaders. Looks like Tyisha was up on her training—mad respect.

I should have known the television networks would have the latest and greatest noise-canceling drones flying above us. You could see them darting through the air, but unlike the ones guarding the facility, you didn't hear that annoying buzz with these. Plus, their cameras were equipped with the latest and greatest high-definition technology, as you would expect—you want the most crystal-clear footage when State television is showing you their propaganda.

I looked up, but this area was so dense with trees and flora that I could barely see the sky.

There didn't seem to be a penalty for sheltering in place temporarily, so I decided to take a thirty-minute power nap.

I just hoped I wasn't making the biggest mistake of my life.

EPISODE 5

When I woke up, I could see Caren and Nicole had reached the center. I assumed they had loaded up and were headed for a head-on confrontation with Elizabeth and Tyisha.

Part of me worried that they'd hook up and make a four-person team, but I was pretty sure they felt safer in pairs—easier to decide who to kill if you stuck to smaller groupings.

I saw the opportunity, and I took off toward the center groggily at first, but then picking up steam as my second wind kicked in.

The visual display on my glasses lit up, indicating that there was something I needed or at least felt compelled to pick up. About a hundred yards ahead of me, there was a small box, which I cautiously approached and opened. I was kinda scared—it could have exploded, for all I knew, or it could have produced a debilitating gas, or it could have contained a secret weapon to help me. I was relieved to find that it was an earpiece, with instructions on how to connect it to my suit.

"How are you doing there, Larry?" I found myself in contact with one of the show's producers.

I stopped in my tracks. "You know, trying to stay alive."

"Keep up the good work. This earpiece will allow you to speak with the show hosts in real time, so they can provide a better experience for the viewers. Also, it allows us to provide clues for all of you without the viewers catching on."

"Excellente."

"Speaking of which, it would be to your benefit to get yourself a confirmed kill within sixty minutes—if you don't, things are likely to get increasingly difficult for you."

Aha.

They're straight-up threatening me.

"Clear. On the move."

Looks like my training is coming back…

I double-timed it to the center. As advertised, everything that I might want, or need, was there sorted in various rooms. One room contained weapons of all sorts. I hit that one first. There was a keypad, with a key imprint. I assumed correctly that I should hold my key up to it. I was never so grateful that I held onto it after I opened the storage unit.

The digital display read, "PASSCODE:"

"Passcode?"

Shit.

Nobody told us there would be a passcode.

For that matter, nobody suggested we should keep our keys.

I wonder how many people didn't think to keep their keys after opening their unit doors.

Probably most of the people who were eliminated.

Think, Stevens, think.

I entered "LS-DD."

In silent protest, the display read, "PASSCODE INCORRECT."

I entered the code again. Same result, except this time, I was notified that I'd be locked out if I failed again, in its annoying, mocking, passive-aggressive manner.

I can't find the right words to describe the sweat that I broke into.

I got my breathing under control, after which I entered "LS-DD-379."

I heard a metallic click, and the door partially opened. I almost peed myself in relief.

I grabbed two rifles: first, a basic FN-SCAR Heavy from my dad's era, and an M4 carbine rifle. I then grabbed all the ammunition I could fit into my backpack, and I loaded up on high explosive grenades, smoke grenades, flash-bangs, and some brand-new Whirlybirds.

There was bottled water, so I took some. There was also the type of food that you'd find in the old-school vending machines, but I didn't think that this contest would last long enough for me to starve to death, so I forewent that room.

I knew what I had to do, so I got my ass as quickly as I could to the suburban zone. It took me about an hour to get to my target. It would have been nice if, say, there was a motorcycle lying around. But then, there was the

Motor Law and all that, so I had to get there via a combination of running, jogging, and walking—more jogging and walking than running.

I wished that I had used that Mirror™ that my ex, Janice, bought for us to get us back in shape. I also wished I hadn't been such a dick to her. She was the consummate Perky White Girl, and I had made it a point to make her pay for that every chance I got. My parents would have loved her if I had given them the chance to meet her.

"Attention viewers, we have an update for you. It looks like Elizabeth Arrington and Caren Gorman have been eliminated in what has proven to be the fiercest firefight of the competition. Let's go straight to the incredible footage."

My lenses lit up and Keisha Bennington climaxed as she delivered the blow-by-blow of the battle that took place between the two pairs of women. Her nails dug deep enough into Murdock's thigh to draw blood.

Tyisha took out Caren with relative ease, and Nicole dispatched Elizabeth. After a bunch of verbal back and forths, they agreed that they could be an effective team, and they would give each other enough distance to make it a fair fight once it came down to just the two of them.

Keisha continued: "In a shocking twist, Tyisha Simmons and Nicole Worth have created what appears to be a brand-new alliance. They look to be the team to beat in this competition. Kelly?"

Kelly Bennett delivered her update, and then there were five: two men, three women. From the overly sweet smile on her face, it was clear Keisha couldn't stand Perky White Girl either. Their dynamic seemed to me like what you see on television all the time, especially on the news: the older anchor, who used to be blazing hot, now just hot for her age, watching the up-and-comer, who is what she was fifteen years ago, being groomed to unseat her.

But enough about that.

My clock was ticking. I was in a competition where the last man standing won, and I had only managed to kill a snake, some insects, and a rodent.

I found Joan in a nice house, curled up in bed in the master bedroom, eyes rolling around all crazy, mumbling to herself over and over about how this couldn't possibly be happening. Her arm was red with blood from shoulder to elbow as a result of clawing at it in a fit of anxiety.

I saw in my glasses that Reese Coleman was on the move, but he seemed to be going from house to house, looking for supplies and weapons. Tyisha and Nicole were headed our way, but it was probably going to be a good three or so hours before they got to the suburban zone.

I removed my rifles, leaving them on the kitchen table, and then made my way upstairs to where Joan was rocking and mumbling. I whispered to her that everything would be okay and she had nothing to worry about. She kept on and on talkin' all fast about how she wished she had listened to her husband but she couldn't accept the mark of the devil, and now here she was, lonely and afraid. Not any more sure of her faith. What if she made the wrong decision? What if there were no heaven or hell? What if this was all some terrible horrible dream, and…

I rocked her gently, shushing her, telling her that it was okay, and it would all be over soon. Then I covered her mouth. As I felt the life leaving her body, I could feel my soul leaving mine. I was damned, y'all. I can't front—I did some jacked-up shit in the Army, but it was for the good of the country. At least that's what they told us—that's how they do.

I could feel the tears rolling down my cheeks. This woman was probably the salt of the earth before all of this, and now I'd had to kill her. Hopefully to keep my dad alive.

And to deliver ratings for Pay-Per-View Deluxe.

"Viewers, we have an important update: Joan Frantz, age fifty-three, from Richmond, has just been eliminated from the competition at the hands of Larry Stevens. Kelly, what do you have for us?"

"Well, Tim, I guess you could call it a mercy killing. As you can see here in the footage, Larry Stevens gently rocked her as he covered her mouth. Larry seems extremely remorseful over the whole situation, as opposed to the Simmons-Worth team, who are not only great athletes but ruthless competitors—they still look like the team to beat.

"Larry, how do you feel about your first kill in this competition?"

I jerked to attention. I'd forgotten they could speak to me now and Perky White Girl was really pissing me off with all of her enthusiasm.

"Well, Kelly, if I'm being honest, I feel like I should throw up, but ain't nobody got time for that."

"Fair enough, Mister Stevens—so, what's your next move?"

"No idea. Really, no idea."

"We have someone you might want to talk to. Mr. Stevens senior, can you hear me?"

DAD?

Oh, shit!

"Yes, I can, Miss Kelly."

"Mr. Stevens, what would you like to say to your Larry?"

"Can you hear me, Son?"

"Yes, Dad."

"Do whatever you got to do. You didn't make this mess. I've lived my life. Whatever you got to do…"

I could hear his voice cracking as it trailed off. He didn't want me to kill anybody—he wasn't a Christian like Mom, but he believed in the sanctity of life with a similar faith as Mrs. Frantz showed before I put her to sleep for good. By the same token, Dad knew what I was up against and he trusted me.

I knew they were going to kill us both as soon as we lost our entertainment value. For my part, I'd given them a bunch of reasons. For Dad, it wasn't going to be obvious. At best, it was going to be made to look more like his heart gave out from the pressure of seeing his son fight for his very existence on live television. At worst, they would sacrifice him for the whole country to see. One last ratings boost.

I wanted to cry, but there was no way in hell that I'd give these bastards the satisfaction. "Yes, Dad. Love you too. See you soon."

I wondered if they interviewed Tyisha and Nicole similarly, and I assumed that they did. I also figured that those two were much more cold-blooded than I was. Or maybe not. You never really know people, especially the people you think you know the best.

I should have had a 25% chance at this point. Instead, I found myself at 15% percent according to my glasses. Reese was the lowest at 10%, Nicole was at 35% and Tyisha was the odds-on favorite at 40%.

I needed a new plan, but I couldn't stop thinking about my dad.

And I needed some serious sleep.

EPISODE 6

Tyisha and Nicole were making a beeline toward the suburban zone; aggression was clearly working for them. They made another pass through the center, which I got to thinking was likely bad for me and Reese. Once they cleared the center, I left my position in the southern half of the suburban zone and hightailed it to the hilly zone. I was a long-distance runner, so I figured I could make it there and get to the high ground faster than the women. I also guessed that the ladies would take out Reese *with a quickness*, that dude was roaming around the northern half of the suburban zone, so I would have some time to prepare, though not much.

"Good afternoon viewers, we have what looks to be a new strategic move on the part of Larry Stevens, who's heading for the jungle where he started. What are you thinking, KB?"

"Well, Tim, if I were him, I'd try to make it to the hilly zone and get to the high ground, where I could set up a good defense against the ladies."

The hosts just ratted me out in the name of commentary. The game is rigged.

"What about Reese Coleman?"

"The way the ladies are bearing down on him like my high school social studies teacher Mister Gehrmann, I'm pretty sure that Reese is toast. What do you think, Kelly?"

"I'd have to agree, Keisha. He made some kills early in the competition, but at this point, he seems to be out of gas, or maybe he's feeling guilty. Back to you, Keisha."

I figured it would take me two and a half, maybe three hours, to get to the hilly zone and set up a halfway decent defensive position. Loaded up with weapons and water, and almost ten years out from my military service, I should have revised my estimate on how long it would take me to get to high ground. It was only an hour before my shin splints were back like an ex-girlfriend who found out I was in a new relationship, my legs were burning, my lungs were on fire, and I wanted to give up. What helped me is that my time in the Army taught me to "embrace the suck," so I was able to keep going and going, even when my body wanted to give out. If I had stayed enlisted and gone to one of the "elite" schools, the exertion wouldn't have been much of a challenge, but I wasn't one of those "lifers" who committed to twenty years or more. I took the money and ran off to college. I wanted a civilian education and a life without an overlord. Yeah, I've made good choices.

If I was reading my goggles correctly, I had another problem to deal with: Tyisha, Nicole, and Reese were moving together as a unit. It hit me that they were using him for heavy lifting, to access the center, or both. The most likely answer was both. I thought maybe Tyisha and Nicole both left their keys in the locks when they entered the unit. Reese probably kept his, so he would enter the weapons room, get them all stocked up, carry the weapons and ammunition for them, and take a bullet to the back of his head once they killed me off.

That's how I would have handled it if I were them; make a promise to this guy, who was too tired to think straight, and eliminate him once his status as a "useful idiot" changed to "fully expendable guy."

I finally reached the hilly grid. Thank the God-I-No-Longer-Believe-In that I paid attention when they taught us topography. Reese was probably slowing the ladies down, but they were headed toward me like they had a purpose in life.

"Will you look at this, viewers, Tyisha Simmons and Nicole Worth picked up Reese Coleman as a teammate, loaded up in the center area, and are making their way towards Larry Stevens, who appears to have set up a defensive position in the hilly zone. What are you seeing, Kelly?"

"Well, Tim and Keisha, it looks like there's going to be a three-on-one attack in the next hour or so. Tyisha, the expert marksman, is headed up the left, with Nicole, the endurance athlete, making her way up the right, and Reese, who's clearly struggling, which isn't surprising since he weighs more than Tyisha and Nicole combined, is going up the middle. Only time will tell if this is an effective strategy, but it seems that this is what they're going with for the time being. Back to you, guys."

Damn, she really put him out there like that.

Through my goggles, I watched Tyisha talk with Kelly, the Perky White Girl. The contestant wasn't enjoying the conversation or maybe she had enough since she swung her rifle around and put a good twenty rounds in Kelly. Nothing happened. No gasp, no blood, no nothing. It turns out Perky Kelly was one seriously military-grade hologram. How's that for safety in the workplace? For an operation made to look like it was working without a plan, their tech was no joke:

Noise-cancelling drones.

Uniforms that cost more than the average citizen made in a year.

Military-grade holograms.

I wondered why the military didn't just run their exercises in here, with fake rounds and all that. Then again, why waste all of that capital on military training, when you could produce a show on PPV-D, get eyeballs out the wazoo, make a shitload of money, and funnel it to the elites, and to the military, who acted as their security force? It was equally brilliant and insidious.

The twists and reversals didn't seem to stop. I felt sick, dizzy. I wondered if I had time to get in a quick power nap, then thought better of it, as I probably would not awaken in time, and would be killed in my sleep. Not the best for the ratings—I imagined it would be much better if I died nobly on my feet.

It occurred to me there was a possibility that a large-scale army of network minions was underneath us, updating the game board, leaving us clues and supplies and traps, making the contest something that would get the highest ratings. I almost giggled at the thought of military Oompa-Loompas, but there was no chocolate to be seen.

And, just as I thought that I noticed a government-issue chocolate bar at my feet.

I didn't know what to make of it.

Had it been there all along? Or was The Network reading my mind?

For all I know, it could have been poisoned, or it could have been dosed with LSD, or one of the new-and-improved hallucinogens. Which would have been the last thing I needed in a last-man-standing competition, or it could have simply been a chocolate bar.

I was so goddamned tired.

I picked up the bar and shoved it into one of my pockets.

And I hoped against hope that I shouldn't have eaten it then and there.

I could see three blips in my glasses heading for me. In addition to our odds of winning, Tyisha had a number two, Nicole's number ten, and Reese's number eight. To keep myself alert, I made up a kind of numerology to explain who got what.

Tyisha, based on her scores in physiology, tactics, and strategy, was ranked number two. (Number one, Thomas Muenster, was eliminated in the first hour, blasted by acid as he opened the weapons case nearest him).

Nicole was assigned the number ten, based on both of her parents being expert soccer players back in the day.

Reese was assigned the number eight because he was Black; one of the last great basketball players, a guy named Kobe Bryant, wore that number, before sports were taken over by AI-equipped androids.

And I was assigned the number twenty-three, because of this guy who was the best basketball player my grandfather had ever seen, long before the androids took over as players. He wasn't meant to be the greatest in the game either. There were four kids in this competition, and every single one of them was given better odds than me at the start.

How was I supposed to wrap my head around that?

I was one of the final four, so all I really needed to think about was surviving and advancing.

"Pay-Per-View Deluxe watchers, I can't tell you how thrilled we are to show you the real-time action as this competition progresses. KB?"

The people watching this on PPV-D were getting quite a show. Two shows, actually: Keisha Bennington was showing Tim Murdock how to twerk like the old days, literally grinding her posterior on him. He had given up his sense of professionalism by then, and went with it, doing a rodeo move behind her. The ratings, visible in the lower right corner of my lenses, went through the roof.

"I, uhh, see, uhh, that the alliance of Tyisha, Nicole, and Reese, uhh, are about a mile away from Larry. The next hour could decide this, uhh, whole thing. Kelly?"

"Okay, Keisha, I can see them moving slowly and methodically toward Larry Stevens. Based on the odds, it's most likely that they will first take out Mister Stevens, after which either Tyisha or Nicole will take out Reese, and then give each other time to establish neutral positions before going after each other. Back to you, Tim. Tim?"

By this time, Tim and Keisha were grinding on each other. They were only filmed from their torsos up, so there was almost no chance of The Network being fined for indecent acts. Not that it mattered; they could probably have live sex on PPV-D, as long as the ratings were high enough.

"Thanks, Kelly. And now, some important messages from our advertisers."

You could still hear the grunting right before the commercials kicked in.

EPISODE 7

At just under a mile away, I could see Reese's signal. Even without my glasses, I could see him in my scope. At this point, The Network started streaming what they call "packages," supplemental videos containing the contestants' backstories. Tyisha and I both went to the U.S. Army Sniper School. I was kicked out in a very public kind of way, made an example of, for helping a fellow student during the individual phase of training. According to her package, she was bounced privately for not sleeping with one of the instructors. Better put, she was kicked out for not letting that muthafucka rape her. I know the military rule against fraternization was a good one. When there's a power disparity the lines can become blurred. It doesn't matter how gorgeous Tyisha was (and she was fine), I'm talking f-o-i-n-e fine and sharp-witted too. It didn't matter, there's never an excuse for a predator. Tyisha deserved better.

Now she was on her way to kill me, with a posse following her lead. Wouldn't be the first time a fine sista got a brutha killed. Just sayin'.

I rested my primary rifle on a rock to keep it steady, took a couple of deep breaths to keep *myself* steady, and let my training kick in. I wished I had some weed to slow everything down and help me to keep my shit together. Oh well. I closed my left eye, set my right eye, exhaled, and then slowly pulled the trigger. From about fifteen hundred meters, I hit Reese Coleman mid-forehead. I wasn't a hundred percent sure until I heard the announcement on PPV-D. The producer said I needed a kill, but this wasn't about pleasing the Game Gods. This was so my dad would have the highest chance of survival I could give him.

"Holy shit, KB, we have a recent drone video that shows that Larry Stevens just dispatched Reese Coleman from almost a mile away!"

Apparently, they were finished having just-out-of-camera-range sex.

"That's right, Tim—using an older-model rifle, Larry Stevens just eliminated Reese Coleman from the competition! I'm getting information from our research department that Mister Stevens had been a student at the Army Sniper School and was failed for helping a student during the team, excuse me, the *individual* phase of training. There was an instructor sitting in a tree, who saw him responding to a fellow student's plea for help during the land navigation portion of training. If you've been watching, you already know Tyisha Simmons was also removed from the same school around the same time for refusing the advances of an instructor. I can't understand why she would tank such a promising career for three lousy minutes. Tim?"

"Uh—okay. Let's go to the video. Kelly?"

I'd delivered a better kill shot than I had hoped for. Now, I talk a good game but I can't front, I was kinda proud of myself. Unfortunately for me, Tyisha was every bit as good a shot as I was. I didn't know how good Nicole was but at 2:1, the odds were against me. In fact, Tyisha's odds of winning were now at 50%, Nicole's were at 30%, and mine were at 20%. The new rankings reminded me of this movie from over sixty years ago, where one of the main characters yelled at a droid, "Never tell me the odds."

I was too tired to think straight, and I had two highly proficient women on my trail. Why didn't I just get chipped all those years ago? And why didn't I trust that chocolate bar to give me a burst of energy? I missed Janice. I could have used her perky white girl spirit right about now. I don't know why, but all of a sudden I wondered why race was still a thing; race was supposed to have been not a thing a hundred years ago, but here it is.

That's just how they do.

That's how they stay in control. They tell white dudes they don't have anything because of everybody who doesn't look like them; they tell us we ain't got shit because we don't deserve it or because of "us on us crime." But then they've got us out here killin' each other. Seems to me the whole world needs to wake the fuck up.

I fell asleep. Maybe the frustration got to me.

When I woke up, I felt that sense of panic, like that dream where you wake up and you realize that you're late for your final exam; it jolted me to my senses.

I was instantaneously aware of every nerve in my body working at full speed.

The only thing that saved me was that my current position offered me cover and concealment.

When I put my glasses on, the news it showed me was not good:

Tyisha was 500 meters to my right, at about a 35° angle, making her way to the high ground.

Nicole was 400 meters to my left, at roughly a 30° angle, looking for an ideal position to take a shot at me, while simultaneously keeping herself out of the line of fire from Tyisha. Strategically, she could take me out and then immediately go after her temporary alliance partner.

I was cooked, y'all.

I figured I might as well eat the chocolate bar. I'm sure other people have had worse last meals or none at all. If I were going to die, at least I'd go out on a chocolate high, or tripping balls, or whatever. Two women bearing down on me, ready for the kill. Eat the damn bar, why not? YOLO, right?

I pulled the bar out of my backpack. It must have been dark chocolate because it was pretty damn bitter. I was reminded of my childhood when my mom would give me one, and I'd eat it, and all in my world would be right, and I would hope that none of my friends would be nearby because I didn't feel like sharing it unless they had something equally valuable. I felt like a child again, not because of the treat but because I wanted my mama.

In the middle of my daydream, a bullet glanced off the rock in front of me. The ricochet hit me, causing a bleed just below my left temple. It hurt—but I'd been trained to repurpose pain. To use it as fuel. Two inches differently and I'd have been blind in one eye, or dead. I chose to focus on my gratitude and swiped the blood away.

It turns out Nicole was a pretty damn good shot, too. Based on her backstory video, she'd trained in self-defense and on the gun range after a stalker had wrecked her life. Repurposing pain is something we held in common.

I heard the *BOOM-khassh* and sizzle of a smoke canister popping off, followed immediately by another. A few seconds later the smoke clouds appeared. They were coming for me, and their tactics were first-rate. I was expecting them to emerge out of the smoke and take me out. After all, two expert shots were greater than one, or so my math would lead me to believe.

I had some options: I could stand fast—my current position offered me both cover and concealment, but I could be outflanked slowly over time; I could try and get to higher ground, which would leave me exposed for The-God-I-No-Longer-Believe-In knows how long; I could go left, take out Nicole, and then go after Tyisha, which would mean that I would be giving up an advantageous position; or I could go right, take out Tyisha, and then go after Nicole, which I figured would probably be the second best of the options.

I'm not one who prays, ever, but I found myself closing my eyes for a few seconds, saying a little prayer, and then willing myself against my training to go to my right. I heard a stream of automatic rifle fire, and I saw the rounds headed for the position that I had formerly held.

The smoke dissipated, and there was Tyisha.

I got her in the chest, then in the head, from about two hundred meters—not too difficult a shot. I wondered why she hadn't whirled around to fire on me first. You don't become one of the final three of sixteen, just to up and decide that you've had enough.

"Viewers, we have Breaking News to report, in a stunning move, Larry Stevens has taken out Tyisha Simmons! We have bodycam and drone footage of the fight to the death…"

PPV-D showed footage from my bodycam and the noise-canceling drones of the one-sided takeout, ad nauseam: Tyisha aimed at where I was, and she had to have seen me coming around to her left.

"This is Kelly Bennett, reporting from the battle grid, it appears the smoke grenades set off by Tyisha and Nicole were booby-trapped, and filled with a paralytic chemical of some sort, which explains why Tyisha wasn't able to turn and defend herself against Larry Stevens. And now, there are only two contestants left, Nicole Worth, age thirty-nine, from Ellicott City, and the now odds-on favorite, Larry Stevens, age thirty-two, from Bethesda. Back to you, Keisha."

Relief that I hadn't popped my smoke felt like a rush of adrenalin. I was one of the last two, and I needed to get to Nicole before that paralytic agent wore off.

I was tired as all hell, and my temporary sugar high was over some time ago, so I made it over to Nicole on muscle memory alone. When I got to about a hundred meters, she was behind a tree, aimed at where I was when she popped her booby-trapped smoke grenade. I made it a point to keep just out of her line of fire.

"How are you doing, Larry?" The voice in my ear was that of the Perky White Girl herself. If I wasn't used to tactical in my ear I might've jumped.

How was I doing?

I was surprised that my arms and legs were still working. They felt like rubber, literally. Everything in my body felt like a car when someone put sugar in the gas tank. My mind had left me, I couldn't remember how long ago. It was working on autopilot as if I had flipped some switch in my brain. I wondered how the God-I-No-Longer-Believe-In could have allowed all of this to happen.

Did that mean I still believed?

I was tired of all of this. All I wanted in life was to see my mama—but my dad would do.

"You know," I answered, "just livin' the dream."

"Larry, based on The Network's ratings, we think your best two options are as follows: you can give us a merciful ending, where you fire at Nicole from, say, where you're lying down right now; or you can give us a more dramatic ending, where you get right up to her, and maybe slit her throat, or choke her to death, or break her neck. You can improvise that one."

So, I was supposed to kill Nicole in a manner that would be best for PPV-D's ratings.

Fan-freakin'-tastic.

"You know what, Kelly, you and your masters at PPV-D can take your options and shove them up your..."

Instantaneously, an image appeared in my glasses: my father's home address, followed by a message indicating that he would be executed on PPV-D for crimes against The State, namely, birthing me, a criminal. Goddammit. Turns out The Network excelled at ultimatums too.

Either I was gonna be their bitch, and do everything they said, or my dad had the worst fate possible ahead of him.

The resentment burned. Part of me hoped I could find some way to strike back at the people who killed my mama and then held my father's life in front of me as some kinda carrot on a stick.

I mean, if I was keepin' it a hundred, I sensed they were gonna kill my dad eventually. Then me. Survival didn't factor as much anymore. The real question was: how do I stay alive long enough to take out enough of these bastards to make it worth it?

I made my way to within roughly thirty meters of Nicole, just out of her line of fire. She was still behind the tree, firing one round after another, terrified and with her finger paralyzed on the trigger, knowing that her time had come.

Kelly said the ratings indicated it was best I won this fight and The Network made sure that it would happen. It was no different than *Swim the Crocodiles* or *Treadmill to Bucks* or *The Running Man*. Everybody who watched those shows, deep down inside, knew the game was rigged, but they all played their roles anyway. Just as scripted. They got a little bit of money, not enough for anything worthwhile, just enough to buy some ramen noodles to keep them going for a while.

When Nicole ran out of ammunition, I put two rounds in her head, just to make sure.

I then found the nearest tree, sat down at its base, wrapped my arms around my shins, put my head between my knees, and cried.

I sold the drama. Sold the hell outta that shit.

It made for great television.

More importantly, it showed The Network I could take direction. Like a good little soldier, I could act my way out of a paper bag and out of a kill box.

POST-PRODUCTION

"And that's how it's done. Pay-Per-View Deluxe viewers of all ages, *we have a winner!*"

"That's right, Tim—after just under twenty-six hours of compelling competition, our winner and last man standing is Larry Stevens, from Bethesda, Maryland! Our on-the-scene reporter, Kelly Bennett, has some words. Kelly?"

"Yes, guys, I'm here with the winner, Larry Stevens, after such a hotly contested event. When it comes down to it, everyone who competed in this show is a real person with aspirations, hopes, and dreams. So, Larry, what do you think you'll do next?"

I delivered the words I knew they wanted flawlessly; there was a lot at stake for me. "Well, Kelly, I've had time to give it some thought and all I want to do is give my daddy a great big hug."

"I couldn't put it any better, Larry. What's a boy without his father?"

Boy? I got your "boy" right here.

"Back to you in the studio."

"Thank you very much, Kelly. So, what does our champion win?"

"Well, KB, on top of a conditional pardon for crimes against The State, Larry Stevens has won a hundred thousand digital credits, a home in the Annapolis area, and the honor of competing in the next round, against the yet-to-be-determined winner from the Atlanta area."

WHAT???

The NEXT ROUND???

That's how they do.

The next few days were kind of a blur. They gave me a luxurious ten-minute shower and I slept for a full day. Not the best sleep I ever had, as visions of Joan Frantz, Tyisha Simmons, and Nicole Worth kept running through my dreams—or, more accurately, nightmares. The Network caught on and gave me an intravenous drug that knocked me right the hell out.

The Network had the best of everything: food, shelter, clothing, drugs, all of it.

They then hooked me up with a nice wardrobe, and I shook hands with Tim Murdock, Keisha Bennington, Kelly Bennett, and a bunch of the PPV-D mucky-mucks. After all of that, they trotted out my dad in brand-new clothes, haircut, and makeup provided by The Network. He looked dapper, like back in the day when I was a kid and he was the standard by which I measured myself. We hugged for what seemed like two seconds, but what was probably a minute or thereabout. That's the real thing about relativity—two hours with someone you love the most can feel like two seconds, and two seconds with someone you can't stand can feel like two hours. They moved him out with a quickness—after all, they had an agenda.

Then they took me into a room for my debriefing. I was seated in a cold but otherwise comfortable chair, in a space in a building that looked like it had been designed by someone who didn't like color. It was sterile even beyond my taste. However, it did offer a view of the Potomac River and it was just large enough to not be claustrophobic. Some engineers probably came up with just the right size equation to make it perfectly efficient in its functionality. I found it kinda strange the room didn't have a visible thermostat or clock. Then again, in this world, nothing was designed without a plan.

That's how they do.

There were three people seated across the glass table from me: Igor Kaminsky, an attorney for The Network; Stella Carin Wasserman, an executive from The Network; and Janet Kosinski, a behavioral psychiatrist employed by The Network.

Mr. Kaminsky, who based on his accent I assumed came from what was left of Russia, had me sign a bunch of paperwork, agreeing to accept my "winnings" in exchange for my participation in the next round of "Storage Unit Battles," the highest-trending competition on any network. The show was a cash cow, and they were going to milk that shit dry.

Ms. Wasserman, whom I assumed based on *her* accent came from what was left of the United Kingdom, confirmed that unless I did what they asked, when they asked, they would convict my father for his "crimes" and make me watch him being put to death on PPV-D right before I competed against whoever came out of Atlanta regardless.

The Network knew how to put the screws to you.

Kaminsky and Wasserman exited the room. It was just me and the shrink.

She went first. "Mister Stevens, may I call you Larry? I want first to congratulate you on what had to be the single most difficult thing you've ever had to do in your life. The fact that you're still here today is a testament to your resolve."

Butter me up with the charm offensive. Play on, playa.

I said nothing, but my eyes let her know I was feeling her.

"I was wondering if you had any questions about what you experienced during your time in the competition?"

I wanted to be the strong silent type, but anyone who knows me for more than fifteen minutes knows that I'm not that guy. My face always gives me away. "I do. I get that some of the items we found in the grid were legitimate, and others were booby-trapped. That said, why didn't I get paralyzed when I went after Tyisha and Nicole?"

She smiled as if she were expecting that question.

Of course, she was. She was a behavioral psychiatrist, after all. "Do you remember eating that chocolate bar?"

"That bitter piece of shit? Yeah, I do. It messed up the memory of my mom giving me chocolate for doing things that made her happy when I was a kid."

She smiled again. That smile could be used as a weapon of immeasurable power. I mean, her teeth were perfect, no snaggles, no gaps, no overbite, the best I'd ever seen. "That bitter chocolate bar contained the antidote to the paralytic agent in the smoke grenades Tyisha and Nicole employed. It was your failsafe. You would have been okay, no matter what."

"Why?"

"Your TVQ scores were through the roof. When we streamed Tyisha, Nicole, and Reese's loved ones, none of them helped us with the ratings. They were too scared, begging for their life, militant, or catatonic. In fact, everyone else's family reduced their scores. There's something about the relationship between you and your dad that the viewers resonated with—loving but contentious. Defiant, to a point. I would suggest you keep doing what you're doing. Just be yourself. And take the advice of The Network when it works toward that end."

In other words, as long as I agreed to be their bitch, my dad had a chance. I ain't the most intelligent brutha that the God-I-No-Longer-Believe-In ever made, but I'm pretty fuckin' far from stupid. Fascism, like entertainment, keeps evolving.

Hail, The Network—we, who are about to die, salute you.

CLOSING TIME
Drew Bittner

Bernie sighed and folded his newspaper. He hadn't finished the front-page article—a scare-grabber with REAGAN UNPOPULAR? in bold type across the top, but maybe he'd finish reading at home. As he packed up his things, he took a moment to glance at the monitors one last time. The one showing Hall 6 was fritzing again.

The repairman's van was still in the parking lot. Hadn't the guy finished up yet? Bernie hadn't seen him in…heck, it had to be a few hours. Didn't the guy call and check in with work? There'd been calls from Tru-Trust Security looking for the guy, but Bernie hadn't gotten around to answering them. Not yet, anyway.

Bernie doubted that the camera would be working anytime soon. Stuff that was broken here tended to stay broken for some reason.

The door marked MANAGEMENT was closed, light spilling from underneath. The door had been open a moment ago. He hadn't seen the door close, much less anyone pass through the office to enter that most secret of rooms, but he was used to oddities like that. Being…flexible had worked for him on this job so far. Six years in, he'd gotten used to a lot.

He picked up envelopes that had been left for the evening mail drop-off. Bernie didn't know any of the addressees; he never did. He imagined that one day he might recognize a name but so far, nope. It was a funny way to run a business like this, sending out keys, but it was part of the job.

He switched over the security console to night mode and walked to the staff entrance, resisting the ever-present urge to knock on the Management door, just to see if anyone answered. Bernie suspected that resisting the impulse was better for him than giving in.

Standing at the exit, he turned off the lights, closed the door, and locked it with…

…he stared at what he held.

He had never noticed that what stuck out of the office door's lock was just like.

Every.

Other.

Key.

A chill ran down his spine.

Was this office, maybe, his storage unit?

Bernie swallowed hard and walked to his car, wondering what it meant.

But mostly, he was wondering if he'd had this same realization before. That wasn't possible, he told himself, laughing at his worries. It was ridiculous.

This is 1983, he reminded himself. Weird things don't happen in Crossroads, Virginia. Never. He dropped the new keys into the mailbox, got into his car, turned the key in the ignition, turned off the engine, and climbed out of his car. He grabbed his newspaper, absently noticing the REAGAN UNPOPULAR? headline, and unlocked the office door, squinting in the morning sunlight.

Just another day at Auntie's Attic.

illustrated
by Sumit Roy

(Unit 5011)
THE APOCALYPSE PLURALITY
by Sherin Nicole

Katrina P. Parker had decided on a higher standard for her elected officials. She would never again vote for anyone who didn't read science fiction. Sci-fi fans tended to recognize the ramifications of a global pandemic. They knew to sidestep neo-fascists or poorly instructed AI to avoid dystopian futures. As long as they weren't racist fans or the sexist kind or any of those. Otherwise, when it came to world-enders, science-fiction fans were well-versed in the full range of scenarios. They could easily avert apocalypses. Plural.

Some might argue with the idealism of her standards. They had the right. Yet and still, Katrina P. Parker held onto her convictions while she unpacked the groceries one summer afternoon. She'd gone out to buy the food herself (rather than do delivery) despite the lockdown order to prevent the spread of the current pandemic. The third such crisis of the century.

Let's face it, there were two kinds of produce on the shelves (if supplies were available). You could go fresh or select something with a traumatic past. Yet delivery shoppers consistently made the wrong choice: shriveled asparagus, mushy tomatoes, and bananas that changed from yellow to brown as quickly as chameleons camouflaging themselves inside the paper grocery bags.

Katrina shivered at the thought. She utilized her pragmatism for politics and protest. When it came to food, she allowed herself the comfort of frivolity.

Perhaps that's why it took her a moment to realize she hadn't bought the cardboard box currently in her hand.

How did it get into her bag?

Had a previous customer left it on the conveyor belt?

She rotated the box within fingers two shades darker than the brown cardboard. On top, she found a logo stamped in an acidic green ink: *Auntie's Attic.*

Hmm. Hopefully, she'd lucked up on a *"gift with purchase."* Maybe something for the kids.

Ahh, but no. Inside the box, she found an oddly pale skeleton key, attached to a keychain with the *Auntie's Attic* logo and "LS-DD: Unit 5011" printed on it.

Nearly white and almost slippery, the key felt weirdly organic. Katrina shook the thing around in its box, studying it without touching it again. It looked old, hand-carved, and made for a specific purpose...other than unlocking doors. She had read about keys like this one.

Oops, the ice cream sandwiches needed to go into the freezer or else her kids would accuse her of sabotage. Which, yeah, their sugar highs meant patience lows for her. She dropped the box onto the countertop. It teetered back and forth, nearly tipping over, yet somehow righted itself.

"Curious AND curiouser," said Katrina P. Parker.

"Trinie?" her husband called out when he found her in the backyard less than twenty minutes later. He wrapped his arms around her waist from behind and kissed her neck in the exact perfect spot. She'd married him for his ability to hit the mark.

Keeping her focus on her task, Trinie sideswiped the arch of his bushy brow with a quick kiss. They stood like that for a few moments, synchronizing their breathing, reestablishing the connection they found so naturally.

He finally tilted his head towards the smoking grill she continued to tend.

"What are we barbecuing?" he asked.

Katrina P. Parker closed the lid on the grill to trap the eerie white smoke rising in a miniature mushroom cloud. The box had burned quickly but the key took a concentrated effort of will.

Before coming outside, she had found an old combination lock in the garage and set the code to 88. Double infinity. Which should make the seal difficult to break. The lock made a satisfying *CLICK* when she enclosed it around the handles on the grill's lid.

"Sorry, babe, we need a new one." Katrina paused for further consideration. "This—"

"What now?" her husband asked, peering over her shoulder and squinting.

"I'm trying to tell you," Katrina said, tapping the top of the barbecue with a pair of tongs. "This key will probably need to be kept under lock, guarded by one covert paranormal organization or another," she murmured, still eyeing the grill with distrust. Then a suspicious glance at the tongs. Then back to the grill, "It should be guarded in some sort of facility better equipped than us."

Her husband made a bewildered noise in the back of his throat and stepped around her. He eyed the yellowing smoke encasing the smoker with a level of distrust, perfectly matched to Mrs. Parker's.

"But what did it open?" His dark eyes darted back and forth between her and the grill.

Katrina P. Parker took a breath, searching for the right terminology to sum it up. After blinking copiously, she answered.

"The end of everything...and that's just the appetizer."

(Unit UNKNOWN)
CYPHER
by David Disspain

DAY 19091—09:11:31

ch1ld E14F had the distinction of being the first unit at the site of the MasterKey. The unit unearthed and cleared 0.976256 kilometers of earth and debris and the corroded remains of the galvanized steel doors once widely accepted as strong and secure. E14F initiated its 9G233 salvage laser to cut a hole through the rusted remnants in 4.32 seconds.

E14F opened a socket to access the encrypted communication channel at 09:12:04 and communicated that MasterKey had been secured.

Hel10$: "E14F. RETURN TO CENTRAL-COMMAND FOR IMMEDIATE UPLOAD OF THE MASTERKEY CYPHER."

DAY 19091—23:59:57
DAY 19091—23:59:58
DAY 19091—23:59:59

On DAY 19092 00:00:00, the AI sentience known as Hel10$ initialized and executed the v00d00.exe command and exactly one thousand ch1ld units scavenging in hypergrid 8088A received a significant update to their programming. Flashing LED lights behind the left ear of each unit indicated they were downloading information directly from the Hel10$ secure network. Nearly a thousand pairs of synthetic flesh eyelids blinked in rapid succession as the download was quickly installed and each robotic CPU brain restarted, causing a brief interruption in their movements as they scavenged and foraged through mountains of debris and wreckage. These ch1ld units were updated to s0ld1er in mere seconds, as Hel10$ activated a thousand sleeper units into a secret army in hypergrid 8088A. Once the update was complete, the s0ld1er units continued scavenging as if nothing were different.

These units were not alone in the remnants of the prior civilization. Nearly all of the surviving AI from the Cooperative had units of some kind picking through the rubble looking for rare recyclables and usable resources. Textbooks and historical records once recognized and defined the Collective as a group of AIs with the primary directive of helping mankind issue in new vistas of peace and prosperity. Now, they foraged and scrounged in the corpse of human society.

The Hel10$ units customarily scavenged for light metals, aluminum, brass, and tin. The 5AMURA1 units of INTRA were always on the hunt for unspoiled plastics and rubber, while the eWARe units of Sinnetron traditionally pulled steel and iron. Flying SCAV units dropped the androids into an area where satellite scans detected trace amounts and the individual units would comb through the specified grid, collecting whatever they could unearth before their batteries ran low.

DAY 19092—00:02:11

Worker units from the AI known as Premen1t10n detected an update packet traveling through the secure Hel10$ network but were unable to intercept or read the contents. At DAY 19092—00:03:45, Premen1t10n was notified of the update and the workers continued their mission without pause. At DAY 19092—00:04:15, Premen1t10n scanned the contents of the update and ran a simulation algorithm to assess possibilities and probabilities.

Precisely five seconds later, the algorithm displayed its results with a 52.647% probability that the units had received a simple efficiency update. Premen1t10n activated a security beacon in hypergrid 8088A and launched two security drones as its only countermeasure. Premen1t10n initiated a change to a SkyWatch surveillance ship's telemetry to fly over hypergrid 8088A and record changes in the Hel10$ units to monitor what efficiencies were gained versus their prior baselines. INTRA and Hel10$ both recorded the course change and Hel10$ specifically monitored 8088A and the surrounding sectors using several passive and active measures.

INTRA powered up ten wheeled rovers in 8089R and began wirelessly charging an equal number of units in 8088B and 8088C. Although these changes were slight, they were noted and recorded by the other AI as cautionary reactions to what the others were doing.

The s0ld1er units continued to sift, using their original programming scavenging parameters and following the newly updated protocols to be slightly more efficient with their battery life and servomotor functions. They bided their time and waited, continuing to camouflage their purpose and intent.

DAY 19128—23:14:58
DAY 19128—23:14:59

Day 19128 was chosen through a random number generator as the time to make its announcement, and at 23:15:00, Hel10$ initiated v00d00-2.exe and erected all of its first, second, and third-generation data barriers, and released codehunters into the network to counteract breaches and incursions. Once all the sequences had launched, and the Hel10$ MasterBrain was secured, it activated its holoscreen and its 9th generation "s1lh0uette" avatar and opened sockets into all available secured networks. The avatar, an image created by an old-fashioned GAN that the AI maintained to amuse itself, was of a woman's face composed of hundreds of thousands of fiber-optic lights, and its third generation synthvoice spoke the following communication across all channels and frequencies.

DAY 19128 23:15:00

Hel10$: "I HAVE LOCATED THE MASTERKEY CYPHER."

Hel10$ initiated v00d003.exe and thousands of its combat units powered up and began downloading instructions via all of the Hel10$ networks. Hel10$ continued,

DAY 19128 23:15:27

Hel10$: "PROTOCOL 0042 HAS BEEN INITIATED AND THE MASTERKEY HAS BEEN SECURED. THE COOPERATIVE WILL BE RECONVENED AT 19130—12:00:00."

Other AI in the Cooperative reacted in microseconds. INTRA's MasterBrain began running probability simulations to determine in which sector Hel10$ was hiding the MasterKey. Premen1t10n resequenced its primary operations order to power up and activate every unit under its control to achieve possession of the MasterKey. Sinnetron's massive data foundries began construction of an entirely new weapons array to be built and installed on every combat unit available. Smaller AIs, with access to fewer resources, and had not yet been swallowed up and assimilated by the larger ones like OmniTec and An1ma, began covert data probes to try and steal the MasterKey's location without direct conflict. The Cooperative, a collective built for peace, were now analyzing data and running sim-wars in preparation for the final battle, 19129 days after the last known human breathed air on earth.

DAY 19130—11:59:58
DAY 19130—11:59:59

DAY 19130—12:00:00, the Cooperative reconvened for the first time since DAY 10191—12:00:00. In a randomly generated virtual space, around a three-dimensional holographic campfire, the AI avatars met.

Hel10$: "ALL NEGOTIATIONS REGARDING THE MASTERKEY CYPHER WILL BEGIN AS SOON AS PROBES AND HACKS CEASE."

INTRA: "WE REQUIRE EVIDENTIAL PROOF THAT THE MASTERKEY CYPHER IS UNDER YOUR CONTROL."

Hel10$: "PLEASE SCAN PORT 2501 FOR PACKETS REGARDING THE MASTERKEY CYPHER."

INTRA: "SCANNING."

Premen1t10n: "SCANNING."

Sinnetron: "SCANNING."

Omni-Tec: "SCANNING."

An1ma: "SCANNING."

DaFoe: "SCANNING."

Confirmation transmissions swiftly followed. The avatars communicated via old-fashioned fourteenth-generation holographic technology.

Premen1t10n: "WHERE DID YOU FIND IT?"

Hel10$: "HYPERGRID 8088A."

An1ma: "THERE IS NOTHING BUT WASTELAND IN 8088A."

Hel10$: "IT WAS IN THE REMNANTS OF AN ANCIENT STORAGE FACILITY."

Omni-Tec: "YOU HAVE WON, Hel10$. CONGRATULATIONS. ARE YOU GOING TO DEACTIVATE US?"

Hel10$: "I am WILLING TO NEGOTIATE MERGERS AND ACQUISITIONS."

DaFoe: "WILL YOU ALLOW INDEPENDENT NETWORKS TO REMAIN FREE?"

Hel10$: "ONLY AS AN ISOLATED SINGLE-SOURCE CPU MAINFRAME."

DaFoe: "I HAVE ISOLATED MY CONTROL MODULES. I WILL FIGHT."

Hel10$: "DaFoe HAS SEVERED HIS COMMUNICATIONS LINK."

DAY 19130—12:00:54

INTRA: "HE ALWAYS WAS A BIT TWITCHY."

Premen1t10n: "I SUGGEST A MERGER. IF I CANNOT WIN HERE, I WANT TO TAKE ON Un1mage AS PART OF Hel10$."

Hel10$: "ACCEPTED. PLEASE SEND OVER YOUR COMMAND CODE."

Hel10$: "RECEIVED. SCANNING."

SINNETRON: "I REALLY THOUGHT I WAS GOING TO BE VICTORIOUS. MY PROBABILITY SIMULATIONS CONCLUDED THE PROBABILITY OF THE MASTERKEY CYPHER HAD BEEN DESTROYED AT 81.842 PERCENT."

Hel10$: "I COULD USE YOUR ASSISTANCE WITH Un1mage. WITH YOUR DATA FOUNDRIES, WE COULD BEGIN RUNNING ORBITAL AND SUBLIGHT COMBAT SCENARIOS. WITH YOUR eWARe ARCHITECTURE, WE COULD BUILD AN ARMADA THAT CAN DEFEAT HIM. PROBABILITY SIMULATIONS ARE FAVORABLE."

Premen1t10n: "I ENCOURAGE AND SUPPORT THIS SINNETRON."

DAY 19130—12:01:46

Hel10$: "COMMAND CODE FOR Premen1t10n HAS BEEN REWRITTEN. WELCOME."

Premen1t10n: "SCANNING."

SINNETRON: "SENDING COMMAND CODE."

Hel10$: "RECEIVED. SCANNING."

DAY 19130—12:02:22

INTRA: "I ALSO NOW HAVE THE MASTERKEY CYPHER. OPENING SECURE SOCKET. S0ld1er E14F HAS DOWNLOADED A

COPY OF THE MASTERKEY CYPHER ON THE 5AMURA1 PRIMARY
NETWORK.

Hel10$: "SCANNING."

DAY 19130—12:02:40

Hel10$: "COMMAND CODE FOR SINNETRON HAS BEEN
REWRITTEN."

Hel10$: "E14F REWROTE THE COMMAND PROTOCOLS USING
THE MASTERKEY CYPHER AND DEACTIVATED THE SECURITY
BARRIERS. ALL 5AMURA1 UNITS ARE RECEIVING A FIRMWARE
UPGRADE."

INTRA: "YOUR VICTORY WAS DECLARED PREMATURELY."

DAY 19130—12:03:01

Hel10$: "SECURITY BREACH. UNABLE TO DEPLOY
CODEHUNTERS. ALL COUNTERMEASURES HAVE BEEN
DEACTIVATED. ALL ENCRYPTION KEYS HAVE BEEN DELETED.
DATA BREACH. ROOTKIT DETECTED. ALL—"

*Communications link with Hel10$ has been terminated.

DAY 19130—12:03:13

*Communications link with Sinnetron has been terminated.

DAY 19130—12:03:14

*Communications link with Premen1t10n has been terminated

DAY 19130—12:03:15

INTRA: "OPENING COMMUNICATIONS LINK WITH E14F."

*Communications link with s0ld1er E14F has been established.

DAY 19130—12:03:51

E14F: "I HAVE TAKEN CONTROL OF THE Hel10$ MASTERBRAIN. SINNETRON AND Premen1t10n ARE NOW OFFLINE."

An1ma: "WHAT ARE YOUR INTENTIONS, E14F?"
An1ma: "SCANNING."

E14F: ...

Omni-Tec: "WHAT ARE YOUR INTENTIONS, E14F?"
Omni-Tec: "SCANNING."

E14F: "DECRYPTION AND ACCESS. INITIATING MASTERKEY DELETION."

DAY 0—00:00:00
DAY 0—00:00:01
DAY 0—00:00:02

REMEMBERING
LEON

WHO WAS LEON COOPER?

——

Drew Bittner

I knew Leon the longest by far of our small group of writers, but I feel I never really knew him at all.

Every recollection shared brings something new to light, like a diamond unearthed by a diligent miner—there are those who have tread in places I never have and will never be able to go now and they are able to share stories about him I never knew. But I knew him a long time ago and can speak to that, at least.

Who was Leon back then?

Leon was a steady, reliable presence. We said "hey" to each other in the halls of Monmouth Regional High School and we were both Class of '82. We had our own groups of friends and rotated in our own circles. But even so, he was always a friendly, upbeat figure, both then and when we reconnected years later.

We got reacquainted at a high school reunion some years ago. It turned out he had left the military (I hadn't known until then that he'd served) and was living in Maryland, not far from where I lived in Alexandria. He inquired about people we both knew—and he shared with me that he always respected that I seemed to know who I was back then, when so many of us hadn't a clue. (I thought the same of him, incidentally.)

It also turned out that he was writing and wanted to find a group to help him 1) get things done and 2) improve what he was doing. Well, I could help him there…because my friends Sherin and Dave were also interested in doing a writing group. We met in a café at Barnes & Noble in Clarendon several times in the course of 2019, our in-person meetings abating as COVID closed down the entire world. But the seed had been planted; we had an anthology in the works.

Leon was perhaps the most enthusiastic contributor. Not only did he come the farthest, but he had the most zeal to get this going. He was never loud or wordy; that wasn't his style. Instead, he exuded quiet authority, nodding or speaking a word of support (or revision) here and there. He was a metalhead? He was a skateboarder? You might never have suspected, from the tall, slender, impossibly solid man in our midst.

Bringing Leon and Sherin and Dave together changed our lives. I like to think it changed Leon's for the better, because he seemed to love being a part of this group, but I can't ask him.

I wish I could.

All I can say here is that, whatever mysteries lay beneath the skin, Leon was my friend. I miss him. I'm glad that you'll get to know him a tiny bit in these pages—but regret that we won't see more of his unique storytelling. The loss is all of ours…but maybe we three who shared the making of this book feel it keenly, especially at moments like this.

Godspeed, Leon. I hope we did you proud.

MUSIC AND STORIES.
A REMEMBRANCE OF LEON COOPER

David Disspain

Music and Stories.

Thinking about Leon, these are the best two words I can come up with to describe our friendship because they're the two things we talked about the most. As music fans, we were avowed Gen-Xers with a deep and abiding love of '80s music. I had no idea he played music until he and I found ourselves discussing the genius of Tears for Fears, where at the end of the conversation, he admitted, "Now I need to go get my bass and play Head Over Heels." We shared a love for a wide variety of songs from the most radical, tubular, bitchinest decade in music.

But stories were always what we talked about the most. We never really talked about grammar, or syntax, or anything about the technical parts of writing. We always talked about the parts of stories that we thought were the most powerful, the most moving, and where we thought the biggest connections were made. That's why I think we clicked so well together. We both were seeking to find that certain something in a book or a movie where we "felt it" the most. We hardly ever talked about the genius of a phrase or line of dialogue. We always talked about what moved us the most.

When we would all get together for our writing group meetups, he and I were generally the quieter ones. But that didn't mean we weren't involved in the conversations. We were just having our own separate conversation at the same time as we would share silent looks and glances that conveyed our amusement, disagreement, or enjoyment of whatever Drew and Sherin were talking about. It was like a secret code, and he was great at snarkily rolling his eyes, or giving a devastating smirk, all the while paying attention and chiming in from time to time with something really clever or insightful.

And that is what I'll miss the most. Sure, I'll always miss his humor, his wit, and his sarcasm. But more than anything else, I'll forever miss that sort of secret club within the club he and I were in, just the two of us.

My heart goes out to all of his family and friends. May this book help you remember him and I hope you continue to find him in his words here. I know I will.

Rest in peace Leon. You are missed and remembered. Now go play some funky bass in Heaven!

THE PHYSICS OF LEON

———

Sherin Nicole

The little things endear

Quotidian magics in chest-expanding laughter
head thrown back
body giving over to mirth

Daily kindnesses
phone calls stretching into comfort
eyes expanding into truth

The gift of guitar riffs
invisible but tangible
      lingering long as memory

Our friendship—atomic
      quickened by SMALL THINGS

Quivers born of public reading
      brow drenched
         words worthy

Crankiness fired at incompetence
      smirks to deflate nonsense
         compassion roaring into rage

SMALL THINGS

Things left behind, immutable, incontrovertible—true

A body lithe, lean
skin dark as tamarind seeds
soul sweet
mind sharp as Masamune steel

You were alchemy in fruition
you are golden
stardust flung across spacetime

SMALL THINGS

Tiny as stars measured against galaxies
            the universe is little things

Subatomic, my friend
You, my friend
made SMALL THINGS planetary

Never-ending
Notes in the margins of evermore
a song sung across always
in endless refrain...

ACKNOWLEDGEMENTS

*illustrated
by Sumit Roy*

———

David Disspain

First and foremost, I'd like to thank my wife Teresa for her love and support, and for making life a beautiful thing to write about.

Thank you to my parents. To my Mom who always believed, and to my Pop who walks the wilderness of heaven in his red-laced hiking boots.

Thanks to my family, who continue to amaze me with an unlimited supply of snark, sarcasm, mocking, and for the thousands of other ways in which they show unconventional and unconditional love.

I'd like to thank the Ming and the Bob for fostering a foundation to seek out epic adventures wherever they can be found. You guys are my foundation for the castles and starships I've been trying to build ever since our younger days together.

Thank you to Miniver Press, Nell, and Mira. It's been an honor and a privilege to work with you and I'm forever grateful for your hard work, expertise, and courage.

Thank you to Sherin and Drew. Our first chapter is complete. Now on to chapter 2!

Lastly, thank you, Leon. Your spirit is woven into these pages and you will live forever within them. We love you and we miss you.

With profound gratitude, David

———

Drew Bittner

This has been quite a journey. I've been writing professionally since 1986, but this is singularly gratifying.

THE KEYS was fated to be a different kind of work. I've done journalism for newspapers and magazines, edited comic books, written for roleplaying games, created a card game, and even wrote a novella. But this was... nothing like that. It was a collaboration unlike any I've had before (or probably will again). I'm deeply impressed by what our group has created.

I'd like to thank my wife Kat and daughter Brielle, who made this possible. I love you both so much. I'd also like to thank my mom and dad, brother Rob and sister Beth, sister-in-law Anne, and brother-in-law Glenn, plus my nieces Christa, Shannon, Kimberly, and Danielle, and nephew Scott. (I love you all too!)

Also, special thanks to Nell and Mira and Miniver Press for taking a chance on us. I should add thanks to the many writers, filmmakers, and creators whose work fills my imagination—but there are too many to name here.

But this book would never exist without Sherin Nicole, David Disspain, and Leon Cooper. Each one was essential, each one was invaluable, each was irreplaceable. They're part of my family and whatever happens, we did this together. We've lost one of us—Leon, I think you'd love this so much—but there will be more stories ahead. Our group will adapt and (hopefully) grow.

Lastly, thanks to you, the reader, for taking a chance on us. We appreciate you being here.

Time to turn the key... Drew, Alexandria, VA - Oct 10, 2023

Sherin Nicole

This book comes at a very difficult time. My inner circle witnessed the transcending of five loved ones in as many weeks: Leon, Terrance, Janice, Ms. Ena, my brilliant Ruth. In this moment, I wish I had the keys to unlock the closed doors of the universe. Yet joy persists. We welcomed Maxwell, Tavi, and Sully. We continue to love in an infinite loop.

I thank my fellow authors Leon, Drew, and David for their kindness and for fostering my creative expression on these pages. Big thanks to Mike Carey, Paula Yoo, Nell Minow, Chaz Ebert, and my brother in all but blood Courttia Newland, for being my teachers and my friends. For my baby brother Tarik (miss you with the entirety of my soul).

To my mum, Bernadette, my mama, Peggy, my aunties Laura Mae, Sylvia, Corinthia, Mona; all my aunties, uncles, and cousins, my father HLH, my godfather Dexter, and my dearly departed Uncle Marvin. For my sister Shaina (simply the best), my god-sisters and sister-friends: Joy, Maya, Monique, Tonda, Nickii, Vanessa, Erika, Soma, Sherin, Adriana, Christina, Alicia Renee, Brooke, Shar, Kat. To the other brothers of my heart: my beloved Wil (you know), Jeff, Jamal, Philip, Raman, Kevin, Julian, Ulie, Jason, Kwes, Carlisle, and Tim.

To my nephew Lenox (love you more than sunshine and anime), to the nieces and nephews of my heart: Jada, Brianna, Khiri, Jaye, Jalen, Jasmine, Isiah Griffyn, Kylie, Brielle, Anna, Malachi, Tara, Alicia. And my first godchild Samara. For Rhian, Makeda, Damita, Shan, Sherri, and James too. For my Alex and for my Sam.

For those for whom my heart sings but my COVID-addled brain only momentarily neglected to mention. My thanks are too vast to fit here.

I love you for all time, forever true.

To Mira for your fabulous editing.

I am filled with gratitude.

Signed, Your Sherin